HER DARK SILENCE

A THRILLER

JASON KASPER

SEVERN RIVER PUBLISHING

Severn River Publishing
SevernRiverBooks.com

ISBN: 978-1-64875-494-4 (Paperback)

ALSO BY JASON KASPER

Spider Heist Thrillers
The Spider Heist
The Sky Thieves
The Manhattan Job
The Fifth Bandit

American Mercenary Series
Greatest Enemy
Offer of Revenge
Dark Redemption
Vengeance Calling
The Suicide Cartel
Terminal Objective

Shadow Strike Series
The Enemies of My Country
Last Target Standing
Covert Kill
Narco Assassins
Beast Three Six

Standalone Thriller
Her Dark Silence

To find out more about Jason Kasper and his books, visit
severnriverbooks.com/authors/jason-kasper

1

June 7, 2021
Charleston, South Carolina

Clara registered her son's distant shriek through a fog of sleep, opening her eyes to see only darkness.

She pulled the sleep mask off her face, then reached to her nightstand and fumbled to turn off her white noise machine. It went quiet, yielding to the slap of rain against the window momentarily lit by a flicker of lightning.

Her son called out again downstairs, his young voice unintelligible. Clara rubbed her forehead, thinking that her husband must be struggling to pull off the morning routine alone. She started to sit up, but stopped short with a grunt as a puppy leapt atop her stomach, racing to lick her face. She pushed him away as her husband rushed into the room, saying, "Thor! Off the bed! *Off!*"

The puppy leapt off the edge of the mattress, landing with a thud beside her husband as he approached the bedside. Jeremy was already showered and fully dressed in business attire as he stopped beside her.

"Hey," he said softly, "how did you sleep?"

Clara sighed, struggling to sit up. Her head was pounding, ears ringing in a high-pitched dial tone. She felt the exhaustion of sleep deprivation, a full-body headache of sorts, and wearily pulled the weighted blanket off her shoulders. "Had a heart attack around midnight, then drank to catch a few hours."

Jeremy sat on the bed beside her, gently pushing the hair out of her face.

"Sorry, babe."

Before Clara could reply, her son Aiden bounded into the room. The four-year-old's face was alight with excitement, his energy barely contained.

Grinning, she braced herself to receive his tight hug. "Good morning, buddy."

"Dad said he's making homemade pizza tonight."

"That's great."

Her son released her, and Jeremy said, "Aiden, why don't you go let Thor outside?"

"Sure," the boy replied. "Mommy, I want to help you make coffee. Don't start without me."

"I won't, buddy."

Aiden darted out of the room with the puppy loping after him, and Clara met Jeremy's concerned gaze.

"I'll be right down," she said.

His eyes softened, and he leaned down to kiss her forehead.

"Take your time. I'll meet you downstairs."

As he rose and left the master suite, Clara looked to the window. The sky was a rolling tumult of storm clouds unleashing torrents of rain on the landscape below.

She inhaled deeply, then released the breath in a beleaguered sigh. Sliding her legs off the bed, Clara wearily rose to begin the day.

* * *

Jeremy was turning off the stove by the time she arrived downstairs, her bare feet crossing the hardwood into the palatial kitchen. She saw he'd already prepared three portions of eggs and avocado, and Aiden was setting an airtight container of coffee beans on the granite countertop.

Clara and Aiden made coffee, the boy dutifully helping as Clara ground the beans and filled the French press. Then the family ate together in the dining room as the puppy disappeared under the table, circling their feet in anticipation of scraps.

Jeremy was a vision of crisp professionalism, his blond hair neatly combed over a pressed button-down and sober necktie. Clara felt like a vagrant by contrast, still in her pajamas with her hair pulled into a hasty ponytail. But no one cared what she looked like at work, and Clara didn't usually put on makeup until a dinner out or weekend foray demanded it.

After breakfast she saw her husband and son off in the three-car garage, buckling Aiden into the kid seat in Jeremy's Maserati and kissing them both goodbye. She watched from the kitchen door while Jeremy backed out of the garage and into the pouring rain.

Clara hit the button for the garage door, waiting as it closed. She turned to hear the puppy whining, his toenails clicking on the hardwood in feverish anticipation.

"I'm coming, I'm coming," she said, rounding the kitchen island to see him spinning and hopping in ecstasy.

She filled his bowl with puppy chow, then set it down as he dove in and began eating, tail wagging furiously.

Then Clara opened the door to the garage once more, checking that the rolling door was closed and taking a lustful glance at her own car.

The gleaming red Cadillac CTS-V looked like a luxury sedan on steroids. The spotless hood had a raised bulge to accommodate the supercharged engine. They quite literally didn't make them like that anymore, she thought, grateful that she'd spent years enjoying what would likely be the last manual transmission 8-cylinder in the Cadillac arsenal.

She closed the door, locking it and testing the handle. Then she walked past the three ground entrances to her house—front porch, side door, and back porch—to make sure deadbolts were engaged. Satisfied, she activated her security system in home mode.

Leaving the puppy to his breakfast, she carried her coffee thermos up the stairs to the third floor and opened the door to the large spare bedroom she'd made into her office. A row of four windows overlooked the backyard, allowing her a full view of the pool and hot tub before spreading into the landscape of the other extravagant homes in the gated community.

But Clara's interest was drawn to the walls without windows, each adorned with whiteboards covered in scrawling dry erase notes and cork boards filled with neatly aligned notecards bearing cryptic handwritten headers.

She walked behind her vintage chestnut desk, positioned in a corner facing the door, and sank into her chair with a wistful sigh.

This was Clara's happy place, her sole refuge in a world that felt increasingly alien and distant. It was the only place she was ever truly relaxed, surrounded by every artifact and treasured possession of her twenty-eight years of life and happily lost amid the work that had come to mean everything to her.

She heard Thor loping up the stairs after her. Clara's only concession to the puppy lay in the corner of her office: a dog bed in which he spent most of the day curled up, asleep. He dutifully took his position there now, laying down his head to watch her. By now he knew the routine. Clara would sit at her desk all morning, rising only to use the restroom. No eating, no work breaks.

She tapped a key and watched her desktop monitor glow to life. Clara didn't check email—that would come later, when her morning shift had elapsed and she reluctantly addressed the drudgery of business particulars. She opened a Word document on her computer desktop and scrolled to the bottom of the file, finding the spot where she'd left off and briefly consulting the cork board. Scanning for the next notecard in the sequence, she found the header she'd written in marker: *ELISE CONFRONTS BRENDAN.*

That was her current scene, and she'd battle with it from now until lunch—or at least, she should have.

Instead she found her fingertips stationary on the keyboard, her mind a gridlock of fatigue. It wasn't a matter of time available, and certainly not discipline. Clara had enough of both to power through any challenges with her current manuscript. But the lack of sleep over the past month had siphoned her energy and ability to comprehend, much less write, her manuscript. If she were an office drone, that might not have mattered much to her overall performance. As an author, it was a devastating blow. There were no rote tasks in writing a novel; it was a meticulous, step-by-step process where every word and intuition mattered, and any author limitations were in plain view on the page.

Which in her case, was currently blank.

Pushing her chair back from the desk, she grabbed her phone. Checking the time, she swiped to her recent calls and tapped the contact marked *KYLE SOLER*.

The call connected, and she heard Kyle's familiar drawl. "What's up, girl?"

Clara smiled at the sound of his voice. His accent went beyond merely Southern, diverging into the deep backwoods lilt that implied pickup trucks and deer hunting, but neither applied to Kyle—these days, he preferred hunting of a different sort.

She answered, "Not much. Another rough night. How are you holding up?"

"Come on now, every night is a rough one for me. That's why they invented alcohol. Still feel like you're getting worse?"

"Definitely. I don't know what's going on, but I don't feel like it will turn around on its own. And I don't want to be drinking every night in front of Aiden, you know?"

"Yeah," he said, "I hear you. So there's something I wanted to tell you about. Don't get your hopes up, but I talked to Alan Smith yesterday."

"How's he doing?"

"He's doing good, real good. Living in Virginia Beach, a couple hours from me. He works at the Jeep dealership, and that's why I called him—my Pathfinder's got 180,000 miles and I'm tired of having to fix something every two weeks, so I asked if he could give me the good-ol'-boy special."

"Can he?"

"Oh yeah, he was thrilled to help out with a trade-in. So anyway, I asked how he was getting on. He said back in January, he got some crazy medical treatment from a doctor in Savannah. Says it turned his whole life around, and if any of our boys were hurting, to pass it along."

Clara smirked. "Kyle, you've ridiculed everything I've ever tried besides drinking."

"You do it right, and drinking's all you need. I just know you've been having a tough time lately, and you were the first person who came to mind."

She grabbed a pen. "Sure, I'll check it out. What's the name?"

"Jannesson." He spelled the name. "Dr. Marcus Jannesson."

She scrawled a note and said, "Thanks, I'll check it out."

"All right, girl, I got a client coming in now. Time for me to get medieval. Get back to your latest masterpiece."

He hung up before she could say goodbye, and Clara turned off her phone and slid it into a desk drawer. Rolling her chair back to the desk, she let her hands settle on the keyboard and faced her book once more.

But the words wouldn't come.

It was a cruel twist of fate, especially to her. Clara had never encountered the slightest hint of writer's block. Nor was that her current problem —if she'd been able to average even five hours of sleep a night, she wouldn't have been able to stop writing. Right now, she just couldn't *think*.

The timing couldn't have been much worse. This manuscript was particularly important, her magnum opus—or one of them, anyway. Clara had made the leap into professional author status with surprising quickness, her trio of thriller novels gaining a solid following in the last two years. Her latest release had made her a *USA Today* bestselling author, and her publisher was confident that the next installment would be a *New York Times* best seller.

But Clara considered the success to be largely hollow, less a credit to her abilities as a writer and more to her publisher's heavy-handed restrictions on what she could and could not write. They were concerned with how every book would fit into a smug marketing plan that was almost entirely reliant on flaunting both her background and a deceptively attractive author photo.

Clara, by contrast, was concerned with her long-term development as an author. And with each thriller she wrote, she sensed more complacency creeping into her writing. She was getting too comfortable, penning action scenes that were becoming second nature. So she'd decided to push her boundaries, taking on a passion project to write a story that had been burning a hole through her. It was no thriller, but a literary novel about a mother, about parenting through tragedy and, ultimately, redemption.

She turned her gaze to a printout of an email between her agent and publisher, detailing the publisher's reservations about her current novel, signaled by a low advance and stern insistence that it must not stifle the schedule of her thriller series. Clara had pinned the email to her board to fuel herself for the current manuscript—she wanted nothing more than to knock this book out of the park and then shove that fact in her publisher's face.

But along with her eagerness to challenge herself came an effect she hadn't anticipated. There were simply too many unanticipated turns in the storyline, and every time Clara thought she knew how the book would turn out she'd uncover a new wrinkle, requiring her to expand the story in complexity and, more significantly to her submission deadline, length.

With a deadline looming in ten days, she was fighting the clock—but still, the words wouldn't come.

She considered the awful truth behind her situation. Plot considerations aside, the novel had a built-in barrier to its completion, one that Clara hadn't anticipated. This particular story allowed her to pour more emotion and trauma into the writing than her thrillers ever had, bringing with it a resurgence of symptoms she'd largely suppressed for the past year—most notably, insomnia. After long ago battling her disease without success, she'd stopped trying to fix herself completely. Her husband had thought she was completely better, but Clara knew the truth. Her disease had simply dwindled to a constant drumbeat in the background of her mind, and she'd fed it with constant work and distraction to get through the day in the hopes that she would sleep each night.

Clara rose from behind her desk, passing a sleeping Thor on her way down the stairs. By the time she reached the second floor, her transition was complete: now she was no longer an author, but a mom tending to her family's needs. She collected clothes hampers and began feeding the contents into her front-load washer. Once the first load was running, she made her rounds through the house to pick up Aiden's toys and put them away. These mechanical actions seemed the only productivity she'd achieve that day, tasks of manual labor that required only the slightest trace of cognitive involvement. Typically, writing was her refuge from reality. But when she couldn't write, Clara instead resorted to these domestic tasks with grudging resignation.

After nearly an hour of cleaning, she deemed the house orderly enough for the time being. She'd accomplished something that morning, at least. Then she returned to her office and took a seat before her computer, finding the cursor still blinking against the file. The story was no further along than when she left it, the morning's coffee proving insufficient to set her mind into motion. She closed the file in frustration.

Clara opened a web browser instead. Clicking the search bar, she looked to the note on her desk and typed in three words.

Dr. Marcus Jannesson

After hitting the search button, Clara opened the first link that appeared on her screen.

2

"It's called cetraphaline," Clara said, maneuvering around Jeremy to fill the electric kettle that night. "I think this could be the one."

Jeremy seemed ambivalent, not pausing from loading the dishwasher as he replied.

"I thought you'd ruled out meds."

She returned the kettle to its base and pressed the button for boil. "I'm not talking about pills. This isn't some addictive opioid or anxiety drug."

"It sounds like a med."

"It's an anesthetic," she said, drawing her phone to consult an article, "that in high doses produces, quote, 'a temporary transpersonal dissociative experience.' Dr. Jannesson's PTSD patients have been reporting, quote, 'transformational resets in their thought patterns, including positive shifts in their contextualization of prior traumatic events, following a single one-hour treatment.'"

She stuffed the phone in her pocket, triumphant.

Jeremy asked, "Clinical trials?"

Clara rolled her eyes. "Come on, man. You know how it is—it's going to be years before there's any official determination. Doctors have been using stellate ganglion blocks for over a decade, and even now in 2021, they *still* don't understand why it works for PTSD."

"But stellate ganglion didn't work for you."

"It worked," she shot back, retrieving a mug and setting it next to the kettle. "It just wore off."

"Don't get me wrong, your sleep is the worst it's been in...a while. Probably since you stopped therapy last year. But I'm afraid that this treatment, this—what's it called?"

"Cetraphaline."

"I'm afraid cetraphaline will end up like everything else you tried back then—ineffective, and potentially counterproductive to your healing. And with the deadline for your manuscript, do you have time to be trying another treatment?"

"If it works, it'll be worth the time. The sleep loss has been devastating to my productivity. It feels like I'm thinking in slow motion; writing is like trying to run underwater."

"What about this doctor, this Jameson?"

"Jannesson," she corrected him, retrieving a plastic storage box from the cabinet and setting it on the counter. "Marcus Jannesson. He was a successful neurosurgeon, and left that behind to focus on PTSD after all the post-9/11 vets came back without any good treatment options. Now he's anti-big pharma, believes in holistic health. Says the overmedication of PTSD patients is a national tragedy."

She began removing the contents of the storage box—tea, two airtight containers, and a pill bottle—and lining them up on the granite counter as Jeremy continued loading the dishwasher behind her.

Finally he said, "Clara, I love you. But you can't heal if you're in denial that you'll ever have to."

The water in the kettle began hissing as it approached the boiling point, and Clara felt her body tense.

"What's that supposed to mean?" she replied, her voice sounding raw.

"It means until you *accept* who you are now, you can't *improve*. And you'll never do either if you're expecting some miracle therapy to fix everything for you. You've been doing great for nearly a year now, and that happened when you stopped trying all those treatments. I don't know what's been going on the past few weeks, but it'll pass."

She plucked a teabag from the box—chamomile with valerian—and dropped it in the mug. "I don't know what's going on either, but this is the worst it's ever been. I don't want to wait around hoping it just goes away.

And this isn't just about me. There have been four, Jeremy. And I need to find something that works—really works—before there's a fifth."

He finished pouring soap in the dishwasher, then put the bottle away. "There's no curse."

"Of course not. But that doesn't mean there's not a very real problem, and it's up to me to fix it."

"You're not responsible for them, Clara. Not anymore."

The electric kettle chimed, and Clara poured the steaming water into the mug. "I became responsible for them after Dakota."

Jeremy hesitated, knowing he was now treading on thin ice. Clara had tried to be objective whenever their conversations traipsed onto the topic of Dakota, but it was an emotional pressure point that ran far too deep.

Finally he said, "I thought we were past this. The obsession with fixing yourself was like playing the lottery instead of getting a job. I don't want to see you go back to that—it wasn't a healthy way to live."

"It's not healthy to be scraping along while averaging three to four hours of broken sleep a night, either."

Clara spun to face the counter, using a spoon to remove the sopping wet tea bag and deposit it in the trash. Then she opened the two airtight containers, both filled with powder, and used a teaspoon to measure her additions to the tea: three grams' worth of ashwagandha root extract and six grams of glycine. Stirring the mixture, she said, "Look at all this crap I'm taking just to have a chance of falling asleep, and that's not counting the CBD."

"But you've been doing great the past year, ever since you stopped looking for a cure."

She deposited her spoon into the dishwasher, considering a response. Clara was too far into her current novel to quit now, and sensed that if she did, things would get worse instead of better.

She released a loud exhale. "Well if I don't figure out something, this is going to tank my writing career."

Then she opened a bottle and shook out two pills—400 milligrams of L-theanine—and washed them down with a sip of hot tea.

Jeremy closed his eyes and sighed, then looked at Clara with a mixture of concern and resignation.

"Clara, I've known you since we were fourteen, and nothing's changed in that time. When you set your mind to something, there's no stopping you. My concern in this case is that you're setting your mind to the wrong goal."

"Agree to disagree," she said firmly.

"Can we call this the last attempt at a new therapy?"

She almost laughed. "Of course we can, Jeremy. There's nothing left to try."

3

Clara awoke with a start, her heart hammering at a breakneck clip. She tore off the sleep mask and sat up, listening over the staticky hum of her white noise machine. Was Aiden crying? The only sound she could make out was rain gently drumming against the window. Clara's pulse soared and her breathing constricted as she realized her violent return to consciousness was nothing more than the usual routine. Which was to say, a random and unpredictable spike in adrenaline with all the physiological effects of mortal danger.

She threw the weighted blanket aside and stood. Continuing to lie in bed would only intensify the panic. There was never a dream, never a flashback. In that, she was lucky—Kyle suffered similar sleep disturbances, but his awakenings followed long and paralyzing dreams in which he was immersed in the many sources of his trauma. Weighed against that, Clara didn't have it so bad.

What she did have, she thought, was this: her dark place, the black surroundings of a house that became a prison in the bowels of the night. She checked the time, saw it was half past midnight. That much was a fortunate reprieve. She'd have time to drink, indulge in her "power hour" of self-medication, and return to bed around 1:30 a.m.—but only if she started now.

She left the bedroom, and the white noise machine faded to the fever pitch of both ears ringing loudly. Irreversible hearing damage, wasn't it grand? She barely noticed the ringing during the day; at night, when she couldn't sleep, it was deafening. Clara navigated her way to the stairs, locating the rail by feel and descending to the ground floor. Her pulse was rocketing now, chest seizing up with crippling intensity. All the sleep experts agreed: when you woke up unexpectedly, you should go to a quiet, dimly lit space and engage in a relaxing activity until you felt tired again.

That was hilarious, she thought as she crossed the kitchen. There were no relaxing activities at times like these, and if she did anything but what she was about to, her body's crisis state would continue until the sun rose, erasing the shadows to make way for the exhaustion that would seamlessly cross into the next cycle of darkness.

Removing a heavy rocks glass from the cabinet, she went to the freezer and wrestled a huge ice cube out of its mold. She dropped the ice in the glass and then moved to her only bastion of hope in the night ahead: her bar cart.

Clara twisted the cork off a bottle of bourbon and poured by the dim ambient glow that penetrated the rain from the security lights surrounding her neighbors' homes, homes that never bore a conscious occupant at times like these. She filled the glass above the cube, probably crossing three shots' worth though she'd never bothered to measure. This was her first round, which she'd finish in twenty to thirty minutes before pouring a second.

She corked the bottle and raised her glass.

"Here's to you, Clara," she whispered, taking the first sip. The warming tingle of alcohol drifted down her core, bringing with it the soothing familiarity of comfort, of relief. Her body's skyrocketing response to some half-remembered terror hadn't subsided yet, but help was close at hand. She drifted to the staircase, placing a hand on the rail to feel her way upward.

Clara continued up two flights, arriving at her office. She crossed into it with a sense of hope—she knew how these nighttime encounters ended, and it was far preferable to any possible alternative.

Sitting at her desk, she felt for the leather coaster bearing an embossed American flag. She set the glass atop it, letting her fingers flutter across the keyboard until her desktop monitor glowed to life. Adjusting the brightness to the minimum setting, she sat before her work in progress.

Clara took another long sip of bourbon, forcing alcohol into her bloodstream. She began to type, seamlessly falling in tune with the manuscript. But her raging heartbeat prevented her from relaxing into the writing process, presenting an unwelcome irritation to progress. She took another drink.

The lines began to flow, her word count increasing in inverse proportion with the remaining bourbon. Her writing was stark, fluid, the prose singing forth from her fingertips. Then she was in the story itself, an observer hastily transcribing the proceedings as she heard her characters talking to one another. She'd crossed the threshold; she was a silent party to the story as it unfolded, the dialogue cracking in her ringing ears with utter clarity. Clara reached for the glass and took another sip, feeling the diminished ice cube hit her lips with a slurry of water.

Time for her second round. If she waited too long, the drift toward sobriety would require a third drink, and that would spell another forty-five minutes to an hour awake. She checked the clock: five past one in the morning. Right on schedule.

Clara left her office, carrying the glass down the stairs toward her bar cart. Her pulse had calmed somewhat, heartbeat slowing to a manageable rate. The ringing in her ears had now subsided to a faint background noise.

She turned on the landing, feeling for the rail.

Yes, there had been a few nights that she didn't remember going back to bed. And there had been times where she remembered going to bed, but returned to her manuscript the next day to find that an inspired scene had devolved into incomprehensible jargon, an awkward stream-of-consciousness parade of misspelled words that not even Clara herself could decipher.

But for the most part, she'd learned to moderate her use of alcohol with an anesthesiologist's precision. Too much drinking would unnecessarily impact her productivity the next day; too little would result in her being unable to sleep, forced to drink even more in order to put herself down. The sweet spot was just the right amount to calm her frayed nerves, to put her mind in a blissful state where she could achieve some truly good writing before returning to bed and sleeping soundly. And Clara had gotten increasingly good at drinking that right amount.

Because by now she knew the alternative. Drinking had its drawbacks, yes. But it was preferable to the soul-crushing experience of watching the sun rise while sober, and facing the new day with no respite from the previous one.

She'd vowed never to do that again.

As she approached her bar cart for the second time that night, a painful memory flashed through her mind. The breaking point had occurred after a twelve-round treatment with a therapist who'd convinced Clara that drinking further repressed her difficult memories rather than allowing her mind to process them. So Clara had agreed to stop drinking, to face the consequences in an attempt to achieve some gradual improvement.

The results had been catastrophic.

After two weeks, her sleep was whittled to an hour a night. She transformed into a zombie, her beloved Cadillac sitting unused because Clara didn't trust her ability to operate it. And contrary to what the therapist had insisted, there had been no "processing" of emotion or memory. There had only been long nights where her pulse hammered at a dead sprint, her body coursing along on a panicked fight-or-flight response to a threat that was no longer there and hadn't been for years.

The experiment with constant sobriety had culminated when Clara found herself sobbing uncontrollably, sitting on the ground floor of her house so she wouldn't wake her family upstairs. The sunrise had entered through the windows with a pale glow that transformed her surroundings from the dark prison of her mind to a well-appointed, grand Southern home. She hadn't slept, not for a minute. The long succession of sleepless nights had by then put her brain into a vise of constant pressure. It was Aiden's third birthday.

She'd put on a lackluster performance, trying to be the mother that Aiden deserved and failing miserably. Her son had spent more time asking what was wrong with Mommy than he did enjoying his party, which was attended by Charleston trophy wives casting concerned glances her way and whispering conspiratorially among themselves. Was Aiden's mother drunk? High?

Clara had decided then and there that her forced bout of sobriety was at its end. After putting Aiden to bed that night, she had two glasses of bourbon and slept for six hours straight.

And when she returned to her therapist to report the cataclysmic failure of his suggestion, the counterproductive response she'd had to everything in his treatment plan, he'd reacted in the same way as every one before him.

He reached for his prescription pad.

Antidepressants, anti-anxiety, antipsychotic, mood stabilizers. Pick your cliché—they were all the same. These pills were the ultimate fallback, the medical equivalent of a doctor throwing up their hands in defeat. Every therapy led toward that dead end, the final surrender to medication.

That's when Clara realized the truth. None of these so-called experts knew anything more about PTSD treatment than she did; they were masters of a narrow domain, and when that domain failed to help or even made her condition worse, they tried to pawn her off on the pharmaceutical industry.

Every treatment began the same way, too. There was a condescending twenty-minute lecture about the evils of alcohol, to which Clara always gave the same response: you show me something that works, and I'll stop drinking today. Weeks later, they were reaching for the ubiquitous prescription pad, or pointing her toward someone who could.

Clara filled her glass with bourbon, stopping a fraction of an inch lower than the previous pour to account for the reduced volume of melted ice. Ordinarily she'd restock her glass with a new cube, but her manuscript was waiting, and the characters continued to talk in her head whether she was writing or not.

Recorking the bottle, Clara took her drink and hurried back upstairs.

4

Clara accelerated up to the rear bumper of a Toyota Prius, then braked to tailgate it.

It wasn't her fault—if you weren't going to break the speed limit like a normal driver, just stay out of the fast lane until you had to pass someone. Better yet, if you're driving a Prius, stay out of the fast lane altogether. Particularly on Interstate 95.

The sun blazed high in the sky, a welcome sight after the days of rain that had smothered Charleston. Not that the weather mattered much to Clara—rain or shine, she was usually in her office, grinding away at the next book.

The Prius gradually overtook the semi it had been halfheartedly attempting to pass, then put on its turn signal and slowly drifted into the right lane.

Clara reached for her stick shift, emblazoned with six gear positions surrounding the V logo of Cadillac's Performance Division. She down-shifted to fifth and popped the clutch, flooring the gas at the same time.

The CTS-V's engine roared amidst the thin whine of the super-charger, and Clara was sucked to her seat as she whipped around the Prius, barely clearing its bumper when she deemed the lane change to be of insufficient urgency for her taste. Then she was off again, passing through the hundred-mile-per-hour barrier with no more effort than it took to sip coffee from the thermos in her cup holder, which she did now.

She let off the gas at a hundred and fifteen miles per hour, letting her momentum carry her all the way to the next obstacle—another Toyota blocking the lane a quarter mile ahead, keeping perfect pace with a vehicle in the slow lane beside it. Amateurs, Clara thought.

She didn't have many chances to drive like this anymore. Since moving to Charleston—a move that corresponded with becoming an author—her thirty-minute commute with long stretches of country road had dwindled to a walk up the stairs to her office, and the CTS-V sat unused more than ever. And when she did get to take it out, Jeremy was more often than not in the passenger seat, subtly bracing his hands on the console and door handle as he warned her to slow down.

Jeremy couldn't even drive a manual transmission, and that was just as well. He treated his Maserati like a school bus, letting Aiden eat in the kid seat and scatter crumbs with reckless abandon. Clara couldn't stand driving the Italian car—it was responsive enough, and the sound of the exhaust note was divine by anyone's standards. But she could never get past the fact that her twelve-year-old Cadillac beat it out by 132 horsepower and a full second in the sprint from zero to sixty, all while costing thirty grand less and being made in America. None of that mattered to Jeremy, of course, who merely needed a status car for work. He drove it like a soccer mom anyway, rarely breaking the speed limit and even then by no more than five miles an hour or, if he was feeling particularly edgy, ten.

Clara liked driving like a bat out of hell, and always had.

Even her first four-cylinder Pontiac in high school was flogged mercilessly on the backroads and interstate, operating at redline so often it was a miracle it lasted as long as it did. Her father had taught her how to drive a stick, and automatic transmissions seemed impossibly boring after that. So Clara had saved money with a vengeance to afford the down payment on a used CTS-V, and then taken a significant loan to cover the difference. Paying it off had taken years, and now the title in the glovebox represented the fulfillment of a dream that began with wistful nightly research and fantasy sessions while she was in college.

Clara hadn't met many guys who were into cars, and exactly zero women.

Until she met Dakota.

She let off the gas, fumbling for her phone and taking a picture of the sign reading *Exit 5: Savannah*.

Slowing to negotiate the offramp at seventy, she texted the picture to Kyle with the message, *Guess where I'm headed?*

Her phone rang almost immediately, and Clara smiled. She pressed a button on the steering wheel to answer the call, and Kyle's Southern drawl sounded through the car's Bose speakers.

He asked, "You in the V?"

"You know it."

"She perfectly waxed?"

"Come on, Kyle, what kind of woman do you take me for? Three coats of Pete's 53 at all times."

"That's my girl. You really doing this thing?"

"Have an appointment in thirty minutes."

He laughed, a throaty giggle that never ceased to amuse Clara.

"I hope it works for you, but you might be better off spending that money at a liquor store. Look at WWII vets...they came home, they didn't talk about it, they drank. No one tried to fix them."

"Maybe," Clara allowed, "but they didn't have cetraphaline."

"You go ride that dragon then, girl. Lemme know how it goes."

"I will." She ended the call, then pulled up the navigation app on her phone. The journey was supposed to be two hours, but Clara was on track to arrive an hour and thirty-seven minutes after leaving her house. Not bad, considering all the left-lane sloths she'd had to battle on the way.

The sound of Kyle's voice never failed to put her in good spirits, but her mood darkened at the sight of a homeless man ahead, standing on the corner to beg. The light was red, and Clara downshifted as she braked, hoping it would switch to green before she had to come to a complete stop.

No such luck.

She brought the CTS-V to a stop next to the man. He was a true vagrant, unshaven and disheveled, holding a piece of cardboard with five crudely scrawled words.

VETERAN. BLIND. HOMELESS. GOD BLESS.

Clara kept her eyes forward, muscles tense in anticipation of him approaching her car. When he didn't, she glanced over as subtly as she could, unsure if the man was actually blind.

Seeing his eyes erased all doubt—both irises were milky and opaque, gazing out at an unseen world. He shifted slightly to face Clara, the rumbling growl of her idling engine leaving no doubt that he was being ignored.

The light turned green, and Clara floored the gas.

Her CTS-V ripped off the line, roaring to sixty with a shift to second gear in just over four seconds. Then she slowed, trying to forget the man as she consulted her phone's final directions to her destination.

5

The nurse drove the needle a fraction of an inch into Clara's arm, and when a flash of blood filled the chamber, she slid a catheter off the needle and into the vein.

Connecting a clear line of tubing, the nurse adjusted the saline drip of the IV bag tethered to a rolling stand. "And don't worry about these lights. For the treatment, we'll darken the room so it's nice and relaxing for you."

Clara smirked. It was hard to imagine a more relaxing setting than this —the room was appointed more like a spa than a medical facility. The walls were paneled with teak wood, a Himalayan salt candle glowed on a corner table, and the zero gravity chair was probably the most comfortable thing Clara had ever sat in.

All of this made her even more confused about the nervousness she felt.

Objectively speaking, there was no reason to be uncomfortable. A year earlier, Clara had undergone medical treatments ranging from the claustrophobic—her brain MRI came to mind—to the invasive. A stellate ganglion block required the doctor to slowly plunge a needle into her neck, and Clara had undergone the procedure on ten separate occasions. Today, by contrast, would be nothing more than a standard IV and a couple shots.

So why did she feel scared?

The door opened, and Clara recognized Dr. Marcus Jannesson at once.

He was a hulking, broad-shouldered white man in a checkered blazer, with a receding hairline and an auburn mustache that transitioned to gray in a neat goatee. He wore thin glasses, and the eyes behind them were youthful and intelligent as he greeted her.

"Hi, Clara. I'm Marcus Jannesson."

She shook his outstretched hand, unsure what to say and settling on, "Nice to meet you."

He took a seat in the chair opposite hers, crossing one leg over the other and addressing the nurse. "Debbie, could you give us a minute?"

"Of course."

The nurse left, closing the door behind her.

"So." Jannesson leaned forward. "Tell me a little about why you're here."

"PTSD," Clara said.

He smiled. "It's just PTS, Clara. Not a disorder. It is an entirely normal —and unavoidable—human response to trauma. The stigma surrounding mental health issues is nothing more than public ignorance of our evolutionary biology. Can you tell me about the symptoms you've been experiencing?"

She paused, swallowing hard. "Mostly insomnia. I never have dreams or flashbacks, but I have a really hard time getting to sleep. After that, it's a crapshoot on whether I stay asleep, or for how long. And it's been getting a lot worse over the past four weeks or so. I'll just burst awake randomly, and it feels like I'm having a heart attack."

"What do you do when that happens?"

"I drink. It's the only way I can get back to sleep."

Jannesson nodded, as if he'd been expecting to hear that. "Alcohol releases naturally occurring opioids that produce feelings of reward and pleasure, and sometimes those positive emotions aren't achievable any other way for people afflicted with severe PTS. How much does it take to go back to sleep?"

Clara thought for a moment. "Six, maybe seven shots' worth."

"Well I see why you came in. That's no way to live your life."

"Not with a child to take care of, it's not."

"Any other symptoms, Clara?"

"Sure," she said. "Hypervigilance, constant muscle tension. I don't like crowds, I don't like when anyone stands close to me besides my husband and son."

"What about emotional detachment from other people—friends, loved ones?"

Her eyes burned. "Yes."

"Suicidal ideation?"

"No."

"Clara," he said, "it's just you and me here. No one's going to lock you in a padded room. Any suicidal ideation?"

"Yes. At night, when I can't sleep. It seems like a really good idea then."

He nodded. "Totally normal for cases like yours. Almost universal, in my experience. What treatments have you previously tried?"

"A year ago, I went through the whole alphabet soup: CBTI, CPT, EMDR, and SGB. Plus acupuncture and a few other things that turned out to be money pits. Everything has ended in someone trying to push a prescription on me when their method doesn't work."

Jannesson gave a frustrated sigh. "The great tragedy of our era, and the shame of my profession. Well." He brightened. "I'm a big advocate for cannabidiol. Aside from the obvious medical benefits, I like the fact that big pharma hates it—try though they may, they can't patent a plant. Have you tried full spectrum CBD?"

"Every night," she said, "1000-milligram strength, half a dropper under the tongue for sixty seconds before swallowing. Along with glycine, ashwagandha, and theanine."

"Excellent, Clara. That's excellent. That combination can be very effective in treating insomnia, so I'm glad you're on top of it already. But you need some real relief from the root cause of your suffering, not just mitigation of the symptoms."

Clara shifted in her chair. "Well that's why I'm here—cetraphaline is the last stop now that I've tried everything else."

"Within the next few years, I think cetraphaline will be the first stop, not the last. Are you familiar with how it works?"

"I'm not gonna lie, Doc. I read every single word on your website, and I didn't understand any of it."

He laughed. "That's not surprising, unless you have a background in neurology. There is some evidence that cetraphaline rewires your brain in beneficial ways, and most of my patients describe the treatment as connecting with the Real, or the infinite, or the divine."

She shifted in the chair. "I hope you're not going to get all spiritual on me, Doc. That's not really my area."

"Nor is it mine. I think the way cetraphaline works is much simpler. From what I've seen, the high doses provide access to our entire subconscious. And that ninety-five percent of your brain stores every memory, thought, and interaction from your entire life experience. By opening those neural channels, cetraphaline allows patients to make connections that would take a dedicated psychiatrist months, or even years, of therapy sessions to uncover."

"Have you ever taken it?"

"I have, though not for PTS. I just won't advocate a treatment that I haven't personally tried."

"What was it like for you?"

"Beautiful. Moving. And I...I came out of the treatment knowing I needed a divorce."

"For my husband's sake," she said, "I hope I have a very different experience. Do you have any family now?"

He shook his head. "My work is my life, no family for me. But I'm confident that your experience with cetraphaline should tell you whatever you need to know. Obviously everyone is different, but more often than not my patients come out of that chair a different person than when they sat down. I don't think you'll regret coming in today, despite how unconventional the treatment is."

Clara shrugged. "After everything I've tried, you can stick needles in my eyes. You want to try any experimental stuff, go right ahead for all I care."

This made him laugh again. "Everything's experimental, Clara. I'll come see you after the treatment, and then I'd like to set up some follow-up calls in the weeks ahead to see how you're doing. Would that be okay?"

"Of course."

Jannesson stood. "Well, it was great meeting you. I'll send the nurse back in, and you can get started." He opened the door. "Debbie? I think we're all set here."

He left as the nurse entered, now carrying a box that she set down on the side table and opened.

First she handed Clara a sleep mask. "You'll want this over your eyes, sweetheart."

Clara put it on, and her world became pitch black. She closed her eyes.

Then the nurse said, "Twenty minutes after the first shot, I'll come back in with the second injection. If you need anything in the meantime, just call for me—I'll be in the next room. Ready for the headphones?"

"Sure," Clara said.

The nurse positioned the headphones, and Clara's ears were filled with a melodic rhythm of flutes and windchimes. Over the music, she heard the nurse ask, "All ready?"

"Ready when you are. Let's ride the dragon."

Clara felt the nurse pull up a sleeve, and the cool moisture of a disinfecting swab on her shoulder. Then the needle plunged through her skin, hitting a nerve and sending a twitch of pain. She felt a squirt of liquid entering the muscle, and the needle withdrew.

"Thank you," Clara said. She wasn't sure if the nurse answered or not, but the door to the room closed a moment later, and Clara was alone.

And then she felt...nothing. Her breathing was calm as she awaited the medicine's effects, but there were none yet. Instead, the song in her headphones transitioned to an Asian melody with wood flutes and birdsong. Clara had the brief thought that she'd have to purge her mind with some classic rock on the ride back. Then the song's tune became staticky and distorted, interspersed with a rhythmic crunching noise that sounded to Clara like glass breaking. The noise morphed into a booming bass drum that increased in volume until it was uncomfortable—what kind of person selected this song for a so-called relaxing playlist?

Then Clara realized that she was no longer listening to a song at all.

The deep booming noise was occurring within her own body, starting in her chest and radiating a shuddering vibration all the way down her limbs and into her fingers and toes. The vibrations increased in strength until she felt her entire body shaking, and the sensation became one of an electrical current surging through her. A muscle in her abdomen twitched, and then her stomach seized up in a painful cramp; suddenly she couldn't breathe at all. The first gasping attempt brought a wave of panic, until Clara was able to force thin, rasping half-breaths through her constricted throat.

Her hands became vises, curling in a numb state of paralysis. She couldn't move, could barely breathe, and still felt like she was being electrocuted. Spikes of discomfort seared from her eyes into her brain, causing an agony unlike anything she'd ever felt. She wasn't sure if she'd be able to call out to the nurse, and resolved not to—she'd lost all control of her life long before this point, and was desperate for a solution. If this medicine fixed her, she could bear any pain, pay any cost it demanded.

But Clara was shaking now, her stomach a heavy stone, eyes aflame. Then she saw herself standing naked in the darkness of her mind—her body was withering into a shriveled corpse that nonetheless stood erect, eyes transforming into the milky opaqueness of the blind man she'd seen on the corner.

The body in her mind's eye began flipping with the blind man, her shriveled corpse for his living one. The haunted white eyes remained as the two bodies flickered from one to the other with increasing frequency until they were both one, the same single figure of death, ivory eyes staring out into nothingness. She heard a deep booming voice echo in her skull.

You will be blind. You will be homeless. God bless.

The voice continued, disjointed and spewing venomous fragments of thought into her mind. *You will be...blind...homeless homeless blind veteran...God...God Clara...*

She resisted the voice, trying to move but no longer cognizant of where her body was, or if it existed in the real world any longer. Clara groped for any shred of light, the slightest memory of who she was or if escape was possible, but there was only the voice.

Blind...God you will be...you have no home...blindness you will...I'm coming for you, Clara, I'm coming and I will find you...Aiden and Jeremy dead...a river of blood in your home...you will be last blind homeless homeless blind...the death you inflicted will find you...the price you pay...the suffering, the suffering will begin, veteran...

Clara heard the door open—had it been twenty minutes? She had no concept of time anymore, and when she tried to speak, her voice came out in a choking rasp.

"Can you check the dose...something's wrong..." Her body was still shaking, twitching spasmodically, her eyes an inferno of scorching pain.

She felt the nurse lift the headphone from her left ear and speak quietly. "There's nothing wrong with the dose. The medicine is working through something, Clara. Do you want the second shot?"

Clara felt horror seizing her in devastating waves, a fear born of this new nightmare she'd descended into. It took her only seconds to answer—she'd answered that question in some form long before coming to this clinic, before she'd ever discovered Dr. Jannesson or cetraphaline—but those seconds were filled with the unspeakable pain she'd been living with. The constant fear and dread, the gnawing anxieties that tore her apart in the middle of the night, her reduction to an animalistic state of survival that nonetheless called for her to kill herself.

"Yes," she gasped. "Give me the shot...the shot..."

The needle plunged into her shoulder and darted out again, the door opening and slamming shut with a shotgun blast that felt like a baseball bat to her skull. Her pain intensified, the electrocuting vibrations in her body reaching a fever pitch until they were continuous, a soprano peak of despair, and Clara's lungs froze. She couldn't breathe, couldn't think or move. She tried to call out to the nurse, but her throat was frozen in the paralyzing grip of an invisible hand, and in that moment Clara sensed that she was going to die, that she was already dead.

Then all pain fell away, and Clara was lost in a soothing rhythm of thought, her body descending into a languid pool of impossible relaxation. She had the sensation of flying, saw lush green hills through wisps of cloud that she soared through with incredible freedom. The view exploded into psychedelic color, infinite fractal patterns that emanated warmth and emotion, pulsating into new configurations that morphed over and over into visions of ever-increasing harmony.

Clara felt a sense of extraordinary momentum and energy, an eternal hope that filled her beyond her capacity to imagine, and amid the beauty was a presence of infinite love. When she saw the face of that love, it was Dakota.

At the moment of recognition, Clara was flung through an eternity of sparkling effervescence that opened into an eternal void. And in that void, rotating end over end like a spinning top, was her car.

Was it? Yes, a glistening Cadillac CTS-V turning end over end in a gyroscopic rotation. The sight brought a deep howling fear in her soul, and her mind reeled with the dissonance—she loved that car, loved that car, didn't she?—and then the car was replaced by Dakota's face, and Clara felt love. The car returned, and then Dakota was back, and the two images flickered from one to the other, the speed of the transition quickening as Clara felt intense fear and love in ever-shorter durations.

But the images were flickering too fast, until they were the same, love and fear now one entity, and the car and Dakota another. Clara had a flash of insight that this was as it was for the universe—all things as one, a cosmic unity whose only distinctions were a result of human perception—and as this thought dawned on her, the voice spoke.

The CTS-V is Dakota's ghost.

Clara's brain locked up then, with the exception of a single conscious thought: *what in God's name is* that *supposed to mean?*

Then Clara's consciousness darted through a rapid-fire chain of memories, each as lucid as if she were living it again.

Clara was an Army lieutenant in Afghanistan, wearing body armor with her rifle slung, dreading the moment ahead. An embedded journalist was being forced on her platoon, and Clara would have to hide her contempt. Clara was alarmed to find that the journalist was both female and beautiful.

"Lieutenant Swanner? I'm Dakota Goldsmith."

Clara was taken aback by Dakota's hazel eyes, sculpted eyebrows, and impossibly high cheekbones. She looked like a model, and Clara's first thought was that Dakota was going to cause a riot among the men of her platoon.

Clara's second thought, occurring after Dakota's next question, was *you've got to be kidding me.*

"You drive a V?" She was pointing to the V logo patch that Clara wore on her body armor.

Stunned, Clara answered, "CTS-V, three pedals."

"Cool," Dakota said. "I drive an ATS-V, six-speed as well."

Then Clara flew through a dazzling universe of color, arriving at a second memory—this one from another day, the day that had defined her existence ever since.

The gunfight was raging in Pantalay Village, and Clara recognized the scene as roughly two hours into the battle. She was running beside the qalat wall, panting hard amid the crackle of incoming and outgoing gunfire. Dakota was crouching beside the wall, snapping pictures of Clara as she ran—my God, Clara thought, this woman was going to get herself killed over these pictures—and no sooner had the thought crossed her mind than a low *thump* sounded from one of the buildings to her left.

Clara recognized the sound, knew what was going to happen even before she caught the thin wisp of smoke streaking toward her. She dove atop Dakota, flinging both of them prone a second before the rocket impacted the building beside them.

Bracing herself for the blast, Clara found herself instead flying backward through space, passing a whirling kaleidoscope of colors that congealed into a single picture: Dakota's view of Clara as she ran, a moment that had occurred seconds before the explosion that nearly killed them both. The view zoomed in on Clara's body armor, settling on the V patch that now shifted from its desert brown into full color.

The images vanished then, having started and ended in the span of ten seconds despite encapsulating every detail, and the voice spoke again.

Your CTS-V and her ATS-V are the same car in your psyche—and it's deeply connected to Dakota. That car is the reason you can't let go—the reason you're three years out of the military and still can't sleep. You used to smile every time you saw that car, but you haven't felt that way since Dakota died. You wore the V patch in Pantalay Village. Now, that symbol represents the most horrific things you've ever seen. In your mind, the CTS-V is a portal to Pantalay, and you're parking it under your son's bedroom every night and wondering why you can't sleep. It is your last connection with the past you want to leave behind. Dakota is free now; let the V go.

Clara was panting for breath now, trying to invoke further revelations. She understood it all now, and wanted to know what else she should do.

But there was nothing—no colors, no memories. She heard the windchimes and bamboo flutes in her headphones and was suddenly aware that she was in a zero gravity chair, in Dr. Jannesson's clinic in Savannah, being treated with cetraphaline.

Clara felt exhaustion and yet an impossible lightness of being. It was as if a dense root structure had been ripped out of her body through her head, leaving behind total and complete relaxation.

She pulled off the headphones and then her sleep mask. The room existed exactly as before, now dark save the glow of the Himalayan salt lamp in the corner.

There was a sliver of blinding light as the door opened, and Clara squinted up to see the nurse entering with a smile.

"Well," she asked, "how do you feel?"

6

The gym echoed with the clanging of metal weights, and Kyle resumed his spotting position behind the bench.

"You ready?" he asked.

The man on the bench shook his head and panted, "No."

"Do it anyway. Go, go."

Kyle and the man lifted the bar off the rack, and Kyle released his hands to transfer the weight to his client.

The man began bench pressing the bar with a series of straining grunts, and Kyle half-supervised the effort with a sense of disdain.

His personal training clients were almost universally like the man struggling to complete a bench press right now. They all had some story about how they'd almost joined the military themselves, but there was always some pivotal figure in their life—a mom, a girlfriend—who'd told them not to, and they'd carried that excuse for the rest of their lives as the sole reason they weren't some kind of war hero today. Whatever that story was, they usually told it to Kyle by the second session. By the third session, they'd be asking him for stories from combat. He'd tell them all the same thing—you want to touch the magic, go find a recruiter.

They never did, of course. That's why they hired Kyle instead: to brag about being trained by a combat veteran, to feel some vicarious association with the military by listening to him berate them on their fitness. That was just fine by him. This wasn't a bad gig, after all. Plenty of money for alimony and plenty of time off to drink and cavort with the steady stream of women he met through the gym and in bars.

There goes another one, he thought, watching a twenty-something blonde sashay past in yoga pants and a pink sports bra, flipping her pony-tail to shoot him a look he knew well. He'd run through enough of the female members here to have gained a reputation. You want a good time, no strings, with a tatted-up muscle man who doesn't realize that sexual boundaries are a thing? You want to be tied up, try out all those toys, the leather, the rubber, whatever porn star fantasies you've never admitted to anyone? Call Kyle.

And they did.

At this point it was shooting fish in a barrel. They had him on speed dial, the freaks in their twenties and the desperate unmarried thirty-some-things who sought any validation they could get, and Kyle was happy to oblige. Three different women rotating through his apartment was a slow week for him; usually it was five to seven, sometimes two in a day and sometimes two at a time. When he wasn't getting laid, it wasn't because he lacked options—it was because his body needed a break.

After a few days he'd get bored of stumbling drunk in his apartment alone, and the parade would resume. Come on in, ladies, the bar is stocked. Kyle hadn't even watched porn since his last divorce. There was no need, not anymore.

An odd wheezing sound interrupted his thoughts, and he looked down to see his client struggling to breathe, the bar pressing against his chest as his arms shook to hold it.

"Really, man?" Kyle said in disgust, grabbing the bar and helping the man hoist it upward. "We're only on the second set."

They racked the bar, and Kyle said, "Gonna be a long session for you today, buddy. We're just getting warmed up."

His client said nothing—he was occupied by gasping for air—and Kyle felt the phone buzz in his pocket. The display read, *CLARA SWANNER.*

"I have to take this. Get in the front leaning rest."

The man sighed wearily and dropped into the push-up position beside the bench.

Kyle took a few steps away and answered his phone. "So how'd it go, girl? You make it out alive?"

"I'm alive," Clara said. "It was...incredible. Absolutely incredible. I'm driving back to Charleston now."

"I want to hear it all. Tell me everything."

"Well, it was transformational, to say the least. Scary at first, and then transformational. Are you sitting down?"

"No. Tell me anyway."

"I'm getting rid of the V."

Kyle felt his mouth fall open. "Then this ain't the Clara Swanner I know, because *that* Clara wouldn't let go of that car to save her life. What did they do to you in there?"

"It was...kind of like a realization. I had some rapid-fire flashbacks, and realized a negative attachment to Dakota."

"Oh." He nodded. "Because she drove the same thing?"

"She had an ATS-V, it's a six-banger, but—yeah, close enough. And the attachment had to do with me wearing the V patch in that gunfight. A voice in my head called this car 'a portal to Pantalay,' and after I came out of the trip, I couldn't even bear to have the key fob in my pocket. I kid you not, the keys are sitting on the passenger seat right now."

Kyle noticed his client struggling to maintain the push-up position, his back bowing with fatigue.

"Hang on," he said to Clara, and then ordered, "Put your knees down and start knocking 'em out."

The man's knees hit the ground immediately, and he began cranking weak push-ups.

His client groaned. "I'm paying you a hundred dollars an hour...and you're...on the...phone..."

"Shut up," Kyle said, "and I've got a special finisher for today's session since you want to run your mouth. You join the military and go to combat, and I'll answer your calls too."

Then he brought the phone to his ear and continued, "Sorry. This is a lot to process. That car has been the center of your universe since I've known you. You could put it in storage, or park it at my place, take some time to think about this—"

"I'll think about it for the next hour until I get back to Charleston, and

34

then it's gone. I'm not even going home first—I don't want it near my house. I'm driving straight to the dealer to trade it in."

"What are you going to get instead?"

"Doesn't matter. I want this car gone yesterday. I don't care if all they have to trade is a minivan in Mary Kay pink."

"Good God," he scoffed, seeing that his client's push-ups had gone from weak to absurd parodies of the exercise. "Hang on."

Lowering the phone, he said, "You want to cheat yourself? Air squat. Any more backtalk and you'll be holding a ten-pound plate while you're at it."

The man said nothing this time, laboring himself to a standing position and then squatting until his knees were bent ninety degrees, his arms stretched out before him.

Kyle raised the phone to his ear. "Did you relive anything from combat?"

"A little, yeah. But everything from combat was insignificant compared to what I realized. I feel like a totally different person—I'm serious. You have to do this. We need to tell the platoon; I'll pay for every single one of their treatments if I have to."

Kyle was emphatic. "Uh-uh, no way, girl. You see the results first. It worked for Alan, but he's always been kind of a weirdo. I hope it'll work for you—Lord knows if it does, I'll head down to Savannah myself—but the last thing those kids need is false hope. Just give it a week or a couple, see how you do."

"I guess. Yeah, that's probably a good idea."

"Course it is," Kyle said. "It came from me. Text me a picture of your new car when you get it, would you? I want to see what you end up with."

"I will. Thanks, Kyle. Thanks for...well, everything."

He ended the call, pocketing his phone and turning his attention back to his client. The man was now trembling in the squat position, his face flushed as he panted for air.

"Get back on the bench," Kyle ordered, taking up his position as spotter. "You owe me two more sets."

7

———————

Clara pulled through the gate of her neighborhood, the road lit by the headlights of her BMW M235i. It was a peppy turbo six-cylinder, and by far the best of all available options. There was nothing on the used lot with a manual transmission, but Clara didn't care about that anymore. The CTS-V had become an object of disgust that she didn't want to bring near her house, much less her family, ever again.

Jeremy and Aiden were waiting on the front porch, and Clara smiled at the sight of them. She'd barely stepped out of the car when Aiden raced down the steps and into her arms. Clara hugged him tightly and said, "I love you, buddy."

"I love you too, Mommy! I wanna see your car!"

She let him crawl over the front seat, then turned to face Jeremy.

They clung to each other in a long, wordless embrace, punctuated by Aiden shouting inside the car, "My kid seat is back here!"

Clara pulled back from Jeremy and kissed him, then buried her face in his shoulder.

"I'm so sorry for everything I put you guys through."

She felt Jeremy shaking his head. "You didn't put us through anything, babe. I'm glad you're home."

Clara met his eyes, feeling a sudden rush of validation that her marriage had just been saved. The thought of him leaving her had become a recurring one, sometimes bringing with it a full-fledged depressive episode.

But Jeremy was looking at her with a renewed sense of curiosity—Clara had tried a lot of treatments, and she'd never returned much different than when she left. She said, "This was exactly what I needed. Thank you for supporting me through all this. I haven't been the wife or mother that you and Aiden deserve, and I'm going to make it up to you."

She pulled the BMW into the garage with Aiden in her lap, his hands gripping the leather-wrapped steering wheel as if he were piloting a spacecraft.

They went inside the house to Thor's excited yelps, the puppy beside himself at the sight of Clara. She knelt to greet him, ruffling his brindle fur as he pranced. Clara owed this creature a little love too, she thought; she'd refused the prospect of a dog until Aiden's desire had overshadowed her resistance, and for the first time she felt a deep empathy for the puppy that she'd largely ignored before this point.

Jeremy and Clara went through the bedtime paces, giving Aiden his bath and then reading a succession of children's books—about dragons and knights, talking animals that learned the true meaning of friendship, a boy facing his fears on the first day of kindergarten—before tucking him in.

Clara remained in the room after Jeremy departed, lying on the bed beside her yawning son.

"I'm so proud of you, Aiden. Me and Daddy love you so much."

He was fading fast, one arm absently stroking Thor's fur, the puppy now curled beside him. Before they'd gotten the dog, Aiden had a favorite blanket that filled this role. He'd forgotten all about it once Thor arrived, and now the boy and his dog slept together every night, inseparable.

When Aiden didn't answer, Clara saw that his breathing had gone soft and shallow, his hand motionless atop the dog.

She leaned over to kiss Aiden's forehead and then delicately rose from the bed. Clara felt completely at peace, her body loose and craving sleep in a way she hadn't for years. She had no energy to return downstairs and make her nighttime tea, no energy to do anything other than cross the landing to her master suite where Jeremy was waiting.

They made love in their bed, Clara's body achieving a sensuous rhythm as she climaxed effortlessly on her back, on her stomach, then finally on her hands and knees. And after Jeremy had finished, the smell of their love faintly reaching her nose like a distant bouquet, Clara lapsed into sleep.

* * *

Clara dreamt that night, and it was a pleasant dream, one of her fondest memories from the deployment to Afghanistan.

She was seated for dinner in the chow tent, a well-lit enclosure that stood in stark contrast to the other buildings and tents in their platoon outpost. Most areas of the base were work-related by design, with designated spaces for mission briefs, equipment storage, and heavy weapons cleaning. But the chow tent was reserved for meals and recreation, hosting the platoon's flat-screen television and video game consoles. Work was discussed in the tent, of course, but for the most part, it was the only place on the outpost where the soldiers could relax, hang out, and generally pretend they were back in America. With a six-month deployment where there was no vacation time or days off, its value to the men—and to Clara— was immeasurable.

The rest of the platoon wore a mix of duty fatigues and workout attire, and was generally seated by team and squad. Clara was alone at her table, and she watched Dakota enter the tent with a tray of food. Dakota's eyes lit up at the sight of Clara, and she approached to take a seat. She'd never seen what was about to occur, and Clara decided to let her find out the same way she had herself: by witnessing the proceedings with the same surprise as the target.

Dakota sat down. "Hey, how's it going?"

"Good," Clara said. "Everything's fine."

Dakota hesitated, squinting at Clara in a mixture of curiosity and concern.

"Are you...worried about the patrol tomorrow?"

"No. Why?"

"Because you're brooding."

"I'm not brooding."

Then Dakota looked around the tent warily, noting the hushed conversations. The tent was filled to nearly max capacity, yet quiet enough to converse in a whisper.

"Clara, what's going on?"

"What do you mean?"

"Why is everyone so...quiet?"

Clara shushed her, fondly recalling how much she had initially resisted Dakota's assignment to the platoon. It was no secret why Clara's platoon had been "selected" to receive an embedded reporter, due in large part to Clara herself, a female lieutenant dealing with tribal elders in a patriarchal society.

And Clara had absolutely zero desire to be the subject of a *New York Times* hit piece against the military. But upon discovering that she and Dakota shared much in common beyond their cars, Clara ultimately sided with a near-total vulnerability toward her friend. This was no small achievement in a combat zone, however benign; no military leader wanted the press to see how the sausage was made overseas, or wanted to expose themselves to a detached and methodical analysis of their moment-by-moment decision making, particularly when it could cost human lives.

Clara knew that her career could possibly be ruined by such reporting. But in Dakota's presence, Clara didn't think much of her career at all. Dakota simply had a bluntness, a cool-girl element, that made such manipulative thinking impossible. Instead, Clara came to genuinely enjoy having Dakota around, and felt that her presence was calming not only to her but to the platoon that had spent so many months far from the shores of their homeland without reward or witnessing the slightest shred of coherent national strategy.

Because after the first thirty days, it was apparent that there was no geopolitical purpose to be had in Afghanistan. Not for America, and not for any of the invading armies that had taken a foothold there in the previous few centuries.

Clara looked toward the chow tent's entryway, and a moment later a gangly teenage private named Cleveland Lewis entered. He was the platoon baby, the youngest member who'd finished basic training a scant few months before the deployment.

Lewis stopped just inside the entryway, his expression registering the unusual quiet. He dropped his tray of food and turned to race out of the tent—but two of his squadmates waiting behind him tackled him to the ground.

The rest of his squad leapt up from their table, descending on Lewis in a violent melee as the squad leader shouted, "Hold him down!" Joshua Thoma, the platoon medic, produced a field stretcher that had been hidden from view and carried it toward the squad.

Lewis tried to fight his way out, but his efforts were futile against nine grown men who proceeded to bind his legs and wrists together with tape, then roll him onto the stretcher and affix him to it with a ratchet strap across his chest. They pulled his shirt up, exposing his bare abdomen and looking to Kyle for approval.

Kyle shouted, "I want a good clean fight. You get nineteen slaps—make 'em count."

His squadmates proceeded to give Lewis the dreaded "pinkbelly," administering hard open-handed slaps to his exposed stomach. Lewis howled in pain amid the platoon's raucous shouts and cheers, and when the nineteenth slap popped across his abdomen, the men hoisted the stretcher upright to face the seated tent occupants.

Lewis's squad leader was Steven Rivera, a lanky Texan who produced a cigarette, lit it, and then stuck it filter-first into a cupcake. The platoon began singing "Happy Birthday" as Rivera presented the cupcake to Lewis. At the conclusion of the song, Lewis tried to blow out the cigarette candle, sending a cloud of ash onto the tent floor.

As Dakota watched in amazement, the platoon began chanting, "Speech! Speech! Speech!"

Lewis began in his typical understated fashion, his young voice speaking matter-of-factly as the platoon listened.

"I'd, uh, like to thank the platoon for this gracious ceremony. When I think of all the places I could be spending my nineteenth birthday—at home with my wife, at a bar with friends—there's no place I'd rather be than in this desert wasteland with you fine people. While I'll probably never recover from the trauma of spending my formative years under people like Sergeant Soler, I can honestly say that my time in the platoon has been the most...shall we say, *interesting* time in my life. What I'd really like for my birthday is to get the hell out of Afghanistan, go home to my wife, and pretend I never joined the military. After that, any of you guys ever pass through Ohio, you have a place to stay."

The platoon applauded wildly, and Lewis's squad members laid the stretcher down and began to untie him.

As the applause subsided, Dakota looked to Clara and asked, "Is that...normal?"

"Oh yeah," Clara said. "Glad I don't have a birthday during this deployment, because they'd get me too. But when you have to spend months on end in Afghanistan, you find ways to pass the time."

Dakota shook her head. "How'd you ever end up in this racket, Clara?"

Clara shrugged. "Dunno. Daddy issues, I suppose."

This was met with a pause from Dakota. "Seriously?"

She shrugged. "My father walked out on us when I was six, and ever since then I've been trying to prove something. The policy banning women from combat jobs was lifted when I was a junior in ROTC, and the rest was history. Why, how'd you end up in *your* racket?"

"Journalism?"

"No. Being the cool, globetrotting hippie journalist."

Dakota gave a short laugh. "I don't know...at first I thought it'd be nice to visit other countries, have some adventures. But in the end, I really like telling other people's stories. Outside of the news, the public won't know what really happens unless there's honest reporting behind it, you know? But what about you—think you'll make the military a career?"

Clara frowned. "Jeremy and I want children, so I'll probably finish my four-year commitment and then focus on the family. You ever want to stop running all over the world and settle down?"

"I don't have the best track record with relationships. I've got daddy issues of my own, I suppose."

"Go figure. Did yours walk out on you too?"

"No such luck. He was abusive, and we walked out on him." She focused on Clara. "But let's get back to you. As a female combat leader, how did you feel about your reception from the platoon?"

Clara felt an odd sense of amusement. Dakota had mercurial mood swings, to be sure, but she also had walls around what she was willing to discuss, and whenever Clara approached them in conversation, her friend would quickly pivot the conversation to journalistic inquiries. Which was, she supposed, more or less Dakota's job.

Clara turned around, finding Kyle seated at the table behind her. "Sergeant Soler?"

"Yes, ma'am?"

"What did you tell me the first time we met?"

Kyle grinned. "I said, 'Let's get one thing out of the way right now. I don't care if you're a woman or man, white or black, straight as an arrow or queer as a three-dollar bill. Because when we're getting shot at, those bullets ain't gonna care either. I care about one thing: the tactical effectiveness of this platoon. You do right by that, you're good in my eyes. You don't, there's nothing that'll save you because I'll end your career if I don't kill you first.'"

Clara turned back to Dakota. "I knew he and I would get along just fine after that."

The two women finished eating, and Clara checked her watch. Rising from the table, she called out an announcement to the platoon.

"We step off for Pantalay at zero seven hundred tomorrow, and that means all PCCs and PCIs complete by six-thirty."

Kyle followed that up with, "You heard the LT, we've got an early morning. Pack it up and get some sleep—unless you've got guard tonight, in which case you can have some extra coffee before we step off."

Clara felt a deep sense of gratitude for Kyle, who never hesitated in backing her with his own brand of reinforcement.

Carrying her tray out of the tent, Clara moved to her sleeping quarters to prepare for the day ahead.

* * *

Clara's return to consciousness was a long, delirious slide through a dreamlike fog of sleep. She didn't open her eyes until she felt a weight on the mattress beside her, and then a hand stroking her forehead. When her eyelids fluttered open, it was to the sight of Jeremy sitting on the bed beside her, dressed for work, sunlight blazing through the windows.

"Good morning, babe. How did you sleep?"

Clara started to lift her head, then let it fall back against the pillow. "I don't ever want to get out of bed again. What time is it?"

"Time to go."

She sat up. "What? Really?"

Jeremy was smiling. "I thought we'd let you sleep. Your breakfast is on the counter, and Aiden tried to show me how you make coffee. It's not up to the Clara standard, but...better than nothing, I suppose."

She struggled out of bed, rising with a wave of lightheadedness and putting a hand on the mattress to steady herself. "So that's what it's like to sleep all night," she muttered.

"That's what it's like to sleep."

Clara made her way downstairs in time to kiss Jeremy and Aiden good-bye, waving from the doorway as the Maserati backed out of the garage.

She waited until they were out of sight, then closed the garage door. Thor was in a frenzy, whining and circling for his breakfast. After feeding him, Clara wolfed down the plate of eggs and sausage while standing beside the counter.

After retrieving her coffee thermos, Clara went through her final checks downstairs, making sure the rolling garage door was closed before locking the interior door, then looking to the deadbolts of the front, rear, and side entrances before setting the security system. She mounted the stairs, taking her first sip of coffee with a cringe. Jeremy didn't understand the subtleties of measuring whole beans and proportioning water, and the coffee was harsh with bitterness. None of that mattered now—her morning writing shift was ticking away, and by the time Clara entered her office she was racked with a profound sense of energy.

And then Clara wrote.

It felt like she was in an altered state, her mind hyperalert, firing off spontaneous inspiration with unprecedented mental clarity. Gone was the brain fog that had pervaded her working days for the past few weeks, along with the head pressure and full-body fatigue of chronic sleep deprivation. She was astounded at not just her productivity but the startling prose and crisp dialogue that flowed out of her as fast as she could type. Writing a novel this way felt like cheating, some unfair advantage granted to her alone.

She realized there was nothing unfair about this; it was a baseline state that the majority of the population existed in. This was, to put it simply, what seven to eight hours of sleep felt like. To Clara, it felt like a super-power. No wonder her author friends could whip out thousands of words a day without plotting. They'd all been accountants or website designers or entrepreneurs before their first book deal, and none of those careers were known for inflicting mental trauma that would periodically rob them of sleep for the rest of their natural lives.

Meanwhile Clara marveled at her writing, which was fluid and powerful to an extent she'd been incapable of while sober—alcohol, she now knew, had simply calmed the buzzing hypervigilance and impact of sleep loss, allowing her to act more normal with booze than she could manage without.

For her manuscript, the return of sleep couldn't have come at a better time.

She was still behind, but now gaining ground with unprecedented momentum. The story continued to throw unseen twists and characters that demanded to be written, dictating the spontaneous creation of new scenes. But so too was her mind now equal to the challenge, eager, even, to be pushed beyond the creative bounds of her previous books. Clara was beyond certain that she'd rise to the occasion.

Besides, she thought, if this was what *one* good night of sleep did for her, how would she feel with two?

* * *

By the time Jeremy and Aiden returned home, Clara felt like a new woman.

Previously, playing with her son after day care was an activity fraught with racing thoughts, her chest tightening as sunset approached, marking the turn of nightfall.

But not today.

She played gleefully with Aiden as Jeremy cooked dinner, free from the pressing anxieties of what would occur after she went to bed. For the first time in a long time, Clara felt like a mother—not some haunted combat vet playing a part for her family's sake, not a PTSD victim afraid to look within her mind's own corridors.

After they put Aiden and Thor to bed, Clara went through her normal bedtime routine—the chamomile and valerian tea with its attendant supplements, the CBD dosage. She felt naturally tired, but she didn't want to alter protocol until she was certain that she was out of the woods.

Clara took a hot shower, then searched through a drawer of the master closet until she found a sheer babydoll and lace panties that had gone unused since...Clara couldn't remember when. Jeremy had gotten them for her before the pregnancy, and she put them on now, examining herself in the full-length mirror. The babydoll was flattering, delicately enhancing and defining her silhouette while revealing just enough to be, well, irresistible.

She entered the bedroom, and told Jeremy to take off his clothes and lie on the bed.

8

Clara had the vague sensation that she was dreaming, glimpsing the funnel of a storm cloud that she fell through, flickers of lightning illuminating her descent.

Then she was walking over gravel and sand, the Afghan sunrise already pummeling the ground with its heat. Clara wore a boonie hat and desert fatigues, the weight of a pistol against her hip. The air was thick with sand, the smell cut by a faint odor of diesel fuel. Clara was walking, unable to stop, only able to see her surroundings through the eyes of her past self, which placed her location at her platoon's outpost with its tents and guard towers.

She glanced sideways as she walked, seeing most of her platoon clustered around the staging area, where four armored vehicles were lined up end-to-end in their order of movement. Having been designed from the ground up to withstand bullets and enormous blasts, the oversized all-terrain vehicles sat atop massive run-flat tires. Each truck bristled with antennas for communications and jammer systems, the armored turrets occupied by gunners who were currently inspecting and loading their heavy weapons system—either a heavy machinegun or an automatic grenade launcher, depending on the truck—as well as a smaller belt-fed machinegun for more precise fire. Dakota was kneeling in front of the first truck, snapping photos with her ever-present DSLR camera.

The vehicles gave the illusion of invulnerability, but Clara knew the truth—the turret gunners remained largely exposed, a big enough IED could upend any one of these trucks, and certain anti-tank rounds from a shoulder-fired rocket would easily slice through the armor and kill everyone inside. Still, the trucks were far preferable to any current alternative, and besides, the protective capabilities were unlikely to be tested on this mission, or any other.

She caught sight of two figures headed toward the trucks.

The first was Staff Sergeant Earl Kelley, a country boy from Florida who would be in charge of outpost security while the patrol was outside the wire.

Clara called out, "You all set to hold down the fort, Sergeant Kelley?"

Kelley threw up his hands. "Ma'am, it won't be easy staying behind while you guys head into battle, but someone's gotta do it."

"Don't remind me. Who knows, maybe today will be our day." She looked to the second man, a snide team leader from Chicago named Kenneth Brown. "What do you think, Corporal Brown?"

Brown stopped in his tracks and shook his head solemnly, his expression deadpan. "LT, I've got a baaad feeling on this one."

Clara smirked and continued walking. Kenneth Brown made that sarcastic proclamation before every mission, to the point where it had become a punchline in the platoon.

As with all punchlines, it had its basis in a joke.

Clara's platoon had been conducting patrols and visiting villages for months now, and their presence had been as unopposed as the cynical, jaded, and dysfunctional platoon they'd replaced. At most, Clara's platoon would receive an occasional rocket attack against their outpost—but the projectiles were wildly inaccurate, usually propped against a rock and launched with the aid of a timer that would allow the shooter to be well out of the area before launch.

As for direct ground combat, the Taliban fighters in Clara's area of operations seemed content to wait out the US involvement, now well into its second decade. Now four months into their deployment, the greatest threat to the platoon seemed to be the complacency that invaded after dozens of multi-hour patrols yielded little more than the endless begging of the locals. The children screamed for candy and bottled water, the elders screamed for additional reconstruction projects, and the platoon tried to maintain their collective sanity.

Eager to face the enemy at the start of their deployment, the platoon members had now largely resigned themselves to counting down their last sixty days in Afghanistan, having come no closer to fighting the Taliban than the occasional rocket attack that sent them scurrying into bunkers until the all-clear had sounded.

The next person she passed was a stout man carrying a crate of ammo toward the trucks. This was Bob Welch, a senior team leader from Maryland who was second only to Kyle in his ragged desire to locate and kill Taliban fighters.

Clara nodded to him as they passed.

"Hey, Sergeant Welch, how's the forecast today—partly sunny with a chance of ambush?"

Welch smiled. "Enemy always gets a vote, ma'am. If we do get hit, you'll be glad to have me in the ranks."

"Believe me, Sergeant Welch, I already am."

This was no empty platitude, and they both knew it.

Bob Welch was one of a handful of people in the platoon with real combat experience. Some of the other team leaders, as well as Kyle and the squad leaders—most notably Alan Smith and Steven Rivera—had great tales of gunfights from previous deployments. But for Clara and the newer members of the platoon, those stories were as close as they'd ever come to engaging the enemy face-to-face. After years of working to earn her officer's commission and miraculously gaining assignment to one of the few units still deploying to Afghanistan, the only time Clara had fired her weapon was on the platoon's training range.

Now she was on her way to the command tent, where she'd transmit her thirty-minute call to her company commander, Captain McHugh. Her next radio call to him would occur from the passenger seat of her armored vehicle, second in the convoy's order of movement, where she'd be buckled in with a harness and wearing the truck commander's headset.

She was a few paces from the command tent when an Afghan-accented voice called out behind her.

"Lieutenant! Lieutenant!"

She turned to see Fraidon, one of her platoon's two interpreters, jogging toward her.

He was wearing an old set of fatigues without patches and a hand-me-down pair of desert boots from one of her soldiers.

"There is a problem in the trash pit. Please, come."

Don't go, Clara thought. But in her dream, she responded exactly how she did then, the beginning of a day she remembered all too clearly.

"We're launching in less than forty minutes, Fraidon. I'm busy."

"Please, this cannot wait until we come back. Hurry."

Clara relented, feeling impatient and irritated as she followed Fraidon to the trash pit. She recognized her verbal exchange with Fraidon—it was a word-for-word replay of that long-ago morning. But Clara was powerless to intervene in the dream, or to change her actions in any way. She was only a passenger on this voyage.

"She is in heat," Fraidon said as they walked. "And the males want...something else."

They arrived at a small structure of four mud walls where three shaggy Afghan dogs were circling before the lone door, snapping and snarling at each other.

Clara picked up a rock and whipped it into the fray, where it struck one of the dogs in the side. He yelped and the trio took off at a sprint, threading dusty sandtrails toward the tents.

Then Clara approached the open doorway and looked inside.

The interior was piled waist-high, with decaying field rations and fragments of ammo crates piled atop an indistinguishable mass of charred garbage. Ash and diesel fumes filled her lungs as she peered inside, catching her first glimpse of the animal.

The Afghan bitch was a shaggy brindle creature—she'd probably gone into the trash pit to scavenge for food and become hopelessly entangled in a partial coil of razor wire. Now her injuries were unrecoverable. The razor wire wrapped around her torso and throat, having sliced through fur, flesh, and entrails to become embedded in slivers of visible bone. The dog was exhausted from the struggle of trying to extricate herself from the wire and defend herself from the onslaught of males. She was wheezing now, her tongue lolling and eyes wild with terror as she lay collapsed atop the platoon's garbage.

Clara drew her pistol, took a two-handed aim at the bitch's heart, and fired a single round.

The dog went rigid, her limbs reaching out as if in a final leisurely stretch. Then her back legs began quivering in spastic postmortem twitches, and Fraidon, seeming unsure if the dog was dead, spoke.

"Lieutenant, shoot her again."

She felt numb and detached as she obeyed, this time aiming for the head. The bitch's eyes were still open, wide and unseeing, as Clara pulled the trigger.

She burst awake, the gunshot ringing in her ears. She was back in bed, back in Charleston, feeling bewildered at the dream. Sunlight was streaming in through the windows, and she turned off her white noise machine to hear the shower running in the master bathroom.

Clara pushed aside her weighted blanket to begin the day.

* * *

Clara slowly rattled away at the keys as she worked on her manuscript.

She'd slept through the night, and her cognition was just as clear as it had been yesterday. But her mind kept drifting back to the dream, feeling distantly troubled. In the three years since she'd left the military, she'd become an expert in *not* thinking about Afghanistan. Her soldiers, sure. The homecoming to Jeremy, yes. But never the dark events of that day, never the sight of her friends and subordinates lying dead, never the bodies they'd found.

There were no dreams, no flashbacks—until now.

Clara continued writing, pausing to check the clock. She had her first follow-up call with Dr. Jannesson in an hour, and she'd discuss the dream with him then.

Now, she needed to write. But the process was hard; she was slogging along, distracted by the dream as she spewed listless prose onto the page. She couldn't hear the characters talking, much less see them; all she could see was the Afghan bitch, how its panicked eyes had frozen open with the first shot, how the second had torn through one eye and blown the dog's brain over the stinking piles of half-burned trash.

She stopped writing abruptly, then opened a new Word document. And here she began writing again, this time about the dream. Not even the dream, she thought; the event itself, now fresh in her memory. She began tentatively, and then found her fingertips flying across the keyboard, the words filling her screen as the story unfolded. To her surprise, the process felt cathartic, as if each detail was extracted from her memory as she transcribed it to the page, and with it the long-forgotten sensations of anxiety and dread.

Her phone rang—a Savannah area code.

Clara had completely lost track of time, nearly forgotten her follow-up call in the rush to write down her dream.

She answered quickly, relieved to hear Dr. Jannesson's voice.

"Hi, Clara. How have you been holding up?"

"Two nights of continuous sleep. It's been weeks since that happened."

"That's great to hear."

"Well," she began, "there was something odd last night. I had...a bad dream."

"Can you tell me about it?"

Clara drew a breath, considering her words. "It was...an actual event. From Afghanistan. I just kind of relived the entire incident, exactly as it occurred. But I couldn't change anything."

"Was it a traumatic incident?"

"Sort of, but not really. Not in my top twenty from that day, to be sure. It involved a dog, not a person."

"I'm not terribly surprised to hear that."

Clara felt her brows furrow in confusion. "Why not? I've never had dreams before this treatment. Or flashbacks. Not ever."

"And I'm not surprised to hear that either. You see, it's not uncommon for the mind to deeply repress the memories of traumatic events. But that which is repressed must ultimately be *expressed*, whether those outlets are healthy or not. When traditional therapy doesn't work, as happens for many PTS patients, those repressed memories and emotions can come to light in unhealthy ways. Drinking, drug abuse, violent outbursts, and the like."

"So was the dream healthy or unhealthy?"

"Quite healthy," he said easily. "That's why transition from the military is so difficult for combat veterans. If you were still deploying, you may well keep those memories suppressed—your brain would recognize that processing them could reduce your chances of survival in some coming engagement. So you build up those repressed memories and emotions, and then when there are no more deployments, no more imminent danger, the mind rushes to process everything that has come before."

Clara sat back in her chair and swallowed hard. "So my brain is finally processing."

"Yes. Your cetraphaline treatment simply unlocked some evolutionary-based, inner cognitive repression that blocked the process."

"You're saying there will be more dreams," Clara said flatly.

"Very likely so, I'm afraid. In fact, you may experience a temporary increase in disturbing thoughts as your mind purges everything that has been tamped down. I've seen that in a few patients with severe PTS, but not all. But rest assured, this is part of your healing process. Everyone has endured a finite number of traumatic events, no matter how severe the emotional effects—and when your mind is through processing these painful memories, you'll be left with healthy, restful sleep. And that will last for the rest of your life."

9

Clara was apprehensive as she prepared for bed that evening, feeling the onset of dread at the prospect of what dreams the night would bring. She'd shot that Afghan dog the morning of a day she'd spent years trying to forget, and if those events were relived in the same stark clarity as her first dream, then things were going to get a lot worse before they got better.

She said nothing of this to Jeremy, of course. By then Clara was well-versed in projecting abject normalcy—or at least passable normalcy—and she went through their nighttime routine gracefully up until making love in bed.

Jeremy fell asleep soon thereafter, and Clara felt her anxiety fading to quiet exhaustion until sleep pulled her down into its grasp. And when the dream came, there was no foreshadowing as with the first—no descent through a storm cloud, no warning that the horror movie was about to begin.

Instead she found herself seated cross-legged atop a pillow, sipping scalding hot tea while surrounded by the elders of Pantalay Village. Kyle was addressing them with the help of an interpreter, and the gnarled old men were watching him with disinterest. Across the circle of pillows sat Dakota, her hair covered by a checkered cloth that wrapped around the sides of her face, just as Clara wore in deference to the local culture. Dakota was alternately snapping pictures with her DSLR camera and scribbling notes in a weathered notepad.

This type of meeting was known as a "key leader engagement," and by then she knew what to expect. It was her third such encounter at this sprawling and primitive community, but she'd done a dozen other such meetings in nearby villages.

Clara's presence was almost ceremonial at this point. Prior to deploying, she'd spent countless hours training in how to conduct key leader engagements with village elders. She knew the ground rules—how to record, repeat, and address their concerns while maintaining eye contact with them rather than her interpreter, while extolling every possible benefit of their alliance with their national government.

But the village elders would nonetheless look to Kyle instead of her for one reason alone: he was a man.

Whatever hopeful progress in gender equality and political reform that had taken hold in the younger generations of Afghans—and Clara knew by now that it was a lot—meant nothing to the elderly and cynical men who clung to power at every level.

To those ancient and gnarled elders, Clara's so-called tribal counterparts, women were literal and figurative property. The young girls in Pantalay Village ran free with their hair uncovered right up until they turned fifteen. Then they had to wear a burka until age fifty, after which they'd be deemed sufficiently old enough to show their faces in public again. The intervening thirty-five years were spent largely within the home of a husband by forced marriage, their closest glimpse of freedom an annual trip to the bazaar where they were relegated to trailing their male spouse by five paces.

Dakota momentarily made eye contact with Clara, then continued jotting in her notepad. While Dakota was an embedded journalist rather than a soldier, she and Clara shared a growing bond of being the only two women in their base to "leave the wire" and venture into the Afghan countryside. And Clara knew by then that Dakota felt the same way about the hopeless treatment of women in this village and others they'd visited; the two would often commiserate about it in private meetings back at the base.

But Clara and Dakota weren't the only frustrated ones—for most of the platoon, these patrols consisted of positioning their armored vehicles to establish security, and then pulling guard amidst an indifferent village until Clara, Kyle, and Dakota returned from the key leader engagement. Clara tried to keep the platoon engaged in their after-action briefs back at the base, providing summaries of the meeting. But no one cared, and why should they? The results were always the same. The village elders didn't trust the national government or, for that matter, anyone outside of a narrow tribal structure. They wanted more funding and construction projects from the Americans, while complaining about the inadequacies of what they'd already received.

Her train of thought was broken by the sight of an American soldier in the doorway.

It was Rich Johns, one of the platoon's team leaders who was supposed to be outside the building. Clara shot him a questioning glance, and he waved urgently for her to join him in the hallway.

She excused herself and rose, stepping into the hallway with a mounting feeling of concern. That feeling turned to irritation when she saw the second figure in the hall: Fraidon, her interpreter. This was the second time that day he'd interrupted her job duties.

"What's up?" she asked Rich.

"Ma'am, a young boy approached the perimeter and asked to speak to the Americans. He told Fraidon that the Taliban came last night, and they're everywhere in the village. They have families at gunpoint in the mosque. They are about to attack with fifty fighters."

Clara tried not to laugh. Such reports were known as Afghan math: if one Taliban fighter was spotted, the villagers would report ten. She looked to Fraidon, who appeared jumpy, in a state of near-panic.

She said sternly, "Translate to American math, Fraidon. Not Afghan."

Fraidon replied, "That is American math. The boy said two hundred."

That was Clara's first indication that something was truly wrong.

She looked to Rich Johns, seeking a second opinion from an American.

Rich spoke without prompting. "The boy was terrified, ma'am. It may be exaggerated, but I don't think it's a false report this time."

"Then get back to your position. Fraidon, come with me."

Rich departed quickly as she re-entered the room where the village elders were still seated, drinking tea and bantering with Kyle.

"Gentlemen," she said loudly. Everyone went silent and looked to her, expressions of rage boiling at this interruption by a woman.

She continued, "I have just heard there are Taliban in this village waiting to attack. Is this true?"

Fraidon translated into Pashto, and when he finished a dumbfounded silence ensued.

These men hadn't maintained their place in a ruthless power structure without knowing how to keep a poker face.

Clara locked eyes with the oldest among them, the village's senior religious leader. He had a snow-white beard against an impossibly wrinkled, leathery face, and when her gaze met his, he looked away.

"Sergeant Soler," she said, "the meeting is over. We're about to get hit. Get everyone in a defensive strongpoint around this building."

Clara realized then how this would look—a nervous lieutenant overreacting to a false report—and she prepared to reissue the order.

But Kyle was already leaping to his feet, speaking into his radio to the squad leaders. Dakota rose too, rushing to follow Clara into an adjacent room, where a long-range radio sat in a rucksack on the floor, its antenna arrayed through an open window. Kneeling beside it was her platoon radio operator, Jason Sims, tasked with maintaining communications via radio checks every ten minutes.

Clara raked at the cloth covering her hair, casting the shawl aside. "We up on comms?"

Sims answered, "Yes, ma'am, we've got 'em crystal clear."

She took the handset, hearing the shutter snap of Dakota's camera behind her.

"Baker Six, this is Sandman Two-Six."

"Sandman Two-Six, this is Baker Six Romeo. Send your traffic."

Clara felt her jaw clench. This was her commanding officer's radio operator—the good captain couldn't even trouble himself to personally handle comms while a single platoon was on a mission.

"Put me through to Baker Six Actual."

A brief pause. *"Six Actual is unavailable, will relay your message."*

Clara knew what "unavailable" meant—her commander, Captain Jared McHugh, was sitting in the operations center, hearing everything but unwilling to trouble himself with a personal response.

She couldn't keep the anger out of her voice. "Sandman Two-Six requests Quick Reaction Force and all available Close Air Support and Close Combat Air assets be dispatched to our location ASAP. Have credible reports of a large enemy force in the village preparing to attack our element time now, how copy?"

There was a long pause, and in the interim she heard Kyle's voice over her platoon radio frequency. "*Six, this is Five. The streets just turned into a ghost town, and we've got a lot of movement in the trees and windows.*"

She responded, "Copy. How long do we have?"

"*A few minutes, tops.*"

Then the command radio crackled to life, and Clara pressed the handset to her ear.

The voice that spoke this time wasn't the commander's radio operator, it was Captain McHugh himself.

"*This is Six Actual, do you have troops in contact at this time?*"

"Negative, but contact is imminent."

His response was spoken in the condescending tone he used when reprimanding the naive lieutenants under his command, a startling display of his own insecurities that never ceased to bewilder Clara.

"*The assets you're requesting are reserved for troops* in contact. *Not scared lieutenants.*"

She briefly considered saying what she shouldn't over the radio—that no other units were outside the wire of their base right now, and therefore the only ones who could possibly be *in contact* were her men—but she settled on using his words against him instead.

"Copy, Sandman Platoon has *visual* contact on large numbers of personnel maneuvering into firing positions in the surrounding buildings and forest. Civilians have disappeared from the streets. Enemy attack is imminent, we have a report of fifty fighters, how copy?"

"*What I 'copy' is a lot of Afghan math. Call back when you have actual shots fired, Sandman Two-Six.*"

"Well you may as well stay on the line, because—"

She stopped her transmission abruptly. There was an urgent shout from her men outside, then another, and Clara lowered the radio hand mic to listen.

And then the first shots rang out.

* * *

Clara jolted awake, her body trembling with chills. The sheets were sticking to her; she realized she'd sweated through her clothes.

Fumbling sideways off the mattress, Clara shakily sat up and took a few panting breaths. It was still dark out—she checked the clock and saw it was a quarter past midnight.

She rose and walked out of the room, keeping her arms outstretched so she didn't strike a wall. Clara's breaths were as quick as her heartbeat as she descended the steps to the kitchen.

Her problem with the dream wasn't the sudden wakeup—God knows she'd survived enough of those—but rather the fact that the dream had occurred at all. This was no flashback from the outpost. It was *the battle*, the last thing she wanted to relive. At the same time, she was grateful the dream ended when it did. Clara didn't want to sleep now, didn't want to risk returning to that day.

She poured herself a tall serving of bourbon, forgoing the ice and carrying the bottle back to her office.

Clara sat before her computer numbly, drinking to quiet her body's roaring vitals. For a moment she considered working on her manuscript, then realized that particular job function was beyond her current capacities. She opened a blank Word document, prepared to type out the dream, but found she had nothing to say.

So she drank instead, ears clanging with the constant ring of permanent hearing loss. But now she could hear the sounds of that day, the distant echoing of gunfire and explosions creeping through the never-ending high-pitched squeal in both ears.

Her glass was empty, and she poured again.

Then she was shakily negotiating the stairs to the second floor, unsure how much time had elapsed and how much she'd drunk. It didn't matter now; she was properly sedated, her mind heavy with a cloud of alcohol that made sleep possible once more.

Her head was spinning as she lay down in bed, grateful for the reprieve. She adjusted the pillow behind her head and slid the mask over her eyes. Sleep would come soon, heavy and thick, and Clara folded her hands over her stomach and regulated her breathing as she waited for the alcohol to carry her away.

The gunfire crackled outside the building, interspersed with the low *thud-thud-thud* of automatic grenade launchers firing atop the vehicles.

Kyle was at the casualty collection point, directing the soldier carrying a boy in his arms.

The child was dead, Clara saw at once, his face a gray pallor only a half-shade removed from the living. He looked strangely like Aiden in that moment, a few years older but with the same innocence that made her heart tick over in silent agony.

Fraidon spoke beside her.

"He is the one who warned us."

Clara felt a brief pang of disgust that Fraidon had chosen that exact moment to reveal that nugget of information, but she focused on the first casualty of the battle.

The boy was now lying limp and lifeless on the filthy sand floor of a building made of mud, being examined by Joshua Thoma, the platoon medic. For Thoma, this was a fast, rote process of searching the boy for injury or airway obstruction. But there was nothing wrong with him—no visible wounds, no blood-soaked entry or exit wounds from enemy bullets.

Dakota was in the corner of the room, her face pale with horror. But she snapped pictures efficiently, staying out of the way as she documented the proceedings.

Then Thoma abruptly stopped his inspection of the boy and sat up on his heels. "It was shrapnel."

Clara was confused, both to where the wound was and why she *had to know* in the midst of chaos. A small piece of shrapnel could certainly kill someone if it hit an artery, but the boy would have been soaked in dark blood.

"Where? Thoma, where?"

Thoma looked momentarily stunned, either by the question or her accusatory tone. He pointed at the boy's face.

Clara knelt and looked closer, and then she understood.

At the inner corner of the boy's eye, welling up at the tear duct, was a single tiny drop of blood. The fragment of shrapnel must have been miniscule; even on close examination, she could barely see it.

Thoma continued, "It must have gone clean through, and embedded in his frontal lobe."

"Oh, right," Clara said flatly, as if this were the most reasonable fate that could be expected to befall a child of that age. Why had she said that?

Kyle grabbed her arm, and she homed in on the end of a sentence fragment over the din of battle.

"We got a KIA," Kyle said.

"Afghan?"

"US. It's Lewis. Call it in, ma'am."

Clara happened to lock eyes with Dakota at that moment, and she saw that her friend had already started to cry.

But Clara registered the news with an odd sense of detachment, immediately darting toward the room where Jason Sims manned the radio. Sims was watching her as she entered, eyes wide with anger.

"Cleveland Lewis?" he asked.

Clara nodded. They'd commemorated his birthday just last night, and now the nineteen-year-old soldier was dead. She remembered wondering how he'd been killed, not that it mattered. A deep, blossoming sense of shame began spreading through her chest, which in hindsight was her first indication of the burden she'd spend the rest of her life bearing.

Minutes later, Clara would learn that the bullet had hit Lewis's throat broadside, searing two carotid arteries—one inner and one outer—and blasting a gashing hole through his larynx. If he'd survived the initial strike, it wasn't by more than a few seconds.

But she didn't know that at the time, instead calmly transmitting over the hand mic to the command frequency.

"Baker Six, we have one US KIA, stand by for battle roster number."

She ripped open the flap of her admin pouch on her chest, its Velcro surface covered with her V patch, and reached inside for the laminated notecards bearing the roster numbers and blood type of every platoon member.

Clara remembered this moment in time clearly—she'd been fascinated by her calm clarity, the lack of trembling in her hands despite the dull ache in her chest, the boundless pain of losing one of her men in this desolate wasteland.

But in the dream, Clara halted the action abruptly. There was a presence in the room behind her, someone who hadn't been there during the battle. She whirled around, seeing a shadowy figure in the doorway, almost holographically translucent. It was a man but she couldn't make out who, and before she could process this, Jason Sims called to her with an urgent voice.

"LT, the tree! He's in the tree!"

Clara grabbed her rifle, dropping to a knee and taking aim. She was looking for a sniper, absently wondering why Sims wasn't opening fire himself—he was as good a shot as any of them, and not prone to panic.

But the view through her rifle's optic didn't hold an enemy sniper.

Instead, she saw Rich Johns, the team leader who'd warned her of the impending attack alongside Fraidon. Rich had survived the battle unscathed—at least physically.

Because four years after the gunfight in Pantalay Village, he had hung himself from a tree behind his mobile home.

And now she watched him in the midst of the battle, dressed in frayed jeans and a green flannel shirt, the sleeves rolled to the elbows.

Rich's body dangled lifeless from the rope, head craned at a horrific angle from the noose. She caught a glimpse of his eyes, milky-white and staring into an oblivion of death.

A distorted voice came through the radio. "*Sandman Two-Six, send battle roster number when able. Sandman Two-Six—*"

A hand stroked across her forehead, and she startled awake.

Jeremy was standing over her, smiling in the morning sunlight that filtered through the bedroom window.

"Hey, babe," her husband said softly, "how'd you sleep?"

10

Clara spent most of the day lost in research. The cetraphaline treatment had reacted with something in her body chemistry or psyche; she was sure of that now. That was her mistake—trying cetraphaline when it was in the early phases as a treatment option. If she'd waited for side effects to be known, she could have avoided all this.

However, that would mean letting other vets suffer so she didn't have to. And Clara didn't know if she had it in her to deliberately make that choice.

In a way, she was the perfect guinea pig for cetraphaline. Physically, she was nothing special—fit, to be sure, though not as much as when she was in the service. But Clara had an immense pain tolerance to bear the effects of PTSD, to self-medicate with alcohol and present a facade of normality to her family and the outside world. In a way, her author career allowed her to channel that pain through a passionate creative outlet, and that alone gave her a huge survival advantage over the vast majority of troubled vets.

Clara was determined to succeed, and confident that she could. She had close to three dozen surviving members of her platoon to provide a solution to, once she'd found it. And she had a world-class authority in Dr. Jannesson, with whom she had a scheduled follow-up call at three.

And when that call came, Clara was prepared to discuss the results of her research.

She picked up on the first ring, feeling a wash of comfort at the sound of Dr. Jannesson's voice.

"Hi, Clara, how are you feeling?"

She sighed wearily. "I'm not going to lie, Doc, it's gotten worse."

"What's gotten worse—the dreams?"

"To put it lightly. Last night they turned to combat, to...my major battle. At first, it was just like the last dream. I couldn't react, couldn't change anything, just watched as everything unfolded exactly like it did that day."

"Okay," Jannesson said cautiously. "And then what?"

"I woke up, and had to drink to put myself back down. Then the dream resumed, but some things were...different."

"Different from the first dream, or different from the actual events?"

"From the events. There was a, a shadowy figure or something, standing in a doorway. It was like a ghost. Then I saw one of my platoon's suicides hanging from a tree outside—he hung himself last year, but in the dream he was dangling from a tree during the gunfight. Then I woke up."

"Clara, this is—pardon me for saying so—but this is fascinating."

She recoiled. "Why? Haven't any of your other patients had dreams turn out like this?"

"Not to date, but I wouldn't let that be a cause for concern."

She felt her jaw clench. "It's concerning to me, Doc."

"Well, here's what I'm getting at—and bear in mind, dream analysis is far from my specialty. But typically dreams as they relate to psychological trauma follow one of two avenues: they are an exact re-enactment, or complete fantasy that substitutes meaningful symbols for elements of the actual event. Both are theorized to be our brain's attempt to emotionally regulate anxieties of the past or present.

"But what you're describing is a melding of the two. It sounds like almost everything was a real event, even if the chronology was skewed—for example, your comrade hanging himself during the battle. I can see how the brain's intense processing of repressed memories from combat could dovetail with emotions of guilt associated with a subsequent suicide.

"Now, this isn't to say that your brain's reaction is in any way unusual. You see, if any member of society was suddenly attacked by someone in a red shirt, they might forever associate the color red with danger. But for combat veterans with multiple or even countless sources of trauma, the perceived threat might be associated with any number of variables—a time of day, the casting of the sun's light, a season, or a particular spoken word. And the patient often doesn't know the source without extensive therapy or self-examination."

Clara frowned. "But what about the shadowy figure? It was almost like a hologram, translucent. And no one was standing there during the event."

"Of course. That could simply be a symbolic representation of another person, and I'd be curious to know if it reappears in the future. You said you drank before the second dream, correct?"

"Yes. Quite a bit."

"It's possible the alcohol played a role. I'd like you to keep close note of whether the dreams diverge into fantasy when you go to sleep sober. If it's all right with you, I'd also like to increase the frequency of our calls to daily check-ins."

"Of course," Clara said. "There was also some research that I wanted to discuss with you, regarding CTE and—"

She stopped speaking abruptly, certain she'd heard something downstairs. Thor was curled up, sleeping in his puppy bed in her office—some guard dog, she thought.

"Clara?" Jannesson asked. "Are you still there?"

"Yes. Could you hold on a second, Doc?"

Clara set the phone on the desk, then rose and walked to the office door, listening. One of the peculiar things about her hypervigilance was that when she heard an unknown sound, she couldn't think or focus until she identified the source. Since she worked from home, those workday sounds were typically Thor making some racket downstairs. But this definitely wasn't Thor—she could see him sleeping now.

There was an odd groaning noise, barely perceptible over the ringing in her ears. Maybe a lawn mower operating next door?

But then she heard shattering glass, and footsteps thudding in her kitchen. Men's voices were shouting unintelligibly, and she only made out two words amid the melee.

"...she's upstairs!"

Clara slammed her office door shut, locking it. Then she ran to her desk and gasped, "They're coming for me!" before ending the call with

64

Jannesson and dialing 911. She had the feverish thought that she'd set her home security system that morning—or had she? Clara was no longer sure.

The line connected, and a female operator said, "911, what's your emergency?"

Clara whispered, "Home invasion, 65 Great Oak Lane." She heard a keyboard rattling as the operator typed.

"Do you see someone inside?"

"I can hear them. I don't know how many."

"Okay, where are you?"

Clara's pulse was surging in her temples, her head pounding. "Third-floor office."

"Officers are headed your way. Are you armed?"

"No." Amid the rising swell of panic, Clara felt a wave of shame. She'd sold her guns after Aiden was born, but a voice in her head reminded her, *you didn't sell them for Aiden. You sold them because you were dry-firing them in your mouth at night.*

The operator continued typing as she asked, "Do you have any further description?"

"No."

"How many vehicles should be in front of your house?"

"None, my car's in the garage."

"Do you live with anyone else?"

"I'm the only one home."

"Do they know you're there?"

"Yes."

"Stay quiet. Keep yourself safe, okay?"

Clara didn't answer—she heard footsteps coming up the stairs.

The operator continued, "Stay with me, you're doing great. Officers are on the way. Can you still hear them?"

"Yes. Please hurry. I'm all alone."

"Take a deep breath, okay? Do you have any idea who these people are?"

"No." Thor was on his feet, howling loudly at the noise.

"Stay where you are. We have officers coming around the front and back." Sure enough, Clara heard the wail of police sirens increasing in volume outside. But they were too late—the pounding footsteps stopped outside her office door.

Someone tested the handle, and when the lock caught, everything went momentarily silent.

There was a great thudding *boom* as someone kicked the door from the outside.

The door rattled and went quiet, and then a second kick sounded against it. Thor was barking wildly, his cries filling the room. Clara felt herself backing up, and then her shoulders hit the far wall. The kicking continued, each strike louder than the one before it amid the screaming police sirens. Clara dropped the phone, both hands fluttering to her mouth. Her breath hitched, and she stood frozen in horror, waiting to see the door being kicked open.

11

_____

Clara stared out the kitchen window. On the lawns outside, she saw clusters of neighbors conversing. These were her neighborhood's flock of unemployed trophy wives, or at least those not gainfully occupied by yoga or spin class while their kids were in school. They were staring at Clara's house, speculating at the reason for the patrol cars that had sped into her driveway without mustering the requisite courage to approach the door and ask if everything was okay, much less inquire if they could help. She regarded them with a sense of contempt, remarking to herself that they lacked even the most basic life experience required to formulate such considerations—and furthermore, they'd be most likely to swoop in not in the event of a crisis but rather to sleep with her husband should the slightest chance present itself.

Jeremy had rushed home from work that afternoon, and he was now apologizing to the last remaining police officer.

"I'm so sorry for the misunderstanding, Officer Dennis."

Clara turned away from the window to observe the two of them.

They were a study in opposites. Jeremy was in his business attire, chest puffed out as if he would have been able to do anything to help had he been home. Police Sergeant Raymond Dennis, by contrast, was a well-muscled African American man. The police shield on his broad chest was flanked by a winged eagle badge, indicating he served on the SWAT team.

This was an officer who had probably been shot at—if not having killed someone—in the line of duty, someone who probably had more in common with Clara than the vast majority of civilians in her homeland.

Sergeant Dennis said, "It's perfectly fine, Mr. Swanner." Then he looked to Clara. "But on the 911 recording, there were no sounds of a break-in. The dog didn't start barking until the police sirens were audible. And we found nothing out of the ordinary inside or outside your home, no signs of forced entry or even shoe prints on the office door. It's clear you had a distressing experience, Mrs. Swanner, and no one's doubting that. But there are a few more questions I have to ask."

"Sure," she replied numbly.

"Are you on any prescription medication?"

"Of course not."

"Any history of psychiatric disorders?"

"No."

"PTSD," Jeremy said. "Honey, you have PTSD."

Clara shot back, "That has nothing to do with what I heard."

Sergeant Dennis squinted at Clara. "Military?"

"In a former life."

"Your husband might be right, Mrs. Swanner. I once had a partner who was involved in a particularly violent use-of-force incident. He had some issues with PTSD afterward. And you guys in the military, having seen what you've seen..." He gave an empathetic shrug. "It's completely understandable, ma'am."

Clara was first struck by the officer's use of the word "ma'am," feeling for a split second as if she were still a military officer. Then she noted with disgust that Jeremy was nodding, as if he had any idea what the officer was talking about.

Jeremy enthusiastically added, "And you've been under a lot of stress lately, with your manuscript and all."

She fought the instinct to lash out, remaining stone-faced despite her husband's ill-timed comment.

Sergeant Dennis continued, "Well, I'm certainly not going to let the department press charges for filing a false report. But I can't guarantee that will be the case if these...episodes continue. I just want to be very clear with you, Mr. and Mrs. Swanner. Of course, call anytime you need us. But you live in a gated community in a very safe part of Charleston. A home invasion in broad daylight is extremely rare. I'm not saying impossible—get a person hooked on drugs, and all logic goes out the window—but for the most part, these people wait until everyone's asleep before they attempt a break-in. I'd encourage you to consider getting some help, or finding someone to talk to."

Jeremy looked at her with concern, but Clara forced a tight-lipped smile and managed, "I will, Sergeant Dennis. Thank you."

Clara showed the officer out with a final apology for the inconvenience, then walked to the kitchen to find Jeremy peering out the window at the accumulated neighbors.

She took a breath. "Jeremy, I think the cetraphaline reacted with something—some chemical exposure in Afghanistan, or internal damage from burn pits. Or traumatic brain injury. I mean, we had protective equipment that allowed us to survive things that would have been fatal in any previous war. I did some research today, and it's possible I have CTE: chronic traumatic encephalopathy. It's a progressive degenerative disorder from repeated brain trauma, and late-onset symptoms can include—get this—confusion, disorientation, and paranoia."

Jeremy was still gazing out the window, arms folded. He muttered, "Uh-huh."

Clara didn't mention the most telling pieces of her research, that additional symptoms read like a laundry list of veteran issues: social instability, impulsive behavior, depression, and suicidality. A growing list of former NFL players were killing themselves alongside veterans, even shooting themselves in the chest so their brains could be examined postmortem. All had been found to have CTE.

Instead, she continued, "They've found CTE in nearly every NFL player they've examined. And since many symptoms don't occur for years, and formal diagnosis requires an autopsy, they're years away from understanding how veterans are—"

"Clara!" Jeremy shouted, spinning to face her. She went silent, shocked at his outburst. Jeremy had never raised his voice to her, and yet she found herself expecting him to slap her across the face. She considered what that act would mean for Aiden, for herself—she'd long suspected that Jeremy would commit infidelity with any number of the neighborhood wives, to say nothing of leaving her entirely—but her husband composed himself, forcing a breath before he spoke in a quiet but stern tone.

"Stop it. Just—stop it. You don't have some bizarre spin on the symptoms that every veteran in your position is facing. You just don't. And this renewed search for a miracle cure isn't just hurting you. It's hurting your family."

Clara reacted with sheer outrage, betraying her attempts at restraint. "Oh? Explain to me how this is worse for you and Aiden than it is for me."

"I'm not saying it's worse. But you're never *here*. You're either lost in one of your manuscripts, or lost dreaming up some new therapy to try. But you never see the solution right in front of you: your family, me and Aiden. We're always here for you—"

"Oh, so what exactly should I tell our four-year-old son?" Hot tears welled in her eyes, spilling down her cheeks. "About the little Afghan boy who took a piece of shrapnel to his brain because of me?"

Jeremy stepped forward to embrace her. "I'm here for you too, Clara. And you can talk to me about anything."

Clara moved away from him, gawking at the statement.

"Really, Jeremy? You're a friggin' trust fund baby. Don't get me wrong, I think it's adorable that you've led a sheltered enough life to be offended by profanity on network television, but the most carnage you've ever seen is when you cruise past roadkill in your Maserati."

He shook his head resolutely. "That's not fair."

"Neither is the fact that I may or may not sleep on any given night, but that's the reality. And you're not ready to hear about real war when you still get upset every time someone uses the word 'moist.'"

"Well that's the problem, isn't it?" His face contorted with anger, his volume rising again. "You don't recognize someone as a human being unless they're a combat vet. But most people aren't, including all the therapists you hail as the second coming of Christ right up until their treatment doesn't work, at which point you turn on them for having never been to war. I'm surprised you haven't started hating Jannesson yet."

"Dr. Jannesson's treatment was the best thing I've ever done."

"Well I wouldn't know it to look at you, because this is the worst you've been for over a year."

Clara paused. "The *worst* I've been? Well I'm sorry to be such an inconvenience to your gilded existence."

"You know what?" He checked his watch. "I'm going to pick up Aiden. Try and calm down before we get back."

"I'll calm down!" she yelled back. "I'll be real nice and calm, the perfect Stepford wife you've always wanted."

Jeremy wasn't listening. He swept past her into the garage, and Clara heard the bark of his Maserati engine coming alive.

She pulled out her phone to call Dr. Jannesson back and saw that it was after five o'clock; his office was closed, and she'd have to check in with him tomorrow.

As the sound of Jeremy's car faded and the garage door rattled shut, Clara realized she was truly a mess—her pulse was racing, breaths coming in short puffs that failed to fill her lungs. This was no PTSD episode, she knew, just sheer anger at Jeremy. And she couldn't let Aiden see her like this.

Clara turned and walked around the kitchen island, retrieving a glass on the way to the bar cart, where bottles of bourbon stood glittering in the fading sun like penitent servants awaiting her will.

12

The sounds of a sustained firefight were a chaotic symphony, the gunfire ebbing and flowing as cymbal clashes of explosions detonated far and near.

Clara was in the command post, transmitting over the hand mic beside her radio operator.

"Baker Six, this is Sandman Two-Six, request update on QRF."

Captain McHugh responded, "This is Baker Six." His voice sounded tinny and far away as he transmitted from his armored vehicle, one of six in the Quick Reaction Force convoy that had launched from the company outpost. "We're passing Checkpoint Seven, ETA twenty mikes."

Clara winced. It had taken the QRF convoy half an hour to depart base, and they'd already been traveling for close to an hour and a half. In the meantime, the enemy had them surrounded and outnumbered. The platoon's ammunition was dwindling to perilous levels, and no resupply chopper had yet dared to come anywhere near the village.

A pair of Apache attack helicopters had come on station an hour earlier, and those pilots had no such reservations.

Instead they'd come screaming over the village, replying to Clara's every request for fire without the slightest hesitation. Those four attack pilots—two per helicopter—had proven themselves to be aerial gunslingers, blasting long bursts from their chain guns and sending Hellfire and Hydra missiles into windows and tree clusters until they quite literally had nothing left to fire.

This had bought the platoon momentary respite from incoming gunfire, and Clara had hoped this would break the enemy's will to fight.

But the moment the pilots gave their "Winchester" call, indicating they'd expended every rocket and bullet aboard their aircraft, the Taliban fighters seemed to realize it. Their assault against the platoon continued, undaunted by the sound of helicopter rotors that was no longer accompanied by chain gun and rocket launches.

The Apaches had returned to base to re-arm, and in the interim Clara was left with a whole lot of air support she couldn't use—an F-16 fighter jet that refused to engage in strafing runs over a densely populated setting, and whose bombs would remain firmly on the rails unless the platoon was about to be overrun, which hadn't happened quite yet.

A B-1 bomber had even streaked in from an Air Force base in Oman, its massive payload far too intensive for precision air support. In its defense, the bomber had performed a "show of force" pass, screaming over the village at less than a thousand feet, but the Taliban seemed well aware that this posturing was a substitute for the ability to drop bombs, and their fire continued unabated.

What Clara needed was close air support that only the Apaches could provide, and they were still over half an hour from returning to the fight. The next best thing was the Quick Response Force convoy, which wasn't much closer to arriving.

She transmitted back to her commanding officer, "Copy twenty mikes, be advised we remain under heavy and sustained effective fire and are going black on ammo. Request QRF convoy enter the village on Route Budweiser; we'll shift fires and you can consolidate at our position to cross-load ammunition and coordinate building-to-building clearance, how copy?"

A long pause followed, and she knew Captain McHugh was feverishly scrawling notes from the passenger seat of his armored vehicle.

"Sandman Two-Six, that's a good copy."

Gone was his previously condescending tone, replaced with the bald-faced apprehension of a fearful man. Clara was in the middle of the fight, and she sounded calmer than he did miles away from battle. McHugh was probably hoping the enemy would disperse before his arrival, when his tactical ineptitude would be on full display. He'd probably let Clara dictate everything from his arrival until the enemy contact died down, after which he'd be back in charge, back to his normal overbearing, insecure self.

Beside her, Clara's radio operator Jason Sims spoke.

"Hey, LT," he said, "twenty bucks says he'll put himself in for a Silver Star after this one."

Clara set her handset down. "No way I'm taking that bet, Sims."

She transmitted over the platoon frequency via a hand mic mounted on her body armor. "Net call, net call, QRF is twenty minutes out. Apaches back in thirty."

Then she switched to the hand mic that served as her personal link to Kyle.

"Five, this is Six."

No response—he could have been occupied at the moment, or it could have been a momentary lapse in their radio connection. It didn't matter; she'd see him in person soon enough.

She told Sims, "I'll be back in a few—going to make my rounds."

He replied, "Happy hunting, ma'am."

Then Clara was off, moving through the building toward the exit, passing first through the casualty collection point.

It was a gruesome sight. The Afghan boy was lifeless, his body laid out beside the flag-draped corpse of Cleveland Lewis, his boots emerging from below the stars and stripes.

But there were now two additional bodies, each covered by the American flags platoon members carried on their personal equipment at Kyle's mandate. On one hand, three soldiers killed in action was an appalling casualty count for scarcely two hours of fighting, comprising over ten percent of the platoon members present in the village.

On the other hand, Clara was surprised there weren't more.

Bill Gottert was a twenty-six-year-old father of two. He was firing his automatic grenade launcher from a vehicle turret when an AK-47 round struck him in the face. This was no sniper shot, but a wild and untrained burst of enemy fire that had found its mark against all odds—and Gottert had dropped dead in the vehicle interior, leaving his heavy weapons system unmanned until a young private could scramble over his friend's body to resume firing from the turret.

Jim McCurdy had suffered a more gruesome fate.

His squad leader had told her that McCurdy was running a crate of machinegun ammo to another truck when there was an explosion—whether it was an enemy grenade or a rocket, no one seemed to know—and the resulting blast had blown off most everything below his waist. Jim McCurdy had survived long enough to emit a few seconds of screaming that Clara had heard from her command post, and then he fell silent, another life laid to rest in the fight at Pantalay Village that continued to rage.

The American flag covering McCurdy was half soaked in blood, the stars and stripes unmarred as they shielded what remained of his body from view.

Besides Clara, the only living person in the casualty collection point was the platoon medic, Joshua Thoma.

His aid bag was open in the corner, the wrappers of expended medical supplies scattered across the ground after he'd treated the superficially wounded platoon members who continued to circulate in and out of the room.

Thoma himself looked racked with despair, his eyes wide and haunted. Clara felt pained at the sight of him—unlike many in the platoon, Thoma was a college graduate and had come from a family of means that had quite literally cut him out of the will for joining the military. But Thoma wanted to do his part in a conflict where so many had suffered, opting to enlist as a combat medic to gain experience for his ultimate goal of becoming a doctor.

Now he was helpless before three of his dead comrades, to say nothing of the Afghan boy, none of whom he could have treated in the slightest. All three had been dead long before they were carried in, leaving Thoma to treat the walking wounded who proceeded to race back into the fight.

Clara felt the need to say something, to assuage his haunted expression with some words of comfort.

She sided with, "Don't worry, Thoma—we're going to kill them all."

Clara regretted the words as soon as they left her mouth; that hollow platitude may have been a battle cry for the other soldiers, but not Thoma.

He was interested in treating the suffering, not in killing, and his forlorn face seemed to convey that she'd done more harm than good.

But there was no time to think about it now. Clara readied her rifle and darted out of the building, cutting left to run toward her second squad's fighting position. The sounds of automatic gunfire and grenade explosions increased from loud to deafening the moment she left the building, and Clara sprinted through the melee toward her men.

It wasn't that the squad and team leaders needed any help from her in telling them how to do their jobs. They were capable of that on their own, much less with Kyle translating Clara's orders and defensive necessities into immediate action.

Instead, Clara visited the positions because half her job was to project a sense of calm and control to the platoon. If they saw their lieutenant coming unglued, or even hunkering down inside the building beside her radio while they were left to fight outside, the apprehension would spread and detract focus from their job of killing the enemy wherever and however they could. It was incumbent on the platoon leadership not just to manage the tactical situation but to show the soldiers that everything was under control—as much as it could be under the circumstances.

Though as Clara ran by the fighting positions, shouting the Quick Reaction Force's twenty-minute ETA for those who hadn't gotten word, she questioned which end of the leadership spectrum was providing more comfort to the other.

She saw Kenneth Brown poised alongside his team, looking over his shoulder to see her running by and shouting after her.

"I got a baaad feeling on this one..."

Amid the pain and bloodshed, Clara actually laughed.

Everyone knew by now that Lewis, Gottert, and McCurdy were dead, and beneath the gallows humor was the resolution to kill as many enemy fighters as they could. It wasn't just about staying alive anymore; it was about exacting revenge, and the fact that these two tasks went hand-in-hand was incidental at best.

Then she saw Thomas Christy, a rifleman from Minnesota who currently bore a medical dressing on his arm. The blood-soaked gauze was wrapped around a bicep that he nonetheless used to maneuver his rifle within the confines of his firing position at the divot of a mud wall.

Clara was completely and utterly awestruck at the sheer grit of this man, and yet she heard herself instinctively call out to him, "Christy, you pussy, I heard you were malingering out here."

Thomas Christy smiled—how could anyone smile at a time like this?—and shot back, "Nah, just a flesh wound. Think they got me with a ricochet, LT."

Clara told him the Quick Reaction Force would arrive in twenty minutes and then continued running, keenly aware that she could be shot at any second on these jaunts between cover. But strangely, the knowledge didn't bring any implicit fear. Sure, her mouth was parched and her heart raced from the strain of running with body armor through the Afghan heat, but she felt no real sense of terror at the proceedings. There was only detachment, a very distant recognition that her life could end at any moment—the same recognition, she knew, that the rest of her platoon was facing alongside her while she alone coordinated forces outside the battle.

But the thought faded from Clara's mind as she saw her first enemy—or at least thought she did.

There were several schools of thought about whether a platoon leader should engage in the ground combat they controlled, but the most prevalent was this: *if you have time to shoot, you have time to use your radio to do something useful.*

But Clara's usefulness had elapsed. She'd utilized every available air asset, reported the firefight before it actually occurred. Now, every American in Afghanistan was tuned into her satellite communications frequency, listening to one of the few remaining firefights as it unfolded.

Besides, Clara couldn't pass up this opportunity. It was one of those fleeting, angled glimpses where every artifice of time and space had to align for her to see what she did at that second.

And even then, she didn't actually *see* him at first, because the sun was blindingly bright, casting the windows and doorways into monochromatic black patches.

But a spark in the darkness caught Clara's eye—a flash of preternatural orange light that sparked and vanished almost in the same instant—and that phenomenon had a single explanation: it was a muzzle flash, the momentary blast of flame that marked a gunshot.

So Clara's aim fell reflexively into the doorway, but not on the spot where she saw the flame; this was Afghanistan, so the shooter had fired a rifle, and she backtracked her point of aim to her best estimate of where a human form would be positioned to hold that weapon.

She fired six rounds.

The human form was evident then, a shadowy mass that fell forward, dead, spilling out of the doorway and into living color on the street.

Clara didn't stop then. Three of her men had been killed, to say nothing of the Afghan boy and God only knew how many civilians who could no longer be carried to the American position. Her opponents weren't marching down the village streets in formation; they were flitting shadows in an endless urban labyrinth, and the opportunity to see one, much less gun it down, was far too precious to leave to chance.

So she continued firing, sending bullet after bullet into her sworn enemy now personified into a single target. Her rifle bucked into her shoulder, the recoil soft and manageable as every facet of muscle memory served to keep her aim aligned and her trigger squeeze steady.

She kept blasting the now-dead opponent, and God help her, it felt *good*. Not necessarily in the sense of revenge, though that awareness was probably present somewhere in the background. But Clara was in a life-or-death fight, and this conquest over her enemy resulted in a surge of endorphins exploding inside her, some long-dormant evolutionary instinct rewarding her body chemistry for this victory.

The enemy fell dead in the street, his body pockmarked with the bloody smears of her bullets. His AK-47 lay unattended in the dirt. He was a boy in his teens.

Clara continued running, circling the central building as she saw her platoon's defenses in all their ragged glory.

There was her team leader Bob Welch, his gaze fixed on her as he shouted a single order to his own superior officer.

"Hey, Swanner! Get Fraidon on the bullhorn, tell him to call for more Taliban."

Clara gave him the twenty-minute call and then flipped him the bird, a response that seemed alien even as Welch reacted with a cackling laugh, and then she was passing one of the armored vehicles whose tires were shot by enemy gunfire.

Kneeling at the bumper was a squad automatic weapon gunner from the bayou, a former traveling carnival employee named John Peters, yelling, "LT, stay away from the tires! LT, *they absolutely hate tires!*"

She was living aboard an absurd, violent rollercoaster now, bursts of humor amid death, ecstasy mingled with horror, and above it all the sense that the wheels had truly come off this mission. Her mind's laser-like focus was hard to comprehend; she could see and perceive *everything*, nuances of detail standing out in stark clarity like never before as she processed information at a staggering rate. Glancing at a fighting position gave her the orientation of the soldiers there, which in turn translated to sectors of fire and maximum effective ranges projected out into the village.

And most of all she could tell that something had changed in the village —the orchestra of gunfire had shifted, converged into a single point that she ran to now.

The route took her alongside a waist-high mud wall, one of the many crumbling delineations between ancient compounds in the village, and Clara noted with a muted sense of horror that Dakota was kneeling, stationary, her head exposed, snapping pictures of Clara as she ran. My God, Clara thought, this woman was going to get herself killed over these pictures—and no sooner had the thought crossed her mind than a low *thump* sounded from one of the buildings to her left.

There was time for only one of two possible actions as the rocket streaked toward Dakota: try to locate and open fire on the man who'd shot it, or save the oblivious journalist who couldn't distinguish the sound of a shoulder-fired rocket launch from any other explosion in the village that day.

Clara opted for the latter, diving atop Dakota and flinging them both prone a second before the rocket impacted the building beside them.

The blast sucked the air out of Clara's lungs. A shockwave rocked her body and the snowfall of debris and sand dust washed over both women.

And Dakota, in that instant, did something that infuriated Clara—she looked sideways to make sure her camera had survived the blast.

Then she said something that infuriated Clara even further.

"Wow, girl, I didn't realize you felt this way about me."

Clara almost shouted, "Your first job is staying *alive*, Dakota. The pictures come second, got it?"

Dakota nodded, sounding nonchalant. "Yeah, probably a good call."

Clara pushed herself off her friend, struggling upright and continuing to run toward the battle converging in front of her. As she sprinted, she gave a passing thought to Dakota—had Clara saved her friend's life, or had the rocket impacted high enough that the blast would have left Dakota unscathed either way? Clara wasn't sure, and it certainly didn't matter now, as she neared the most intense fighting.

As she arrived at the center of the storm, she saw one of her platoon's armored vehicles rumbling around the corner of the building. In a 360-degree fight, that was a massive relocation of nearly a quarter of the platoon's combat power that she hadn't approved, and only one person besides her could, or would, make that call without asking for approval.

She saw him a moment later—Kyle, shouting directions to a squad leader and darting forward to get a better view down the street.

Clara felt a distant sense of comfort that no one on the battlefield that day, Taliban or American, had more combat experience than Kyle did, and Clara knew that if she was missing anything about the course of the engagement, Kyle would fill her in at once.

She heard the hissing crack of bullets striking the wall of the building beside her and clanging against the two armored vehicles now united at the corner.

Clara skidded to a stop behind Kyle, giving his shoulder a hard shake.

But Kyle's attention was unbroken, fixated on a single building down the street.

She waited half a second for him to see whatever he wanted to see, then slapped the back of his helmet to get his attention as the turret-mounted machinegun beside them thundered alive with a long burst of gunfire.

When he turned to her, she shouted, "Why are we moving trucks?"

He didn't answer her question, instead yelling back, "What's the status on QRF?"

"Twenty mikes."

Kyle looked like she'd just punched him in the throat, the first time she'd ever seen fear in his eyes.

He said, "We ain't gonna make it that long, LT. I think they're massing." The crump of a mortar round detonating on the far side of the vehicle drowned out his voice. The explosion subsided to the clatter of gunfire as he continued, "The enemy is massing in Building 64."

Clara's heart sank. Of all the buildings in the village...of course they'd use that one.

Kyle said, "I'm putting two trucks here and cross-loading ammunition, but we're running out of ammo faster than we can hold them off. There are too many of them, and—"

Another mortar round impacted with a quaking blast, and Kyle continued, "Once they push down the street from Building 64, they're inside our perimeter. If we don't drop it now, and I mean *right* now, they're gonna overrun us."

Clara peered around the side of the truck at the dusty expanse of street leading to Building 64's mud-brick minarets. There it was, the explanation for everything she'd perceived about the course of battle shifting to a single point in the village. The enemy's position wasn't accidental or impromptu; the Taliban had arrived in force, undetected by US intelligence, and were now deliberately executing a carefully planned attack that would end with her platoon being wiped out.

She ducked back behind the truck, uttering three words.

"I'm on it."

She simultaneously gave Kyle a thumbs up, which seemed in hindsight an obscenely inappropriate gesture given what she was about to do. Kyle returned to managing the tactical situation on the ground, and Clara raced back inside the building, toward her impromptu command post.

Jason Sims was kneeling a few feet from the window, firing his rifle toward an adjacent building. He stopped shooting as she entered, shouting over the explosion of a grenade outside.

"LT, I just heard. Want me to call in the drop on 64?"

"No," Clara said. "No, this one has to be me. Put me on the air freq."

He reached toward the rucksack holding the radio and passed her the handset. Clara took it and knelt, pressing the button to transmit.

"Raptor Four-Three, this is Sandman Two-Six Actual. Ground force commander assesses imminent threat to friendly forces, need emergency close air support. Request one-by GBU-12 center mass on Building 64. You are cleared for danger close engagement, ground force commander initials Charlie Sierra."

The voice that responded was clinical and detached, speaking with all the drama of an airline pilot. Which was particularly impressive, Clara thought, since he was flying in a fighter jet over a combat zone during an active gunfight with three dead Americans at six hundred miles per hour.

"Two-Six, this is Raptor Four-Three. Restate target."

Clara transmitted, "Building 64, center mass, danger close."

A pause, and then the pilot transmitted the words no ground force commander wanted to hear.

"Be advised, Building 64 is a mosque."

She felt her jaw twitch, recalling the words of her interpreter before this entire nightmare had kicked off.

They have families at gunpoint in the mosque.

"Raptor Four-Three," Clara replied, "be advised, ground force is going black on ammo and about to be overrun. Enemy is massing in Building 64 to launch their final ground assault, and if you don't drop that bomb right now, you're going to be talking to an empty mic, how copy?"

This time, the pilot's response was immediate.

"Raptor Four-Three inbound for drop. Sixty seconds to weapons release."

Clara tossed down the handset, transmitting to Kyle and her squad leaders via the radio mic mounted on her body armor.

"Net call, net call, bomb strike on Building 64 one minute out."

Then she lowered her hand from the transmit button, muttering three lonely words to herself.

"God help us."

The battlefield noises became strangely muted as Clara considered the repercussions of what she'd just ordered. Her thoughts were interrupted by an eerie response from Jason Sims, and she was momentarily surprised that he'd even been able to hear her speak.

"God?" Sims asked. "There's no God here. There's...there's nothing."

She heard a gunshot then, and jumped—it wasn't outside, but right there in the room. Had Sims just shot her? Clara turned and saw that the reality was much worse.

Jason Sims was standing now, wearing his full dress uniform as he had at the time of his suicide. One hand loosely gripped a semi-automatic pistol, its slide locked to the rear from the last shot it would ever fire, a single wisp of smoke rising from the tip of the exposed barrel.

She backed up as he staggered toward her.

The top half of his face was recognizable, but only just so—one eye was marbled with blood, the iris drifting listlessly downward. But the other eye was locked on her, his jaw hanging free to expose a pinpoint of light at the back of his throat.

Then his lips peeled back gruesomely, loose jaw bouncing as he spoke, his voice a disjointed melody spewing from both his mouth and the bullet's exit wound. The effect was a surreal echo that rose above the din of battle.

"What good did it do? What we're about to, to these...these people."

The radio crackled.

"*Thirty seconds.*"

It was the fighter pilot's voice, transmitting calmly. During the battle, she'd relayed that time hack to her men, but now she was struck with terror, reflexively trying to clutch her rifle but finding her hands empty.

Jason Sims didn't seem to notice, taking another limping step toward her.

"You know what happens now. Look at me, look at what I...I did. Oh God, Lieutenant, what have I done?"

Sims looked at the pistol in his hand, seeming shocked to find it there. He released it, and the weapon clattered to the sandy floor.

Clara's back hit the wall, and she looked toward the door, now her only escape, but it was blocked by a shadowy figure.

She tried to make a move for it anyway, but Sims lunged toward her, clutching her shoulders desperately.

"*Ten seconds,*" the fighter pilot said over the radio.

Sims drew his face near hers. "Tell me what to do, Lieutenant," he whispered. "You always called the shots during that fight...but look what happened. You know what that bomb's going to do to them, what it'll do to us." The blood-marbled eyeball drifted upward in its socket, the pupil warbling in lazy circles. "Those people, Lieutenant. What we did to them. You know what's about to happen. How could I live with it? How could any of us?"

As she struggled to breathe, her body immobilized, the shadowy figure vanished from the doorway. It reappeared behind Sims, a dark and swirling mass in the form of a man.

The radio squawked with two final words from the pilot. "*Weapons release.*"

A five-hundred-pound bomb had just soared off the fighter jet's rails.

Jason Sims's face was inches from hers, his hot breath stinking of gunpowder. "Do you remember what it sounded like, right before it hit?" He gasped and said in a choked voice, "I never stopped hearing that sound."

The time between first hearing the bomb's descent and its impact wasn't long: a single second, a second and a half at most. But the auditory shock was jolting, causing Clara's last thought before the blast to be a terrifying certainty that the pilot had mistakenly sent the bomb dead-center into her platoon's position.

It was the sound of air shredding, almost as loud as if the fighter jet itself were plummeting into the ground. A whistling, howling vortex of sound that crescendoed brutally toward them, toward the mosque full of innocents. It was the sound of death on a massive scale, the last noise that many in Pantalay Village would ever hear.

And in those split seconds, Clara saw something strange. The shadowy figure drew close behind Sims, peering over his shoulder at Clara in her terror. Its head was a churning, smoky blackness, and then two white eyes glowed amidst the dark void as it transformed into the face of a man.

It was Dr. Jannesson, now gazing at her with a look of pained compassion.

The bomb pummeled through the mosque's roof, striking the ground floor and exploding with a deafening crash that shook the entire world around her.

And then Clara awoke.

13

Clara spent the following day in her office, typing furiously—but not on her novel.

Instead she detailed her dream in staggering detail, as if she were writing a fiction scene.

She did this because it was the only respite she had, the only way to claim any power over the horrors of her mind. It didn't cathartically dispel the anguish, but it quieted her mind to a place where she could think again, where she could process her feelings.

As she wrote, she periodically glanced over to the phone, waiting for Dr. Jannesson to call.

She dreaded the conversation. So much to unpack, so much to explain, starting with yesterday's home "invasion." What had the cetraphaline reacted with—something in her system from Afghanistan, some previously undetected brain disease, or something she hadn't considered yet? She was certain she'd heard glass breaking, men charging up the stairs and trying to kick in her door. But the cops were equally certain that what she'd described couldn't have possibly occurred. And that pointed the Charleston PD, her husband, and all the Southern trophy wives of this gated kingdom to one conclusion: Clara was losing her mind.

But hang on, Doc, there's more. How could things be any worse than losing her marriage to Jeremy, and then reliving the horrors of combat in her sleep? Answer: losing your marriage, and then reliving those horrors combined with your former platoonmates turning into zombies. That's a fun little twist, now isn't it? At least the memories of combat had a finite quantity, terrible though they may be. As for the terrors her own mind could apparently conjure...she wasn't so sure those wouldn't go on endlessly.

And Dr. Jannesson appearing in her dream—what had that been about?

When he hadn't called her by three o'clock, she let her hand hover over the phone, summoning the willpower to make the dreaded call. But she had to; whatever was going on with her, Dr. Jannesson alone held the answer. This conversation would go like all those before it: Clara terrified and bewildered, and Dr. Jannesson calmly explaining exactly what was happening in her mind. Maybe she needed another cetraphaline treatment. Because there would be some end in sight; there had to be.

Didn't there?

Clara finally lifted her phone and dialed. She could hear the pulse in her ear against the phone, even above the constant ringing.

A woman answered.

"Savannah Wellness Clinic, how may I help you?"

Clara hesitated. "Hi, this is Clara Swanner, I was down there recently for a cetraphaline treatment. I need to speak with Dr. Jannesson."

The woman sounded uncomfortable. "I'm sorry, Mrs. Swanner. Dr. Jannesson had a family emergency, and is out of town at the moment."

"Oh," Clara said quietly, feeling heat rising up her shoulders to the nape of her neck. "Do you know when he'll be back?"

"We're not sure yet. But once he is, we'll call his existing patients to reschedule follow-up calls. So you can wait to hear back from us, okay?"

Clara agreed and ended the call, setting down her phone numbly.

Her eyes drifted to the framed photo on her desk, the one of her and Dakota posing arm-in-arm, smiling in front of their two cars. The picture was taken stateside in the base's unit parking lot after their return from deployment. Both women appeared happy and smiling, with Clara in her fatigues and Dakota in a low-cut top and jeans. They were a military officer and a journalist who looked like a model, polar opposites to the outside world and yet sharing more similarities than the cars behind them. Both women had returned from Afghanistan, alive but forever changed. And while they projected the image of friends, Clara knew in her heart that everything had changed after that moment in Pantalay Village, when a single confrontation with Dakota had altered the world as she knew it, much less her relationship with her friend, forever.

But she didn't have much time to consider the thought.

The garage door opened, and Thor leapt up from his bed and bounded down the stairs.

Jeremy had arrived home early.

Clara descended the stairs, arriving at the ground floor in time to see him entering alone.

"Hey," she said, "everything okay? Where's Aiden?"

He kissed her lips, then pulled back. "Yeah. Everything's fine. I got off work early, and we don't have to pick up Aiden for another couple hours. I thought we could go upstairs and—"

Clara blurted, "Do you think something's wrong?"

Jeremy's shoulders sagged. "Like...what?"

"What I mean is, obviously this treatment has had some adverse effects on me. I think something went wrong."

Jeremy shifted his weight to one foot, considering the statement.

"Clara, from what I've read about this treatment, it has helped hundreds of vets. A thousand or more, maybe, with no lasting negative effects. If you think something is wrong, I don't exactly disbelieve you. But I can't buy into it either—not because you're not a stunning and intelligent woman, but because you haven't been yourself lately."

Clara felt her throat closing up. Her mind was screaming at her to stop talking, to cut her losses before Jeremy thought she was any crazier than he already did.

"You're right," she said, crossing the line into an outright lie. It certainly wasn't the first time. "I've been under a lot of pressure with the manuscript. Maybe it's just been getting to me."

"I think it has. Maybe you should take a...I don't know. A spa day or something. Just give yourself a break."

A spa day. What a joke. She'd tried a spa day, once. During it, she had undergone a ninety-minute deep tissue massage, and within half an hour her constant muscle tension resumed, unabated.

She leaned in to kiss him, then said, "I can think of something that would relax me more."

"Oh?"

Taking his hand, she led him up the stairs to their bedroom.

* * *

When Jeremy went to pick up their son, Clara recused herself by citing some loose ends she needed to tie up on the manuscript. That was yet another bald-faced lie; she hadn't touched it in days now.

She'd had sex with Jeremy, and done so in spectacularly promiscuous fashion—especially for a weekday afternoon—more or less to divert his mind from her paranoia, from the home break-in, from the fact that he was increasingly suspecting that she was losing her mind. He wasn't wrong; Clara knew she was in a dangerous place now, atop a perilous razor's edge of sanity. And Jeremy had far too many better options for her to be flirting with total vulnerability right now.

The house suddenly felt stifling. She craved fresh air, and reverted to one of the rote mechanical tasks she could perform without conscious thought: checking the mail. She wandered downstairs, feeling as if her mind was swimming in a near-fugue state of confusion.

Exiting the front door, she felt the hot rays of sunshine warming her skin. Since she was normally confined to her office, the outside world now seemed a blinding and dazzling array of majestic homes and manicured landscaping. It was a sterile universe of gated perfection maintained by landscapers and swimming pool technicians who lived outside the community's fence, only allowed entry when their formal duties required it. Clara shuffled toward her mailbox with the absurd feeling that this neighborhood epitomized everything she'd been doing since leaving the military—retreating to an oasis from the outside world, shielded from realities she could no longer bear to face. Unlike her trip to Savannah, she was now in no danger of being solicited by the homeless, be they blind veterans or otherwise.

But as she approached her mailbox, she realized there was an arguably worse option.

"Clara!" a woman called cheerfully.

Jackie Hazley, the bombshell blonde from two doors down, was power walking down the sidewalk toward her.

Jackie was emblematic of the neighborhood wives, which was to say outwardly bubbly and obsessed with physical perfection. For these women, daytime public appearances were preceded by squeezing themselves into costly, moisture-wicking, and above all else skin-tight workout attire, and Jackie was no exception.

She looked resplendent in the labial wedgie of her yoga pants, her flat abs ending in a hot pink sports bra doing its part to support her surgically enhanced breasts. However senseless this facade appeared to Clara, she knew it was like cocaine-laced catnip for men—and with a darkening sense of jealousy, she remembered that Jeremy was probably chief among them. While the neighborhood husbands were sporting trophy wives on their arms when they weren't bedding their mistresses, Jeremy was stuck with the troubled female veteran, a brooding wench who had to drink herself to sleep.

Stopping before Clara, Jackie said, "So what are you up to?"

"Just checking the mail." What type of makeup didn't run under such conditions, Clara didn't know, but Jackie was dolled up in lipstick and eyeliner just the same, her cheeks rosy with exertion and carefully applied blush.

"Oh, right," Jackie replied. "I just had some time before I have to get dinner started and thought I'd burn some extra calories. Can you believe how hot it is?"

Clara squinted up at the sun.

"Yeah, kind of," she said. "We're in the South."

Jackie faltered at this, seeming unsure what to make of Clara. She resorted to a dazzling smile. "You should come to Pilates with the wives sometime. It's a fantastic workout."

"I've got to work."

"Oh," Jackie said, dismayed. "What do you do again?"

"I'm an author."

"That's right. So are you working on your first book?"

"Fourth," Clara corrected her. "I've published three."

"Oh wow, that's—impressive. Do you write under a pen name, or...?"

"Nope. Clara Swanner."

"Okay, all right." Jackie was nodding now, her expression conveying the implicit knowledge that surely Clara was a massive failure so long as her books weren't appearing front-and-center in the local national chain bookstore, right next to Patterson's tenth co-written release of the year. Outside of her own readers, Clara had yet to meet anyone who'd read a single book that wasn't launched with the benefit of millions in marketing dollars. Jackie concluded, "I'll have to read your stuff sometime."

"Sure," Clara said, feeling increasingly irritable. How could she ever compete with this? The rest of the neighborhood wives all stopped working sometime during their first pregnancy, and once their one or more kids were in school, had never worked again.

That wasn't to say their days were empty, because this particular brand of fair maiden kept a stringent schedule: depending on the day of the week, they'd meet the other wives at yoga, or Pilates, or spin class. Then they'd retire to a Starbucks or the smoothie bar, recovering from their workout while gossiping about whatever it was these women talked about—probably whoever wasn't present, with Clara a prime candidate. She was almost a pariah by virtue of being gainfully employed, and that was just the starting point in a long list of reasons that she didn't fit in and never would.

And yet, compete she did, because she'd seen the way some of them looked at Jeremy, and knew that a few of the lustier ones wouldn't hesitate for one second to have an affair if offered the chance.

Clara knew that Jeremy had precious little to lose by divorcing her. In addition to guaranteed custody of Aiden, Jeremy would be free to find not just a younger woman, but more importantly one who hadn't been marred by combat. He'd have a fresh start with a trophy wife of his own, a conquest he'd never possessed, someone who didn't need to constantly produce novels to remain distracted from their own messed-up psyche, a porn-star-in-training who would be thrilled to enjoy the life he could provide. Someone who could be content, a fate that would forever be denied to Clara. The Barbie dolls of Charleston would be lining up for Jeremy's attention, and all of them would be far better wives than she.

"Clara?" Jackie said.

"Yeah?"

"I said, you should bring the family over for dinner sometime soon. It's been too long."

"It has," Clara agreed. "Well, I better get going. See you later."

"Okay," Jackie said hesitantly, and Clara began walking toward her house before the conversation had to drag along any further.

Jackie called after her, "Clara?"

"Yes, Jackie?"

The woman seemed confused. "Your mail. Weren't you going to check your mail?"

* * *

Clara entered her house, tossing the mail on a side table and locking the front door. Her eyes were burning with tears now, and she angrily wiped them away.

Thor padded toward her from the kitchen, whining at the sight of her. Clara smeared the tears from her eyes and muttered, "Don't judge me, dog. Come on, let's get you some food."

The puppy followed her into the kitchen, joyful at his dinner's early arrival. Clara was feeding him for no other reason than she felt numb, powerless, incapable of anything but mindless domestic tasks.

Clara put the dog food away and drifted to the stairs, ascending the steps to her office with the feeling that she was well and truly alone. Or, *almost* alone. Because there was only one person she could be completely honest with, and it wasn't her husband.

It was Kyle.

As her platoon sergeant, Kyle was a tactical genius. He'd previously deployed to Afghanistan with different units, seeing combat action in various provinces. Upon meeting him, Clara sensed that he'd stand a better chance than anyone of getting their men home alive. Upon seeing him manage the fight with her in Pantalay Village, she knew for sure. He'd effortlessly directed the squad leaders, crescendoing their rate of fire from a dwindling ammo supply to hold off the enemy until that five-hundred-pound bomb hit. Their platoon had lost three men that day, but Clara knew in her heart that without Kyle, they would have lost many more.

But combat effectiveness had a fleeting shelf life in terms of being a personal strength.

Kyle had been gently nudged out of the military at the end of his contract, as had Clara—you didn't blow up a mosque in 2016 and have a career to return to, dead enemy fighters confirmed or no—and while Clara could pretend to fit in amidst an alien world of civilians, Kyle was too far gone to ever return to the fold of society.

It wasn't his fault, Clara knew. It had taken her years to gradually piece her humanity back together, until she was able to feel emotions other than anger, impulses that extended beyond animalistic survival. And Clara had only been in one gunfight, horrific as it was.

But Kyle had no concept of how many gunfights he'd been a part of, how many IED blasts he'd nearly died in, or how many people he'd killed. He simply had too many deployments to too many terrible places in Afghanistan, most occurring at a time in the war when combat units possessed free rein to hunt the enemy as they pleased.

And as a functioning member of a peacetime society that didn't need or want ruthless killers in its ranks, Kyle was forever lost. He'd never regain his humanity as it existed for the rest of the population, never even feign normalcy as Clara had learned to do.

Kyle had left the service to find that no one particularly cared about his combat credentials, that most of them were only vaguely aware that America even had forces in Afghanistan almost two decades after 9/11. As with Clara, he'd faced the tirade of memories and guilt that descended on a mind forever removed from war. But unlike Clara, Kyle *wanted* to go back. Combat was his only respite from a world that had long since grown meaningless, and once that thrill of adrenaline and living on the cutting edge of death had been removed, Kyle turned to the bottle.

Clara self-medicated with alcohol in order to sleep; Kyle practically sedated himself with it every night, tormented by the haunting memories of countless fights from the other side of the world. While Clara never had dreams or flashbacks until very recently, Kyle faced them every night. He'd be back in Pantalay Village, or Logar Province, or the Tangi Valley; he'd be applying his own tourniquet after getting hit by a bullet, or seeing his subordinate getting shot in the head a second after moving to a position that he had ordered.

Arriving in her office, Clara took a seat and held her phone, debating what she'd say to Kyle. Like her, Kyle had tried a few treatment options, usually discontinuing when the first session found him screaming at the therapist. He also despised medication—Kyle simply believed there was nothing pills could do for him that alcohol couldn't, and Clara didn't necessarily disagree.

So he'd turned to drink in full, having his first glass in the afternoon and continuing until he blacked out, or came so close that the threshold became a matter of semantics. That had cost him his second marriage, already in shambles well before his departure from the service. Now Kyle paid dual alimony, his recreational pursuits limited to drinking and hosting a parade of women through his bedroom. He'd turned that latter hobby into a virtual art form.

Clara knew all this because Kyle told her, sometimes drunkenly texting her pictures of women tied up on his bed, blindfolded and writhing in anticipation, and sometimes relaying the information with a giggle during an entirely sober phone call. To him, none of this was strange in the slightest, and Clara had never protested, and never would, for one reason alone: there was no one else Kyle could talk to. Not honestly, at least. Not about the disturbing nature of his sexual addiction, not about the extent of his drinking, and certainly not about some of the more violent acts he'd been a party to in combat.

In that regard, he and Clara were much the same. Kyle was the only one Clara could be completely honest with, which became staggeringly clear the night before Dakota's funeral. As Clara and Kyle drank at the hotel bar, long after the attending platoon members turned in for the night, he'd abruptly said, "You don't really care if you die, do you?"

Clara's mental walls had immediately gone up; by then she'd been fantasizing about suicide for some time but deeply compartmentalized that desire beneath the carefully maintained veneer of a normal mother.

Then she realized who she was talking to: a man who'd seen what she'd seen and far more, who was incapable of judgment against her. Clara thought that this was the first moment she'd ever been able to be completely honest with anyone, at least since Pantalay Village.

"No," she said, feeling her constantly tense muscles suddenly relax. "I don't."

He laughed. "Yep, I could tell during that gunfight. I didn't care if I died, either, but the rest of our platoon sure did."

Then he'd switched topics and continued chattering away, oblivious to the profound revelation that Clara had just had. But Clara had never forgotten. Kyle was the one man she could be completely honest with, devoid of any formalities or projected normalcy.

And right now, she needed that desperately.

Sitting in her office chair, eyes fixed on the framed picture of her and Dakota with their Cadillacs, she called him now.

Kyle answered on the third ring. "'Sup, girl?"

"Kyle, I need to talk. And I don't have much time before Jeremy gets back."

She heard the clanking of ice on glass—he was already getting started for the evening.

"Have the tables turned, Clara? Usually it's *me* calling *you* with issues."

Clara swallowed, considering whether Kyle would consider her insane by the end of this conversation.

"Since I got back from Savannah, I've been having dreams. I'll be back in Pantalay, and our suicides are coming to life, you know? Just super disturbing, really messed-up stuff."

"Oh, I know all right. You're describing my average Wednesday."

"Yesterday, I could've sworn I heard people breaking into my house. I called 911, and the police found nothing. Jeremy thinks I'm losing my mind, and I'm worried he's going to ask for a divorce."

"Come on now." Kyle laughed. "Single life ain't so bad. I can teach you how to meet guys and tie 'em up."

Clara closed her eyes and brought a hand to her temple, feeling the onset of a low-grade headache. "Maybe there was something wrong with my treatment. The nurse could have given me the wrong dose, or it could have reacted with something in my system. Or... what if I'm just losing it?"

She winced in anticipation of Kyle's reaction. On the other line, the ice cubes tinkled again. "Good God, Clara, do I have to spell it out for you?"

"Spell what out?"

"During that battle you coordinated our platoon, air support, and the Quick Reaction Force without ever losing control of your voice. We were about to be overrun and you were talking to me just as calmly as you are now. Gave me the thumbs-up before dropping the bomb, as I recall. I'm not having a conversation with some dive bar trollop right now. You're Clara Swanner, a genuine warrior princess. I've seen a lot of people who became killers after multiple deployments, but you're the only person I ever served with who was *born that way*, and showed it on their first gunfight. So I ask you, Lieutenant Clara Swanner of Pantalay, do you think something is wrong, or not?"

"Yes," she responded instinctively, without the slightest hesitation.

"Then there's your answer, girl. Something's wrong, so spare me the self-pity and stop second-guessing yourself."

Clara heard the garage door opening.

"Jeremy and Aiden are back. I have to go."

"Tell you what. I'll drive over to Virginia Beach in the morning, see Alan Smith in person—he's the one who told me about this treatment in the first place, so I'll see if he's had any issues. I'll call you back tomorrow."

"Okay. Thanks, Kyle."

"I'm here for you. And get yourself checked out by a doctor. If the medicine reacted with something in your system, better we know now."

She ended the call, starting to rise before her gaze fell once more upon the photograph of her and Dakota. The image of her friend, neatly framed on the desk, was the reason Clara couldn't resort to medication. She'd tried to do so before, of course; pills had been Clara's first uneducated choice of treatment, and she went through a variety of prescriptions just after leaving the military. Some had left her in a lobotomized trance, others in a dreary, half-present existence where she watched her husband and son like they were actors in a movie. The worst of them made her sink into a depression, calling forth the suicidal ideation that floated as a distant thought in her mind until it was pulsing in her temples, as quivering and ever-present as the ringing in her ears.

Then Dakota had killed herself, overdosing on a bottle of opioids that, it turned out, she'd been self-medicating with for years. Her suicide note was beautiful and moving in a way that only an impassioned journalist like Dakota could have produced, and after her stepfather provided its text to the media as part of a public plea for veteran treatment, Clara had thrown her own prescription bottles in the trash. She found the very prospect of pills revolting after learning how Dakota had died, and vowed never to outsource her survival to a prescription again.

14

After dinner, the Swanner family gathered in Aiden's bathroom for his nightly tub session.

Clara had always enjoyed this part of the night. Aiden loved taking baths, and merrily splashed away surrounded by his floating toys as Thor stood watch over the proceedings, his front paws perched on the side of the tub.

Then they dried Aiden off, moving to the adjoining bedroom to tuck him in. Clara and Jeremy alternated reading from a stack of children's books, and when Aiden began rubbing his eyes with the back of his fist, they kissed him goodnight.

Clara and Jeremy performed their nightly ritual—dishes, tea, and television—and Jeremy lapsed into sleep almost immediately after they went to bed. He'd always been a sound sleeper, his conscious apparently free from everything that plagued Clara at night. She felt secretly grateful that she wouldn't have to spread her legs for him a second time today. Part of it was that she felt troubled about Jannesson. But the other part was the fact that her husband didn't, and wouldn't, believe her, and she sensed a chasm of mistrust growing between them.

She rose from bed, walked upstairs to her office, and closed the door behind her.

Clara wanted to continue researching what could be wrong with her.

But she'd exhausted the list of topics—brain injury, burn pits, chemical exposure—and found herself before the screen without the slightest clue of what to type.

She looked away then, letting her eyes fall to the picture of her and Dakota, dimly lit by the computer screen's glow. Clara stared at it silently, thinking about her cetraphaline trip and the voice in her head telling her, *Dakota is free now.*

Then she recalled her meeting with Dr. Jannesson before the treatment, unsure why her thoughts were drifting to his comforting words that her PTSD was normal; expected, even, for someone in such circumstances.

But as she recalled his words, a different quote stood out to her—hadn't he mentioned that he didn't have a family? She scanned her memories of the meeting, clearly recalling the statement as Dr. Jannesson shook his head: *My work is my life, no family for me.*

But the receptionist at his clinic that day had definitely said he was out of town with a family emergency—what sense did that make? Was she covering for him, or had he lied to cover up something else?

Then she recalled seeing Dr. Jannesson in her dream, calmly peering at her over Jason Sims's shoulder.

Clara began typing into a web browser, looking for background research on Dr. Jannesson. There were press reports and interviews of all kinds, mostly citing his work with cetraphaline and a few old references to his neurosurgery career. The inquiry led her to the Federation of State Medical Boards website, and she clicked the *FIND A DOCTOR* feature.

Entering Jannesson's name returned no results.

Clara sat back in confusion. How could that be? She re-entered the search with variations of his last name, landing on one result when she spelled it J-A-N-I-S-O-N.

She clicked on it to see the contents.

Marcus Janison, MD.
   Education: Yale School of Medicine
   Active Licenses: No Active Licenses
   Actions: 2020-11-17 Revocation of medical license. No document available; refer to board site.

Clara examined that last line several times over. Jannesson's license had been revoked...so how was he still administering medical care?

Deciphering the *refer to board site* comment led her to the website of the Georgia Composite Medical Board, where she again searched Jannesson's name with the new spelling.

This time she found the aforementioned document, a three-page, double-spaced memorandum serving as the official revocation of his medical license. The text was made in sprawling and at times incomprehensible legalese, but Clara's eyes darted across phrases such as *failure to treat a patient according to the generally accepted standard of care*, and *attempted concealment of the act constituting a violation*. The details were hazy, consisting largely of dates, patients referred to by initials, and names of various medications Clara had never heard of. Cetraphaline was never mentioned, which she found oddly disturbing in a way that made her stomach churn.

But the most disturbing turn of phrase came in the second-to-last paragraph: *alleged experimentation on unconsenting patients*.

Experimentation...if Jannesson had been experimenting with administering substances the year before, then what was he doing now, in 2021? And what could he have put into her IV drip while she was passed out? She had no idea, but she was going to find out. As soon as Jeremy headed to work the next morning, she'd be on her way to a doctor—a *real* doctor—for a full set of bloodwork.

The document ended, *NOW THEREFORE, the Board finds that Respondent's continued practice of medicine poses a threat to the public health, safety, and welfare and imperatively requires emergency action and hereby ORDERS that Respondent's license to practice medicine in the State of Georgia be and is hereby SUMMARILY REVOKED...*

Clara saved the files and links to her computer, closing down the screen and slipping out of her office. She faced a judgment call now—it was after eleven, and she could either try to go to sleep naturally in the wake of what she'd just learned, or throw up her hands and head straight for the bar cart.

She opted for the former, telling herself that she couldn't keep living in fear. If the nightmares came, then so be it; she'd been through combat, and she couldn't keep cowing in terror at the thought of what each night would bring. And she was determined not to turn into Kyle, reliant on the bottle for daily existence. She loved and respected the man, but if there was any chance of natural sleep, she was going to take it.

Clara slid into bed beside Jeremy, adjusting the weighted blanket over her and putting on her sleep mask. The white noise machine was still humming along, drowning out the ringing in her ears as she regulated her breathing. She saw Aiden, the most calming force in her universe, and directed her thoughts to his smile, his constant drawings, his hysterical laughter as she played with him. This was a common nighttime ritual for her—Aiden was the best way to keep the dark emotions at bay, to calm herself into a state where sleep was a possibility.

But twenty minutes passed that way, her visions of Aiden increasingly punctuated by thoughts of what she'd just learned about Jannesson. *Alleged experimentation on unconsenting patients.* She'd need legal consultation, no doubt; but first she had to see a doctor, and find out what else was floating around in her system.

Clara rose from bed. She knew what would happen if she didn't: the tension would mount, her thoughts growing increasingly panicked and anxious until she found the bottle. On nights like these it was far better to start and end her drinking early, returning to bed with the prospect of continuous sleep before the sunrise.

So she felt for the rail and descended the stairs to her kitchen. Retrieving a glass, she moved for the bar cart by the ambient light of adjacent houses. The downstairs was ghostlike at times like these, and she always felt slightly uneasy here until the first warming sip of bourbon was easing its way down her throat.

But Clara stopped halfway to the bar cart. She sensed something wrong, although it took her a moment to identify the source. A muggy breeze was wafting across her, carrying with it the smells of damp grass and night air, and her eyes darted across the windows in sequence until she found an open one. It was on the far side of the dining room table, and Clara knew in an instant that it hadn't been open when she went to bed, that it hadn't been open that day at all.

Then she heard a noise in the living room, and knew in a split second that someone was on the ground floor with her.

In a flash, she realized that she hadn't hallucinated the home invasion. Whoever had broken in must have had some alternate intent, maybe to engineer a way past her security system so they could come back for her at night.

She leapt sideways, her free hand flying to the light switch and flipping it up.

Then she whirled to face the living room, reflexively yelling one word.

"Jannesson!"

She raised the glass to throw it—she'd need to buy herself time to race for the steak knives beside the stove—and her eyes darted toward a figure that she sensed before she saw it.

Joshua Thoma, the last member of her platoon to kill himself.

The medic had done so in spectacular fashion, drawing a hot bath and then opening his arteries with the combat knife he'd carried in Pantalay. And she saw that his current state was how he looked at his death—naked, sopping wet, and deathly pale, huge open gashes on his thighs and wrists.

She peeled scream after scream, the glass falling from her hand and shattering on the floor.

Joshua's bloodshot eyes met hers, as if he hadn't known she was there until she made a sound. Then his expression fell into a look of relief, of comfort, and he began walking forward.

He took delicate steps, as if his feet had trouble supporting his weight now that his femoral artery was slashed on each leg. The blood that pumped futilely from his open wounds was jet black, turning a dark crimson as it ran down his body to pool in greasy streaks on the hardwood.

She saw now that his right hand loosely clenched his combat knife, its blade covered in blood from sawing through his flesh and veins.

"I didn't even want to fight," he said in a low voice. "I became a medic to help people—but I didn't help anyone. I couldn't save that Afghan boy, couldn't save any of our men. I couldn't save anyone in that mosque that we...that we bombed."

Thoma faltered then. "I stood with those bodies for the entire battle. You told me we were going to kill them all—and we did, LT."

Clara wanted to look away, to run. But her entire body was rigid, immobilized by the nightmare before her.

Thoma was crying now, tears pouring over his gray cheeks. "I mean,

Christ, Lieutenant—we thought we were saving ourselves, but did we? Look at the cost. Everyone who survived the battle has been living with the weight of what we did to survive. Did we deserve to live? Did I?"

He was still coming toward her, staggering forward grotesquely. Blood and water were flowing off him, and tears poured from his red-rimmed eyes, his mouth agape and wheezing between words.

"It was too hard, there was too much pain. More of us have died by our own hand than by the enemy. You think I'll be the last one? Because I don't. Who's next—you? Kyle?"

He was close enough now for Clara to breathe the pungent coppery stench of his blood through flared nostrils. She wanted to scream, to flee, but she could only manage half-gasped breaths as panic blossomed in her brain.

She saw the tip of the blade quivering in his shaky grasp and wondered if he was going to use it on her.

Instead he hesitated, his tear-soaked eyes widening with incomprehension.

"I'm getting so cold," he said. "It's so...cold here."

Clara woke up then, bolting upright and peeling the sleep mask from her face. She was surrounded by darkness, trying to breathe but unable to pull in any air. Her lungs were seized up, her throat constricted.

Finally she managed one shallow breath, then another. Panting, Clara thought, it was a dream. Just a dream. She told herself that over and over, feeling her heart slamming erratically as she struggled to breathe.

15

Kyle pulled his Pathfinder into an open visitor spot. The brakes groaned as he slowed, and the vehicle shuddered as it came to a stop. He killed the engine, and it rattled to a halt with a series of ticks. Yeah, Kyle thought, probably a good move to get rid of this thing before the wheels fell off.

He exited the vehicle and slammed the door shut, expecting he wouldn't be alone for more than ten seconds. And sure enough, the glass door to the showroom swung open, and the first salesman shuffled out to meet him.

Kyle looked at the approaching man-child, disappointed to see that he was a bearded douche with the points of his mustache waxed. The skinny arms protruding from his dealership polo shirt were tattooed with colorful nonsense, flowers and infinity symbols and stars and cursive song lyrics.

He was eyeing Kyle's forearm tattoos as he approached, trying to make a determination on this new potential customer and settling on the worst possible option.

"Hey, bro. How can I help you?"

Kyle was silent for a moment, eyeing the kid up and down before he replied.

"I ain't your bro, you little millennial train wreck. Go fetch me Alan Smith. Tell him the guy who called about a Pathfinder trade-in is here, and ready to play hardball."

The salesman was staring at Kyle in shock, as if he expected this customer to laugh at his own joke, or suddenly compose himself and apologize for the insult. But Kyle stared at him with unblinking eyes until the man replied, "Yes, sir. Give me just a minute."

He disappeared inside, and Kyle waited with his hands on his hips, turning to survey the parked vehicles spread on the lot before him. The sun was already beating down—it was going to be a hot one.

The dealership door opened again, and Kyle spun to see Alan Smith striding onto the sidewalk with the bearded man-child in trail.

Alan looked good, Kyle decided. He'd put on a bit of a gut, but a wedding ring twinkled on his left hand and his eyes were bright, without the dark circles that Kyle had.

"Mr. Soler, nice to meet you in person."

He extended his hand and Kyle shook it firmly, trading a quick glance of understanding.

"The feeling's mutual, fella. Hope you came to work ready for business, because I'm a hard bargainer and I won't let up until I hit your bottom dollar. We clear on that?"

Alan smiled. "Wouldn't have it any other way, sir. Here at Hall Chrysler Dodge Jeep RAM, we pride ourselves on providing a higher trade-in value than any dealer in the state." He looked to Kyle's Pathfinder, a heap of an SUV whose navy-blue paint was marred with countless scrapes and dents from off-roading. Alan winced at the sight, then said, "Would you mind if my associate Tyler takes your Pathfinder for a test drive while you and I take a look at our extraordinary selection of new and used vehicles at unbeatable prices?"

Kyle removed the keys from his pocket and handed them to the small bearded man. When Tyler accepted the dangling keys, Kyle maintained his grip on the key fob.

"Watch the paint, *Tyler*. I know each and every scrape on that truck, and you better believe if there's one more mark on it when it comes back than it had coming in, I'm going to know. Don't think I won't check. Call me 'bro' one more time and I'm liable to break your jaw."

He released the keys into Tyler's grasp, and the man mumbled, "Yes, sir," as he scuttled backward a few steps, then approached the Pathfinder to begin his test drive.

When he was out of earshot, Alan said, "There's the Kyle I remember. How you doing, bro?"

"Not bad, my friend, not bad at all." He nodded toward the rows of vehicles parked in the vast lot and said, "Shall we?"

"My manager likes to peek out from time to time, so make sure you keep a confrontational posture—shouldn't be hard for you."

"No," Kyle said, "it shouldn't."

He followed Alan to the first row of vehicles, asking, "You got to work with trash like that every day?"

Alan shook his head mournfully. "Some of these kids today, man...you wouldn't believe me if I told you. So how's life?"

"Good, man. But there's something I need to talk to you about first."

"Sure, man. What's up?"

"That treatment you mentioned—"

"I knew it." Alan broke into a broad smile. "I knew this day would come. Kyle Soler, Mr. G.I. Joe himself, would one day get help. Welcome to the club, buddy, and you won't regret it. Not one bit. The medicine is called cetraphaline, and the doctor's name is Dr. Marcus Jannesson. And this treatment *will* change your life."

They walked around the last vehicle in the row, and headed down the second row of cars in the opposite direction.

Kyle said, "Yeah, so about that...how'd you find out about this treatment in the first place?"

"Luckiest day of my life. The doctor did a clinical outreach at my VFW post, talked to all of us back in...January this year, I think it was. Right after New Year's. Explained how cetraphaline worked, the whole nine yards. Even gave us a discounted rate."

"Did anyone else get the treatment?"

Alan nodded. "You bet. Six of us went down to Savannah later that month, did our treatments right in a row. Boom-boom-boom, all on the same day. That night we all went out for dinner, had some beers and talked about what we saw. Different experience for every one of us, and a couple of those guys were Vietnam vets, so I can only imagine what they went through."

"And?"

"And nothing," Alan said with a shrug. "It was the most amazing thing

I've ever done, hands down. Like a rollercoaster ride through everything in your past. I thought about the things that happened in Pantalay and my mind opened up to the whole history of human violence, all the wars and bloodshed. I kid you not, what we were involved in seemed small by comparison. I came out of it a totally new person. That's why I'm telling you, man, you have to do it yourself."

"No nightmares? Flashbacks, nothing?"

"Before the treatment? You bet. After? Not a trace. Sleeping great, drinking way less, never happier to be a car salesman in my life. I think it'll do big things for you, I really do."

"Right, uh-huh. So these other five guys, how are they doing now?"

"Never better."

"You're sure?"

"Yeah, I'm sure. I see them the first Tuesday of every month, like clockwork. Couple of them still have dreams, mind you, but it's way down from what they were dealing with before. This is the way ahead for people like us."

Kyle hesitated, unsure where to take the conversation. In some ways, he knew Clara Swanner better than she knew herself, and certainly better than her husband did, at least in the ways that mattered. And Clara was not prone to hysterics or exaggeration; whatever she was experiencing, it was real.

"All right," Kyle said as they strolled, "so this doctor's practice is in Georgia, right?"

"Savannah. Beautiful town. Plug in a few days to explore after your treatment, if you can make the time."

"But you're in Virginia Beach. How did this doctor come to find your VFW post?"

"You know, that's a good question. Let me think...yeah, I think one of our members went to see him, and asked Dr. Jannesson to coordinate a visit with our post commander. Glad he did, because otherwise I never would have found him."

"Who was the VFW member that tried him first?"

Alan shook his head. "No idea, and that's a good question. After the six of us came back from our Savannah trip, we thought they'd come talk to us about it. No one ever did—but some guys are embarrassed to need help, you know?"

"Yeah, I get it. Listen, can you send me the phone number for your post commander?"

"Sure, I'll text you his contact info. He's a retired Air Force colonel named Mark Hutchins, flew bombing missions in Desert Storm. Just tell him you served with Alan, and he'll have all the time in the world for you. You really should look up your local VFW, Kyle. Real nice to hang out with other vets, I'm telling you. Real nice."

Kyle tried to sound convincing. "I'll look into that. Did you tell Dr. Jannesson about our platoon, talk about Pantalay at all?"

"Of course not. He knew I served in Afghanistan, that's it."

"You didn't give him the names of anyone else in our platoon?"

Alan recoiled. "You crazy? I wouldn't do that. Why do you ask?"

Kyle stopped walking and met Alan's eyes. "Well, after you told me about Jannesson, I mentioned him to someone else from that platoon. Seems that treatment has made things worse, not better."

Alan was quiet for a moment. "I'm surprised to hear that. Who was it?"

"Doesn't matter," Kyle dismissed. "Did you tell anyone else from the platoon about Jannesson? Anyone besides me, who could have gone in for the treatment?"

Alan looked away, his voice going flat. "Yeah, yeah, I did. One guy called me about a car a while back, and I told him the same thing I told you. He never went, though."

"You sure? I'd like to call him and check, just to be safe."

Alan's face looked pained. "You can't call him, Kyle."

"Why not?"

"It was Joshua Thoma." Alan's voice faltered. "And he slashed his veins in the bathtub a few weeks after we spoke."

* * *

Kyle pulled off the lot in a 2012 Jeep Wrangler, the upgrade a result of his trade-in with some cash on top courtesy of his friend and former squad leader, Alan Smith.

Turning right onto the main road, Kyle drove out of sight of the dealership before pulling into a gas station. He pulled out his phone and found the new contact for Mark Hutchins, Alan's VFW post commander.

Hutchins answered on the third ring.

"What do you want?" He spoke in a scratchy voice.

Kyle hesitated. "Sir, my name is Kyle Soler, I served with Alan Smith from your VFW post."

There was a pause on the other line, then a short laugh.

"Sorry about that, son. I didn't recognize your number, thought you were another telemarketer. What can I do for you?"

"Well I just bought a vehicle from Alan, and he mentioned Dr. Marcus Jannesson, the guy who spoke at your VFW."

"Of course, I remember. What about him?"

"Sir, do you recall how he selected your VFW post for his outreach program?"

"Sure," Hutchins replied. "He said one of my members got treated and then asked him to reach out to me. That happens from time to time, guys find something that helps and want to share it with their brothers."

Kyle cleared his throat. "Do you know who that original patient was?"

"I sure don't. Jannesson cited doctor-patient confidentiality, and I didn't press him on it. But the group of guys who took him up on the treatment all said it helped them a lot. If you're looking to go, Jannesson would probably be happy to extend you the same discount."

"Yeah," Kyle said, "I was thinking about it. But if I may ask, sir, did anyone at your post seem to think Jannesson was suspicious in any way? I mean, with him just showing up out of the blue."

"Suspicious?" He thought for a moment. "Yeah, we got a guy by the name of Jim Murrell. He called the guy a quack to his face, along with a few other colorful terms that I'll spare myself the indignity of repeating. Said anyone who listened to Jannesson was crazy, and walked out of the meeting. Hasn't come to any meetings since, though that was probably a long time coming."

"Why'd he do that?"

"With Murrell, who knows? Maybe because he's a crotchety old piece of work."

"What's his background?"

"Murrell was Special Forces in Vietnam, did some CIA black ops stuff he won't talk about. Phoenix Program, that type of thing, so tread lightly if you do talk to him. He's got a pretty dark worldview, but he's one of the smartest men I've ever met, inside the service or out."

"Would you mind giving me his number?"

Hutchins laughed. "His number? Kyle, I don't know that Murrell owns a telephone. But you don't need it. Are you still in Virginia Beach?"

"Yes, sir, I am."

"Then head on over to a shopping center at the corner of Clemson and Maynard. There's a bar—no idea what it's called, the sign outside just says "Pub," so that should give you a pretty good idea of the clientele. You head by there any time after they open at noon, you're likely to find Murrell. Just look for the guy who looks like he's been through hell, and if there happens to be more than one—which there probably will be—ask a bartender."

* * *

Kyle arrived at the pub ten minutes later, walking past a group of geriatric smokers blowing clouds of foul-smelling cigarette and cigar smoke outside the door.

The sign was just as Hutchins had described: three letters spelling PUB, with no further attempts at marketing. It seemed to say, it's a pub, people, so take it or leave it.

Pushing open the door, Kyle entered the darkened interior to find what was technically a bar, though unlike any he'd ever been in.

There was no house music, no cracking of billiard balls, no giggling laughter of women. It was scarcely three in the afternoon, and almost every seat at the bar was taken—yet the room was almost deathly silent.

A few television screens broadcast sports games, but no one was really watching.

Instead the occupants were nearly identical, slouching over their drinks at the bar while a few murmured conversations elapsed between them. The only activity seemed to be from the two bartenders, who appeared to be the youngest people in there by at least twenty years. They were hustling to keep the drinks refreshed, and looked to Kyle as he entered with an expression of muted surprise at not seeing a regular.

Kyle appraised the patrons at the bar, trying to determine which one could be a Vietnam-era Special Forces shooter by the name of Jim Murrell.

This proved no easy task among the clientele of gray-haired men nursing their drinks. Most of them fit the requisite age range, and more than a few fit Hutchins's description of looking like they'd been through hell, some of them multiple times.

And it took little detective work to make out the veterans among them —the signs were everywhere, from ubiquitous veteran hats proclaiming their branch of service or the conflict they fought in, to biker jackets with unit patches sewn on, to honest-to-God fatigue pants.

So Kyle considered what Hutchins had told him about Murrell: Special Forces background, with the added distinction of having served in the CIA's Phoenix Program, which meant he'd been an assassin.

He found his likely candidate at the end of the bar, an unshaven man who stood out by virtue of a complete lack of military affiliation. Black T-shirt, jeans, black boots, his wallet affixed to his belt by a short chain. He was looking straight at Kyle, then turned back to his empty glass with a mild look of disgust.

Kyle approached the man, noting a degree of facial redness that he suspected was ever-present—this was no sunburn, but the effect of years if not decades of hard drinking, his cheeks interspersed with enlarged blood vessels.

"Jim Murrell?"

The man glanced at him with dark blue eyes, wet and bloodshot.

"My name's Kyle Soler, I'm a friend of—"

"I know who you are," Murrell cut him off in a gravelly voice.

Kyle considered whether the VFW post commander had called the bar to warn Murrell ahead of time. He took a seat on the stool beside him. "I don't think we've met."

"And we don't have to, because I can see all I need to know about you. You're one of the young vets, still riding your high off patriotic fervor. But you don't really know war yet."

Kyle smiled at the man calmly. "I've got a few bullet scars that would beg to disagree with you, sir."

"You're still a few decades away from joining my generation." Murrell swept a hand across the bar to indicate the other occupants. "You think you know, but you don't. Not yet. Only half of war is combat; the *other* half is the rest of your life. Guess which one is more fun?"

Kyle's grin faded. He leaned in, suddenly feeling like he could learn a lot from this man.

The bartender appeared, and Kyle ordered a bourbon double on the rocks, along with another round for Murrell. Kyle thought this would endear him to Murrell, but he saw instead that Murrell was looking sideways at him, irritated at the lapse in conversation.

"Spit it out. I've got a lot more time than patience, though at this age I dare say that both are dwindling."

"Sir, I wanted to ask you about a man named Dr. Marcus Jannesson. He came to your VFW post a few months back—"

Murrell barked a ragged laugh. "Jannesson? What do you want from that quack?"

"Why do you say he's a quack?"

"Because I saw him, that's why. I look into a man's eyes, and I see the man. When you walked in here, I saw a killer who wasn't deluding himself about who he is, or should be. War isn't the problem. It's the modern world of comfort and convenience that tries to snuff out every spark of human nature within us, to convince us we're something we're not. Do you know the truth about human nature, son?"

Kyle shrugged. "No, I suppose not."

The bartender reappeared with their drinks. Kyle made a move to toast, but Murrell just took a sip and continued speaking.

"Since the first one of us was born in Africa, we've spread to every continent and killed off every other species of early human. We drove every species capable of feeding us to extinction, and didn't stop until we figured out how to domesticate animals for food. And once we ruled the earth, we started invading each other's land and slaughtering our own. Humans may change, but human *nature* doesn't. We are the most bloodthirsty killers the world has ever produced."

Kyle nodded, taking another drink. "So what did you see when you looked into Jannesson's eyes?"

Murrell spun his glass in a circle on the bar and shrugged. "I saw a man who was not what he claimed to be."

"How so?"

"Hell, son," Murrell continued with a wince, "know how many doctors I've seen by now? I'm always one of fifty patients they see that day, and everyone's got a different complaint. You get three minutes to explain the problem, and three minutes for them to write you a prescription. Then they're off to the next ailing vet. It's a Saigon whorehouse. They're the prostitute and we're the johns, all sitting in the waiting room, ashamed, avoiding eye contact, until a veteran wanders out the door 'cause he's got his fix. They get the next one of us from the waiting room to be serviced. No cleanup, no shower—get in line, in and out, next please. There's no time for sentimentality; there's enough of us waiting to be seen, and when your time is up, it's out the door again."

Kyle nodded. "Yeah, I know that drill well enough by now. So what about Jannesson?"

"Jannesson was the Saigon hooker who wants to pull overtime with you, hear about all the things she doesn't need to know and shouldn't be asking about. Jannesson just wanted to talk, and talk, and talk. That's what made him suspicious—the guy was way too interested in our jobs. The doctors who treat vets don't want to hear the war stories, because they've heard enough. This guy, on the other hand, didn't want to talk about anything else. That doesn't make him a doctor, whether he is one on paper or not. It makes him something...else. Something strange."

"This guy's treated a lot of vets, though. He's regarded as an expert, so how's he pulling it off if there's something shady about him?"

Murrell shrugged, taking another sip and setting the glass down hard.

"First thing I knew about Jannesson was that he's so convinced of his own intelligence that he'd be impervious to reason. And people like that tend to rise to the top. You see, son, it's the politics paradox. The mature and balanced decision maker seldom has the political ruthlessness necessary to rise to the post for which their decision making would be most valuable. Show me a man at the top of his profession, and I'll show you a ruthless man."

Kyle felt his eyes narrow, and he fought the impulse to disagree. "But Jannesson's profession is medicine, and there are a lot of standards in that particular field, ain't there?"

Murrell guffawed and threw back another sip.

"Medical industry is the worst of all. Do you know what the most powerful effect in all of pharmacology is? It's not any medicine. It's the placebo effect. If you believe something will work, it'll work. The treatment becomes a self-fulfilling prophecy, so the doctor just has to make the smoke and mirrors seem effective to get the patient to *believe*. Those VFW guys who sing his praises *believe* they're fixed. Guy like Jannesson could get pretty far on that type of thing, I believe." He looked at Kyle with suspicion. "What's your angle with him—you get treated too?"

Kyle frowned. "No, I've got a friend who saw him, one of the people I served with." He decided not to mention the fact that his friend was a female, unsure how that would sit with an older veteran and particularly one with Jim Murrell's disposition. "My friend thinks Jannesson might have done something besides the treatment, something that caused a lot of bad effects. But I've looked this doctor up, and I can't find anything bad about him."

"Doesn't surprise me. You probably wouldn't."

"Why is that?"

Murrell grunted, taking another drink. "Guys playing a role like that, whatever their motive, are careful. They do a good job covering their tracks. That's why they're successful at what they do—even if you think they're suspicious, there's no trail to follow."

"So if I want to get to the bottom of this, where do I go from here?"

"To the source. When the law can't catch these people, you have to resort to extra-legal means to get the job done. Don't suppose I need to tell you much else about that."

Kyle stared into his glass, the ice cubes suspended in the amber liquid.

Then he said, "No, sir, you don't."

16

The doctor entered the exam room with a clipboard, and Clara looked up from her seat expectantly.

Dr. Catherine Eckl had graduated from the University of South Carolina School of Medicine in 2008, and maintained an active license. Clara knew this because she'd looked her up on the Federation of State Medical Boards website prior to coming in that morning, just as she probably would every medical professional she saw for the rest of her life.

Dr. Eckl was a short woman in her forties, and wore her sandy hair in a tight bun over her white coat.

"Well, Mrs. Swanner, I can see why you haven't been feeling very well."

Clara's stomach fluttered. "What did the lab results show?"

The doctor hoisted the clipboard and lifted the cover sheet.

"Your Vitamin D levels are pretty low, along with iron. That's probably contributing to your fatigue and difficulty sleeping. I'm going to recommend a daily multivitamin, as well as a magnesium supplement. Many patients find magnesium helps their mood, and it's been clinically proven to help with depression. I'd start with 450 milligrams per day, and give it a few weeks before you expect to see results."

Clara was dumbstruck.

"What else is in my bloodstream? Surely you found some...substances. Something."

Dr. Eckl lowered the clipboard with a sad smile.

"We did."

"And? What was it?"

"Alcohol, Mrs. Swanner."

"I could have told you that without paying for blood and urine labs. What else did you find?"

Dr. Eckl sighed impatiently.

"Mrs. Swanner, there are no other substances in your bloodstream. But I must warn you about the dangers of alcohol. It's been shown to increase the risk of depression and anxiety, and that's just in the short term. Long-term dangers include high blood pressure, heart failure—"

Clara cut her off. "And liver disease, and dementia, and increased risk of cancer. Listen, Dr. Eckl, I've received the condescending anti-alcohol speech in every possible variation. I'm looking for substances in my body that aren't offered at a happy hour special."

Dr. Eckl's eyes narrowed. "Well I'm sorry to disappoint you, Mrs. Swanner, but there aren't any. Your hormone levels are consistent with what I'd expect from a mother your age, and everything from your blood pressure to your resting heart rate shows you to be in excellent health. If there's any substance responsible for your difficulties, I think its source is from a bottle. The best recommendations for healthy, natural sleep are for you to limit your drinking, avoid caffeine in the evenings, reserve the bedroom for sleeping and sex only, and set regular wake and bed times. It may seem that alcohol is a sleep aid, but it actually—"

"Disrupts circadian function, suppresses melatonin, and reduces REM sleep. I appreciate that. But my choices don't come down to good sleep or bad sleep; they come down to bad sleep or *no sleep at all.* Now, can I kindly get a copy of the lab results?"

Dr. Catherine Eckl smiled tightly, withdrawing a sheaf of papers from the clipboard and handing it to her. "Of course. Here you go."

Clara rose, took the papers, and walked out of the office.

* * *

Clara was furious as she navigated the clinic parking lot in search of her car.

She found her BMW in the back row, tossing the lab results on the passenger seat as she slammed the door shut behind her. Firing the push button start, she heard the inline six-cylinder spark to life and backed out of her parking spot.

This car was the polar opposite of her previous CTS-V. The Cadillac was all power, a roaring supercharged V8 that rumbled her seat even while idling. This little M235i, by contrast, was coolly sophisticated, a zippy piece of German engineering that she enjoyed driving to a surprising degree—even when she found her left foot pawing for a clutch pedal that wasn't there.

Clara was halfway home when Kyle called, and she answered on the car's speakers.

She said, "Kyle, I just wasted a day getting labs done. Nothing in my system but alcohol. Did you find anything out?"

"Sure did," Kyle answered. "Traded in the Pathfinder with some cash on top, and I'm driving home in a 2012 Jeep Wrangler, courtesy of Alan Smith. Talked to him about Jannesson—apparently the good doctor miraculously showed up at his VFW post on a clinical outreach. Six of them tried the treatment, all six were thrilled by the results. So I talked to Alan's VFW post commander. He said Jannesson called him out of the blue, explaining that one of his patients from that VFW post asked him to come to a meeting and explain the treatment. But he couldn't say who it was due to doctor-patient confidentiality, and nobody's come forward saying it was them."

"And you don't think that patient exists," she said.

"I've got my suspicions, especially after this next bit. The post commander referred me to an old Vietnam shooter, who was awesome. Crazy, but awesome. I want to be him when I grow up. He took Jannesson for a quack from the moment he saw him, but he didn't have any facts, just instincts."

"Well his instincts aren't so bad, but we can discuss that in a minute. Anything else?"

"I haven't gotten to the worst part. Alan said that besides me, he only told one other person from our platoon about the treatment. Get this: it was Joshua Thoma, and that conversation was a few weeks before he killed himself."

Clara mentally recoiled at the mention of Thoma. Now that she'd seen him in a nightmare, she couldn't imagine him any other way: veins slashed, dripping blood and water as he staggered toward her.

She pushed the memory away, braking for a stoplight. "We should see if any of the other suicides were VFW members."

"Already done, sister. I called Alan and asked him to check the member roster. Spoiler alert: none of our suicides were on it. And I haven't been able to dig up anything else about Jannesson. You find out anything new?"

"Sure did. Jannesson changed his name a long time ago, and his medical license was revoked in November last year. How's that for things I should have looked up before seeing him?"

Kyle was silent for a moment. "*Revoked?* As in, he can't practice medicine at all?"

Clara accelerated off the line as the light turned green. "Not in the state of Georgia. And he never had a license anywhere else, so no."

"So this guy's way off the legal grid. We need to talk to a lawyer."

"Way ahead of you—I sent my findings over to an attorney, and have an appointment at ten tomorrow morning. But if Thoma knew about Jannesson, I'm concerned that there could have been others from the platoon. We need to talk to the parents of our other four suicides, and find out for sure if any of them were treated by Jannesson."

"I agree one hundred percent. You want to handle the families of Rich and Dakota? I can call the parents of Thoma and Sims."

"Yeah," she said. "Don't know if I'll have time before Jeremy gets home, but I'll try them tomorrow at the latest."

"Cool. Let's reconvene tomorrow."

"Definitely. Talk to you then."

Clara ended the call from a button on her steering wheel, and floored the gas.

17

Kyle was back in his apartment by early evening, and the keys to his new Jeep lay on the kitchen table next to his glass of whiskey. Normally he preferred his drinks on the rocks, but the clinking of ice tended to be a distraction when he was on the phone with people who didn't understand the finer points of alcohol as a part of their daily existence.

Ending his call, Kyle set the phone down and picked up his glass. He was troubled by his earlier conversation with Alan Smith—the fact that he'd told Joshua Thoma about the treatment seemed a surefire link between Jannesson and a platoon suicide.

But Kyle had just gotten off the phone with Thoma's parents, and it was a dead end. They hadn't known he ever had PTSD, much less whether he was being treated for it. So Kyle had carefully probed them for any information about travel to Savannah, and they knew nothing about that either. Nice people, quite jovial given the circumstances, but a total drought of useful information.

Now the sun was starting to set, and Kyle felt his chest tighten with predictable regularity. This was the way the light fell on a few hundred pre-mission outings, as his men performed radio checks and readied their weapons to load the vehicles or helicopters before launching on a night-time mission. Most of his operations had been night raids, back when the war was in its heyday and no one batted an eye at a US casualty.

At least, that's what he attributed his sunset tension to—this was the time of day that preceded the gunfights, the IEDs, the life-or-death combat in a part of the world that was just about as developed as the surface of the moon. By the time he'd gotten his first platoon sergeant job, it was 2015. The war in Afghanistan had dissolved to sporadic combat outposts launching patrols without much of a coherent campaign strategy, generally in areas known to be free of Taliban interference. Kyle had been fairly certain that his first rotation as platoon sergeant would be the only deployment without major enemy contact.

And instead, he'd gotten Pantalay.

Kyle killed the rest of his drink, then poured himself a fresh glass. Sitting back down at the table, he picked up his phone and prepared to make his final call of the evening.

He found the contact for Craig and Veronica Sims, then took another sip of whiskey and tapped the phone to call.

A man answered. "Hello?"

"Hi, Mr. Sims. This is Kyle Soler, I was Jason's old platoon sergeant."

A pause. "Hey, Kyle. Yeah, I remember you from the funeral. How've you been?"

"Doing just fine, I suppose. How are you and the missus holding up?"

"Well, I can't say we'll ever recover from something like that. Veronica had two miscarriages before she went full-term, and Jason was our only child."

Kyle felt his grip tighten on the phone. "I...I'm sorry. I don't know what to say."

"You don't have to say anything, Kyle. That's our burden to bear. I know it's not any easier on his friends from the platoon, and I know he wasn't the only one to take his own life. Sure do hope he's the last, though."

"So do I, Mr. Sims."

"But with this whole veteran suicide epidemic...I just don't know. How is it no one's found a solution for that?"

"That's a great question," Kyle said. "And that's something I was hoping to ask you about."

"Oh? Not sure how I could help, but go ahead and shoot anyway."

"Did Jason ever mention getting any treatment for PTSD?"

"No, he did not. Never even admitted he had it, at least not to me or

Veronica. Can't say he kept in particularly close touch after joining the military, though. Never talked about Afghanistan, that's for sure."

"What about travel—he ever mention going to Savannah?"

Another pause, and Kyle felt his hopes lifting with the prospect of recognition. But Craig Sims said, "Savannah? No, he never mentioned anything like that."

Kyle's shoulders slumped. He'd just struck out with Thoma's parents, and now Sims's father had turned out to be a dead end as well.

Then Craig said, "But there was a girl shacking up with Jason at the time of his death. First time I met her, I knew she was trouble."

"What do you mean, trouble? As in she was cheating on him?"

"Well, to say she was cheating would be to imply she was monogamous to begin with, and I don't think that was ever the case. Impression I got was that she was a local girl in need of a meal ticket, and my son had full disability from the VA. She's still living in Franklin, just south of Nashville, best I know. She couldn't even be troubled to attend the funeral. But you could try asking her—it's worth a shot, I suppose."

"I'd like to, if that's all right with you. How do I find her?"

"Name's Jenna Tanner, but she goes by the stage name of Krystal. Spells that with a K, presumably because it's trashier that way."

"Stage name?" Kyle asked. "What is she, a singer?"

"Nothing so prestigious, I'm afraid. Jenna is a stripper at the Platinum Lounge."

18

Clara was back in Pantalay Village, though now she fought nothing but the sun's gradual descent into dusk, and one thing more—her own friend, Dakota.

There were no longer any gunshots or explosions, but noise was constant as the pair of Apache attack helicopters circled the village. When their rotors drifted out of earshot, Clara could hear the continuous thunder of fighter jets orbiting high above.

Now that the battle was over, every possible asset had appeared, including the Quick Reaction Force platoon from the local combat outpost, led by Clara's company commander who hadn't believed her initial report in the first place. The battalion had reinforced that with a second platoon that arrived via Chinook helicopters an hour later, and the brigade sent a field surgical team along with EOD, photographers to document the damage, and combat air controllers to manage the now-constant rotation of aircraft stacked overhead.

All that firepower was, of course, worthless now. The battle had ended the instant the five-hundred-pound bomb had reduced the mosque to rubble. If any more enemy fighters were here, they'd long since hidden their weapons and were now playing the part of helpless villagers caught in the crossfire.

Clara had been relieved of ground force command on the spot, with tactical authority being seized by her commander, Captain Jared McHugh. Not that he was anywhere to be found at present—he was currently meeting with the village elders, in addition to whatever district and provincial leadership had arrived. That much was just fine by Clara, who wanted to line up the village elders against the remains of the mosque and execute them, one by one. They had all known of the attack, she was sure, though the senior religious leader was the guiltiest of all.

She thought of how he'd looked away from her when she asked if there were Taliban in the village—an elderly, established Afghan man breaking eye contact with a woman was her tipping point of suspicion. Now Clara felt that if she saw one more glimpse of his wrinkled face, she'd be likely to put a bullet in his forehead with no emotion besides the grim satisfaction of combat justice. Clara felt more compassion for the female dog she'd shot that morning than she did for that man; indeed, more compassion for the dog than for any of the enemy fighters her platoon had killed in the past few hours.

Captain McHugh had barely spoken to her upon his arrival; now that the battle was over, he'd instead made some gravely passive-aggressive comments about her judgment in calling for the airstrike, and said that the brigade had appointed an investigating officer who would be waiting for her when she returned to base. There was no mention of the three members of her platoon who'd been killed in the battle. He hadn't even made the rounds to check on the rest of the platoon, to show the support of their chain of command despite the horrific fallout of the battle.

Instead he'd vanished into the building formerly occupied by Clara, ejecting Jason Sims from the impromptu command post to make way for his own radio operator.

That much was a small mercy to Sims, who'd been eager to rejoin his platoon. Besides, Captain McHugh would have his hands full managing the fallout of endless requests for information from every level of command from battalion on up.

The four-star commanding general in charge of NATO's Resolute Support Mission and US forces in Afghanistan had flown to Kabul before the dust had settled over the mosque, and was now meeting with the Afghan president at his palace. The Taliban had, of course, already released a statement declaring that the Americans had dropped an errant bomb onto a mosque, killing twenty-eight unarmed worshipers. That was how things worked in Afghanistan—the Taliban said whatever they pleased, usually citing precise but totally fictional casualty counts, and while the world stage didn't believe them, American forces had to race to systematically disprove every false claim for the benefit of a largely uneducated and illiterate Afghan populace.

The commanding general's highest priority was obvious: conduct boots-on-the-ground BDA, or battle damage assessment, and thoroughly document each casualty in Pantalay Village. Therein lay the most twisted contradiction of all in the hours following the battle—of all the reinforcing elements that had descended upon the village, exactly *none* had orders to search the wreckage. They were all occupied in securing the village, which, of course, no longer needed any securing. The battle was over. And it had fallen on Clara's platoon to search the mosque's rubble, a task they were currently performing with all the enthusiasm of gravediggers on overtime.

Clara worked alongside her platoon, laboring to dislodge chunks of mud brick construction. They'd begun work with an urgent fervor, hoping to uncover survivors before they succumbed to being buried alive.

But within the first half hour, it became clear that no one inside the mosque had lived past the bomb blast.

The first dozen mangled, bloody corpses had been removed to a perverse and collective sense of relief for Clara and, she was certain, Kyle. They wore chest rigs with AK-47 magazines and grenades, they had rocket-propelled grenade launchers and RPK machine guns with belts of ammunition. If nothing else, that meant Clara wouldn't be going to jail over calling in the strike.

As they dug deeper into the rubble, Clara heard the first cries for EOD. Alan Smith had uncovered a body with a suicide vest, and the bomb disposal experts rushed in to disarm it. Then a second casualty with an explosive vest was found, followed by a third. All told, they'd found eight suicide bombers among the wreckage. These men were the enemy's second wave, sprinters designated to race within the platoon's perimeter before detonating themselves amid defensive positions of Clara's soldiers. She'd felt an odd sense of validation then—her platoon would have been wiped out, or very close to it, if she hadn't ordered the airstrike. It was a mosque, yes, but the enemy had chosen it for precisely that reason. They could have mobilized their force in half a dozen other buildings for their final assault, some closer than the mosque was. This was a smart play from the public relations perspective: even if a bomb killed them all, which it had, they'd gain the endless propaganda value of villainizing American troops and invoking local support for their cause.

And in the wake of this realization, Clara had the odd feeling that she was being watched. She glanced over her shoulder and found Dakota lingering on the periphery of the wreckage, for the first time in their relationship snapping pictures not of the relevant action at hand but instead the surrounding village, a landscape of buildings scarred with bullet and missile impacts from both the ground fighters and attack helicopters.

But Dakota was overlooking the obvious centerpiece of the day: the ruins of the mosque that her own platoon was sifting through.

Clara abandoned her search, first rising and then stomping toward her friend, resisting the impulse to smack the fancy DSLR camera from her grasp.

"What do you think you're doing?" Clara very nearly shouted, addressing Dakota in an insulting tone that she wouldn't dare use on one of her privates.

Dakota looked fearful, but responded in a falsely overbearing voice. "My job, Clara."

"No," Clara shot back, "your job is recording the truth, and that's not what you're doing at all. You want to see the cost of what happened here today, get in that wreckage and start taking pictures of the reality. The truth is in that mosque, not in the village."

Dakota looked pained then, an impossible sadness born of some life-long burden that Clara didn't yet have the wisdom to detect.

"Clara, you don't understand." She lowered her voice. "After seeing that dead boy, I don't want to see any more. *I don't want to see.*"

Clara shook her head resolutely, advancing a step closer to Dakota. "My men don't get a choice, and neither do you. You're part of this platoon, or you're not. Let's go."

Dakota followed then, but not at first. First, she removed the memory chip from her camera, knelt down, and, with a trembling hand, used a lighter to melt it into a molten square of unrecoverable plastic and metal.

Clara watched the process, confused—Dakota was destroying the very photographs she'd almost been killed to obtain. But for some reason, the full import of that action didn't seize Clara at that moment. It was the equivalent of Clara destroying her radio link to higher command, severing the literal and metaphorical scope of her job responsibilities; and whether Clara had realized that at the time or not, the move would cost Dakota her career. It wasn't until after they returned to base that her friend would erase the remainder of her photographs and submit her formal resignation to *The New York Times*.

When her friend followed her, she was no longer a journalist. Now she was an active participant, a willing accomplice who proceeded to search the wreckage not as a witness but as a conspirator.

Clara didn't feel the full sting of remorse for another ten minutes, after the rush of validation had dissolved, giving way to disgust, repulsion, and finally, resignation.

The trickle of enemy corpses had faded to nothing, and their search turned to the other victims that day, the ones Fraidon had warned of when relaying the dead boy's warning along with the words, *They have families at gunpoint in the mosque.*

And this was the other master stroke in the Taliban's plan—not to rely solely on misinformation to convince the people of civilian casualties, but to ensure it, and in the worst way imaginable.

Because the bodies they began pulling from the wreckage weren't families, per se. They were the most defenseless members of Afghan society present in the village: the elderly and the women and children. It seemed inexplicable at first—why hadn't the men protected their families?—until reports of executions the night before came trickling in. The Quick Reaction Force had mobilized search teams, following villagers to home after home where the men and teenage boys had been shot and, in some cases, decapitated.

But Clara's platoon saw none of this; they were covered in dust, feverishly searching the rubble in the dwindling daylight. And the bodies they uncovered then were the true victims.

She was reminded of footage from 9/11, the dust-covered survivors scrambling away from the disaster. Clara had been eight years old when she watched those images on the news. Now she was living the ramifications of that event, fifteen years later and half a world away, immersed in a war with no end in sight.

The first civilian they'd found was uncovered by Jason Sims. She was a girl in her teens, the bulge of her stomach beneath the burqa leaving no doubt that she'd been a late-term pregnancy when the bomb exploded. Clara had watched numbly as Alan Smith helped Sims carry her away, thinking it was the most tragic thing Clara had ever seen. Then the first shattered body of a child was found, and that had unsettled her more than any other corpse in the wreckage.

The bomb blast and subsequent building collapse had resulted in chaos —some of the bodies were remarkably undamaged, their dust-covered faces almost serene. The first child pulled from the rubble was a little girl of three or four, her body coated in pale dust like all the rest. But if that grime were cleaned, the toddler could have been mistaken for sleeping; her cherubic face was placid, eyelids gently closed, mouth slack. Clara had felt bizarrely hopeful that perhaps this girl was alive, had survived the blast against all odds, but when she lifted the girl's body, it sagged as if made of gelatin. There was no way to gauge how many bones were broken or in how many places, or the extent of internal organs liquified by the bomb's shockwave.

Clara had started crying then, sobbing uncontrollably even as her body continued to support the girl's weight in a determined march to the casualty collection point. And then she saw that she was not alone—the faces of many in her platoon were likewise marked by streams of tears that sliced downward through the sand caked on their skin.

Dakota helped move the bodies, her ever-present camera nowhere to be seen. She was searching the wreckage alongside the platoon, face somehow unmarred by tears but otherwise indistinguishable from Clara's soldiers.

The search continued. The platoon uncovered the bodies of geriatric men and women, the remains of infants, the adolescent forms of what had once been hopeful boys and girls with their whole lives ahead of them.

Clara awoke then not with a jolting start but with a gradual return to consciousness that brought with it the worst of realizations. That was no dream, no horrid fantasy that could be dispelled as a nightmare. It was simply a memory of things she couldn't unsee and events she couldn't unlive, a memory that would return to her at odd moments for the rest of her existence. The memory might occur while she was playing with Aiden or making love to her husband, and Clara couldn't simply drop everything she was doing to deal with the emotional fallout. She'd have to bear those consequences deep inside, tamp them down while projecting the role of wife and mother amid a sea of people who couldn't conceive of what she'd seen even if she told them, which of course she never could.

They deserved their peaceful lives, their mundane concerns about work and school, their weekend relaxations. A lot of people had been deprived of those human luxuries in Pantalay Village, and in Afghanistan, and in every country gripped by war. And those who survived such atrocities would forever harbor the memories, deal with them by whichever means they could, whether therapy or the bottle or, for the worst cases, suicide.

Clara rose from bed, seeing the first indications of sunrise outside the window. She'd make coffee early today, she decided. For once she had no desire to write, whether fiction or the account of the dream she'd just had, and wanted instead to busy herself with her rote household tasks rather than contemplate reality any further.

Pulling open her bedroom door, Clara stepped outside and prepared to face the day.

19

She was driving her BMW down the freeway at twenty over the limit, veering around a minivan that drifted over the lane markers as its driver texted, when Kyle called.

Clara pressed a button on the steering wheel to answer.

"Hey, Kyle."

"Hey, girl, what's the good word?"

"On the way to my legal consult now. But I talked to Dakota's stepfather yesterday. He didn't know anything about Savannah, or Jannesson. He's still driving Dakota's ATS-V, though—said it's what she would have wanted."

"He's right about that. What about Rich's parents?"

"They didn't answer their phone; I left them a message on the third attempt. They might just have severed ties with Rich's circle of friends, I don't know. You get anything on your end?"

"Not from Thoma's parents. They didn't know anything about their son going to Savannah, had no idea who Jannesson was when I asked."

"And what about Sims?"

"That's where the plot thickens. Sims's dad didn't know any more than Thoma's parents did, but he put me onto a girl who was living with Sims when he shot himself. Said she might know something, and I intend to find out tonight."

"Tonight? You mean you're going to call her?"

"Nah. She's not on the best of terms with the Sims family, and a cold call from me would probably get my number blocked. I'm flying out to see her—my flight to Nashville leaves in a couple hours."

Clara shook her head. "Kyle, if she won't talk to you over the phone, what makes you think she'll tell you anything if you just show up?"

Kyle gave a delighted giggle. "She's a stripper."

"A—stripper, right. Right, Kyle, now it all makes sense. So you're going to perform some boots-on-the-ground reconnaissance, all in the name of research."

"Just following the clues, girl."

"Well try not to catch any venereal disease in the course of your professional responsibilities."

"Clara, you of all people should know: if I haven't died of AIDS yet, then it must not be real. Talk tomorrow?"

"Definitely. Safe travels."

Kyle ended the call before Clara could, and she weaved through a gap in traffic to accelerate down the fast lane.

Clara left all other thoughts behind as she drove. In times like these, her fascination with cars and obsession with speed seemed painfully clear. High-performance vehicles had their aesthetic beauty, sure, and it was one that Clara appreciated far more than any work of art entombed at some cold and lifeless museum. But operating one of these vehicles was about more than that.

In her life, she was adrift and faithless. In the driver's seat, she could cede control of her existence to a powerful machine, one she usually piloted with reckless abandon. And when she was gripped by speed, there were no thoughts of the insomnia, of the late-night ruminations about her life or the things she'd seen.

Clara had loved cars long before going to combat. But after seeing war firsthand, she'd returned with a physical necessity to drive, to pour on speed on the open road. Helpless in so many other aspects of her own life, and unmoored after her release from war, the pointlessly absurd bursts of acceleration were the only link to desirable adrenaline she had left. Combat had gotten her strung out on that particular hormone, and in the civilian world, speed was her only recourse to achieve it.

All that ended as she parked at the Law Office of Ryan Frahm. The instant she put her BMW in park, Clara was re-immersed in the world of banality, of legislation and order. My God, how she hated it. Combat was traumatizing, but there was a freedom in chaos that she secretly craved, subconsciously desired to fling herself into. After you'd encountered the indescribable endorphin rush of nearly being killed, time after time and all of it in a single exalted day of your existence, what purpose could the bucolic world of peacetime ever hold for you again?

She tried not to think of it as she entered the building, checking in at the front desk a few minutes before her appointment. A secretary escorted her to a meeting room, and she took a seat to wait. Clara was irritated when the lawyer hadn't entered by her appointment time, but the door flung open a moment later, and he entered carrying a file in one hand.

"Mrs. Swanner, I'm Ryan Frahm. Pleased to meet you."

She rose and shook his hand. He was a paunchy middle-aged man with Hispanic features and a neatly trimmed beard.

"Nice to meet you too, Mr. Frahm."

"Please, have a seat."

She did, and he took the chair opposite her. Setting the file on the table between them, he flipped it open and began, "I've reviewed everything you sent me, and done some additional background research into the specifics of his dispute with the medical board."

"And?"

Frahm scratched his beard at the corner of his jaw, then swallowed.

"The long and the short of it is that Jannesson was accused of performing experiments on unconsenting patients being treated for PTSD. These patients complained of experiencing side effects that were not consistent with the medication they'd been administered, and this triggered an investigation by the Georgia Composite Medical Board."

"Right," Clara said, "and they revoked his license."

"It's not quite so simple, Mrs. Swanner. There were three complaints issued, all by patients who received treatment between 2019 and 2020. Before that, he didn't have a single infraction that I could find. And the three patients received in-depth medical examinations to determine if there was any evidence of residual medication or altered hormone levels conducive with unauthorized treatment. There wasn't: all three were in perfect health."

"Then how could the board pull his license for experimenting?"

He shook his head. "They couldn't, and they didn't—not for experimentation, at least." He flipped a paper over, consulting the page beneath. "They did uncover sufficient evidence to charge him with other violations of Title 50, Chapter 13, Article 1 of the Georgia Code. Specifically, failure to treat a patient according to the generally accepted standard of care, and attempted concealment of the act constituting a violation. Those charges are more or less catch-alls for the medical board, similar to how police departments resort to disorderly conduct when they can't prove any more significant charges."

"Okay," Clara agreed, "but he's still claiming to be a doctor when he's not, and using a false name."

"His name was changed legally some time ago, Mrs. Swanner. And while his website lists an accurate medical school degree, it doesn't explicitly state that he is licensed to practice medicine. So there's no false advertising there."

Clara turned her palms upward. "But he is still illegally practicing medicine, Mr. Frahm."

"To understand how he's doing so, it's important to understand the legal protocol governing the use of the treatment itself. Cetraphaline is categorized as a Schedule III drug, which means it has a low to moderate risk of physical and psychological dependence. Same as Tylenol with codeine. Schedule III drugs require a DEA license, which the Savannah Wellness Clinic has had since they opened—which was in 2010, just three years after cetraphaline was FDA approved for use as an anesthetic."

"But I didn't get it as an anesthetic."

"Right, but once a drug receives FDA approval, licensed physicians can use their best clinical judgment in prescribing it for uses other than originally intended." He flipped a page and pointed to a line of text. "Its use to treat mood disorders is known as CNAI: cetraphaline for non-aesthetic indications. This is also known as 'off-label' use, and it is not only legal, but quite common across a wide variety of pharmaceuticals. For instance, there are blood pressure medications used to treat ADHD, beta blockers used to treat anxiety—"

"You said 'licensed' physicians. We already established that Jannesson isn't licensed."

"That's right," Frahm conceded. "But when the Georgia Composite Medical Board began investigating him, Jannesson hired a licensed doctor to maintain compliance. I've checked that doctor's state medical board license, as well as the clinic's ability to store controlled substances, OSHA compliance, insurance coverage, and city and county licensing. Everything checks out. By the time Jannesson's license was revoked last year, the clinic was already operating legally under the new doctor."

"I was injected by a nurse, not a doctor."

Frahm paused, choosing his words carefully. "As long as the licenses check out—which they do—there are no additional regulations that dictate who can administer cetraphaline. Any employee of the clinic is legally permitted to do so. And while Jannesson is not allowed to practice medicine in the state of Georgia, he can still work at the clinic as a non-physician employee, which he currently is. From a legal standpoint, it wouldn't matter if he gave you the injection himself."

"Then what is he doing that's illegal?"

He turned up his palms. "Nothing whatsoever, Mrs. Swanner. He's operating in a very gray area of modern medicine, navigating every loophole in the laws that govern conduct of medical treatment. Now I'll be the first to agree with you that what he's doing is deceptive in the extreme, and highly immoral. But the law is binary, Mrs. Swanner, and I'm sorry to tell you that Jannesson isn't breaking it."

20

For the first time in as long as he could remember, Kyle was at a strip club.

Being here reminded him exactly why he'd never paid for the privilege, save a few jaunts with a fake ID back in high school and the occasional bachelor party. The entire setting was a grim fantasy for desperate and sexually unsatisfied men, all of whom seemed to converge on this pallid appeal to their psyche.

The Platinum Lounge reeked of cigarette smoke cut with cheap stripper perfume, a pervasive stench whose only respite was the occasional whiff of alcohol as Kyle sipped his fifteen-dollar, watered-down shot of bourbon on ice. The house music was turned up painfully loud, the bass notes throbbing in his ears, and the lingerie-clad women chatting up slovenly bar patrons had to lean in and shout to be heard.

Kyle had chosen to sit alone at a corner table, his back to the far wall so he could see most of the room with a sweep of his head.

The best seats in the house, if you could call them that, were a row of chairs ringing the stage. Most of them were staffed by overweight men in their thirties to fifties, sipping Budweiser and Coors while hungrily forking dollar bills onto the stage. Was this what life was like for guys who couldn't get laid at will? A naked woman was awkwardly crawling across the stage on all fours, doing her level best at making bill collection a seductive affair.

He felt his phone buzz with an incoming text, and saw two short sentences from Clara.

Lawyer can't help. Jannesson is in the gray, but legal.

Kyle felt a twitch in his jaw, and at that moment the club announcer's voice boomed over the PA. "Coming on stage for a two-song set, please give it up for Krystal!"

Kyle put his phone away, then reached for his glass and took a sip as Jenna Tanner took to the stage.

And when he saw her, he almost choked on his liquor.

Jenna Tanner was a legitimate "ten," even by Kyle's impossibly high standards. Her face was heart-shaped, her hair forming twin blonde pigtails though he could tell by the roots that she was a natural brunette. Perfect curves and not an ounce of body fat, her lithe body was clad in a low-cut white shirt ending beneath her breasts, and a short plaid skirt over white stockings.

A booming rock song began, and while the previous dancers had gone through their songs with the hollow, awkward ministrations of unpracticed stripper moves, Kyle saw that Jenna had turned stripping into an art form. Her back was against the pole, and she writhed sensuously against it as she squatted down to reveal her panties.

A girl like that should have been dancing in Nashville or Memphis by now, if not Vegas. The fact that she was still working in a small-town club told him that she was probably crazy, or stupid, or had a drug problem. Or maybe some combination of the three.

But he enjoyed the view regardless, watching Jenna with a genuine sense of intrigue. He'd have fun with her tonight, once he got the information he wanted. Alcohol quieted his mind, but sex turned it off entirely—it was Kyle's only means of experiencing life without the humming throb of fight-or-flight instinct, without feeling fear and anger.

Besides, he thought, Sims wouldn't mind.

When his cocktail waitress returned, Kyle handed her a twenty.

"This is for you. I want the VIP room with that girl on stage, and some bottle service."

"VIP is three hundred an hour, sugar. That all right?"

Kyle turned his eyes back to the stage, where Jenna Tanner was now inverted on the pole, her legs spread-eagle as she corkscrewed her body slowly downward.

"Yep," he answered, "three hundred an hour will be just fine."

* * *

The term "VIP room" was a lofty way to describe where Kyle now found himself, seated on a faux leather couch facing a low table and a platform with a stripper pole. The lights in here were low and red, casting the small room in eerie crimson as he waited for his new date to arrive. Kyle felt uncomfortable here—he'd restricted himself to three watered-down bourbons before this, and was feeling the low-grade onset of a headache that begged to be drowned in alcohol.

But Kyle forgot all about that when Jenna Tanner arrived.

She stepped through the door like a model taking the runway, now clad in a garter set under a sheer lavender babydoll that ended just below lace panties. Her makeup was perfect—bold eyebrows, smoky lids, cat-eye liner, and pouty red lips. She exuded sex in a way that transcended conscious effort, and it occurred to Kyle that Sims probably couldn't have cared less that she was cheating on him.

She sat on the couch beside Kyle, a hand resting effortlessly on his thigh.

"What's your name, darling?"

Her pupils were dilated beneath colored contacts with sky-blue irises, and her heart-shaped face was focused on him in a way that told him that beyond any shadow of a doubt, she'd snorted one or more lines of coke in the past ten minutes.

And that was good, he thought; she may be unbearable, but at least chatty.

He said, "Well, sweetheart, I'm Kyle."

"Kyle." She giggled. "Kyle and Krystal, ain't that grand?"

"Ain't it, though? What are you drinking, Krystal?"

"I'm a vodka girl. What about you?"

"Oh," he said, leaning into her perfume, "I like anything wet."

She giggled again, a high-pitched, rapid-fire laugh that made Kyle's stomach warm with anticipation. He'd never had trouble getting girls, but this felt like cheating.

A cocktail waitress appeared and asked, "What'll it be?"

Kyle announced, "Bottle of Grey Goose, bucket of ice, two glasses, and some privacy." He looked to Krystal. "I'm sorry, sweetheart—did you want any mixers?"

She looked over her shoulder and called, "Cranberry juice."

"Perfect," Kyle said, feeling revolted at the thought of that particular cocktail. "That'll be it."

The cocktail waitress departed, and Jenna turned back to Kyle. "I haven't seen you around, darling. Why haven't you come see me before?"

"Just passing through on my way to Chicago. After seeing you, though, I may have to stop in Franklin more often."

"I hope you do. None of the regulars get bottle service, and it's nice for a girl to be treated every once in a while."

"Then I'll have to stop in town on my way back home. Would that be all right with you, sweetheart?"

She curled up against him, keeping the hand on his thigh and draping the other on his shoulder. "I'd like that, Kyle."

The cocktail waitress returned with a drink tray, pouring them a cranberry cocktail and a vodka rocks before setting the bottle of Grey Goose down on the table and leaving again.

Jenna handed Kyle his glass and then raised her own. "What are we drinking to, darling?"

"To new friends," Kyle replied, toasting her glass.

"To new friends," she said, and they both took a sip.

Kyle kept his face neutral, trying to hide his disdain for vodka. If you wanted the closest thing to rubbing alcohol, then vodka was your ticket—and while Kyle preferred brown liquor over anything clear, at present he couldn't complain about alcohol any way he could get it.

Or the view.

He said, "So tell me about yourself, Krystal."

She gave an alluring shrug.

"Not much to tell. I'm a Franklin girl, born and raised. I like having a good time, like to party. You?"

"I'm from Florida, about a half hour east of Tampa. How long have you been a dancer?"

"Six years. Just saving up enough to move to LA." Then she brightened. "You been there?"

Kyle shook his head. "I'm a small-town boy, sweetheart, and I stay away from the big cities unless duty calls."

Her eyes narrowed at the word "duty," and then Kyle saw her glancing at the exposed tattoos on his forearm, settling on a half-sleeve American flag.

"Oh, God," she said. "You aren't military, are you?"

Kyle laughed. "No, I'm a personal trainer. Why?"

"Because the last military guy I dated will remain the last, that's why."

"Really?" Kyle asked. "Tell me about it."

"I don't much want to talk about that."

"Sweetheart, we got nothing but time and bottle service. I spent all day on the road, and could use a little"—he paused a half-beat—"company."

But Jenna's eyes fell to the American flag tattooed on his arm, and she shook her head slightly. "No, I shouldn't have said anything."

Kyle momentarily considered revoking the inquiry for the time being, and letting her get a few drinks on top of the cocaine in her system. He didn't want to push too hard right out of the gate and risk scaring her off the topic.

Then he had a sudden revelation. He was Kyle Soler, a man who could pick up any woman in any bar, whenever he wanted. If this conversation were happening back home, he'd be talking circles around this girl, using any opening he could to keep her talking, to introduce the first physical touch, to break down her walls until there was nothing left but the ride back to his apartment.

And this woman—gorgeous though she was—was a stripper. Three-quarters of the work was already done for him.

He threw his head back with a laugh, then said, "Sweetheart, I'll be honest with you. I can't *stand* the military. I was a Navy brat and had to follow my worthless dad all over the country, all while he was pushing me to join. Moved out as soon as I got out of high school and never looked back."

She seemed to relax a little, and he continued, "I think it's crazy how much people worship those guys. Only thing the Navy did for my dad was turn him into a wife beater."

Jenna latched onto this comment, huffing a sigh of relief. "I know, right? We're all supposed to hail those guys as heroes for going overseas, when the truth is they come back so messed up that it makes life hell for the rest of us."

"I take it your guy was abusive, like my dad."

She nodded. "May as well have been. Nights were crazy, living with him. I'd wake up to find him choking me 'cause he was having a bad dream, or running around the house with a loaded gun because he thought he heard something."

"Good God. Why didn't he get help?"

Jenna shook her head. "The pills turned him into a lunatic, and when he tried the other thing, it was the final straw."

"What other thing?"

"The VA had some doctor call him." She paused to take a long drink. "Offer some treatment for free because he was a hundred percent disabled and nothing else had worked. He asked what I thought, and I said sure, go for it. Whatever gets you out of town for a few days. Well I didn't actually *say* that last part, but I sure was thinking it."

Kyle nodded, thinking that the VA didn't have outside doctors contact anyone—they had their hands full with their own backlog of veterans.

"Where'd he have to go?"

"Georgia. That should have been his first indication that something was wrong, because nothing good comes out of Georgia, you know? I mean this guy was in Savannah, but still."

"You're talking to a Florida boy, sweetheart. You don't have to tell me anything about how much Georgia sucks, believe me. So what happened, you left him?"

"Should have." Another long drink, and then nothing left in her glass but ice.

Kyle refilled her drink, then handed her the glass.

"But no," she continued, "*this* guy had to blow his brains out right in the

137

bedroom, where *I* used to sleep, a week and a half after his so-called miracle treatment. And his crazy parents wouldn't even let me have the house, can you believe that?"

"That ain't right," Kyle agreed, failing to see the logic. He filled his glass with vodka and said, "What was wrong with him? He get screwed up in Iraq?"

"Afghanistan." She spat out the word with contempt. "Only story he ever told me was the same one he told the doctor. Something about him and another guy, one of these so-called war heroes, carrying the body of a pregnant woman they'd killed on accident. Said that messed him up worse than everything else put together. Can you imagine living with someone like that?"

Kyle was having trouble breathing now. He remembered the pregnant woman clearly—she was the first civilian they'd found in the rubble of the mosque, and Sims had carried her body with Alan Smith. If he told the doctor about that, he wouldn't have referred to the other guy anonymously; Sims would have called him Alan, or Smith, or both.

And since Alan Smith wasn't a hundred percent disabled, Jannesson couldn't have used the same lie of being referred by the VA. That explained why he'd gone the VFW route, and now Kyle knew beyond a shadow of a doubt that Jannesson hadn't just killed Thoma: he'd killed Sims as well.

Kyle took a sip of liquor and said, "No, sweetheart, I cannot imagine that."

She nestled up beside him, laying her head on his shoulder and batting her dark eyelashes.

"But that's enough about me, baby. Tell me a little more about you."

He looked back down at her, and it was like seeing a completely different woman. Her makeup seemed grotesque now; he could actually smell it over her perfume. Jenna's hair color was fake, her eye color was fake, even her personality was fake. She'd spent six years tromping around the stage and pole, and the thought suddenly repulsed him. Kyle had slept with some shallow women, but at least they were coming for what they wanted: sex, and only sex. Jenna had probably treated Sims like garbage, and for once in his life Kyle felt zero drive to bed a willing female participant.

He replied, "Well as I said, I've been on the road all day. And I'm tired. And I hate vodka. I best be getting to bed."

Then he shrugged her head off his shoulder and stood, moving for the door.

Jenna called, "Where are you staying? I get off work in a couple hours. It won't cost you nothing."

Kyle stopped at the door, looking back at her seated before the bottle.

"I know," he said, and stepped through the door to leave.

21

Clara had risen alongside her husband that morning, feeling beyond refreshed after eight hours of sleep. Today she hadn't needed to lie to Jeremy; she'd slept through the night without dreams, or at least none she could remember. That was just fine by her. Once Jeremy and Aiden were out of the house, she planned to give Kyle a call to see what he learned from Sims's ex-girlfriend, then spend the day tearing through her manuscript while she still had some rest under her belt.

But as she buckled Aiden into Jeremy's Maserati, she felt her phone buzzing in her pocket. Only Kyle would be calling, and Clara thought he should have known not to do so this early.

She pulled out her phone to decline the call, expecting to see Kyle's name on the display. But it was a Seattle area code, followed by a number Clara knew all too well.

"Sorry," she said to Jeremy, "I have to take this."

Giving Aiden a kiss goodbye and closing the car door, she rushed inside and answered the phone before the caller hung up.

"Hello, this is Clara."

"Clara, this is Liz Johns, Rich's mother."

Clara tried to sound nonchalant. "Oh, hi, Mrs. Johns, thank you so much for returning my call."

Thor was whining at his food dish, and Clara ignored him. Instead she hurried upstairs, wanting to bring the call to her office so she could take notes.

Rich's mom continued, "Well I am just so sorry that it took me this long. Darren and I got back last night from visiting our daughter and her six-week-old baby in Portland. I'm afraid the number you called was our home phone, and I was just getting around to checking the messages this morning."

"No problem," Clara said, continuing to mount the stairs two at a time, "and congratulations on the new grandbaby. Is it a boy or a girl?"

"Boy. Eoin, spelled the Irish way because God help us all, my daughter married a Mick. Sweetest baby boy you've ever seen, and I swear, Clara, he's built like a bowling ball. He was every bit of *ten pounds, seven ounces* in the delivery room."

Clara entered her office, easing the door shut behind her. "I hope your daughter has forgiven the father...my boy was eight pounds, four ounces, and I thought I was going to murder my husband in his sleep."

Clara rounded her desk, immediately regretting the statement—she wasn't talking to Kyle or Rich now, she was talking to a grandmother—but Liz Johns released a titter of laughter.

"Don't I know it, dear. What's your boy's name?"

"Aiden," she said, taking a seat, "and he's turning five in November."

"What a fun age. I hope you're enjoying every minute, because the next thing you know he'll be—"

Rich's mom went silent, and then Clara heard a choking gasp.

"Oh God, Clara, I miss him so much."

Clara rubbed her forehead, feeling her neck tingle with shame. How could these parents not blame her, she thought, when she certainly blamed herself. "I know it, Mrs. Johns. We all do."

"It just doesn't...doesn't get any easier, you know?"

"No, it doesn't." Clara felt tears in her eyes. Rich's suicide had been a terrible thing, as all suicides were—but there was a desperate, bottomless sadness that surrounded a parent who had lost their child. The pain in Liz's voice was so total, so endless and complete, that Clara realized at that moment she'd never be able to go on without Aiden.

Liz continued, "Sometimes I get so *mad* at him. You...you raise your children in this life, you try to prepare them with everything they need to take on the world. And to see the pain that Rich had at the end, to be able to do nothing to help him, as a parent, that's just...as a parent..."

"I know," Clara said. "It's been unbelievably difficult for me to cope, and I only knew Rich for a short time. I can't imagine the pain you and your husband feel."

Liz gave a short sob, then sniffled and said, "But I don't mean to hold you up, dear. You wanted to talk. I'm assuming it's about Rich."

Clara paused. "It is," she said, "and I'm terribly sorry to have to ask."

"Don't be sorry. We all have to get on with life, however we can. What is it I can help you with?"

"I'm not sure if you know this, but did Rich ever mention anything about traveling to Savannah, or—"

"Oh of course," Liz said, "of course he went to Savannah. Darren and I paid for his trip, and believe me, it took no small amount of convincing to get Rich to go."

"Really? Why?"

Liz sounded surprised. "Why, to see Dr. Jannesson, of course. Have you heard of him?"

"I have," Clara said cautiously, feeling the gooseflesh ripple up her spine. "I mean, I've heard the name in passing. How did you find him?"

"Darren and I were desperate. Rich was on a downhill slide, his depression getting worse every week, and nothing seemed to work. Eventually I found Dr. Jannesson, but not soon enough."

"What do you mean, 'not soon enough?' Jannesson didn't treat him?"

"No, he did. Gave him the injection of...cetraphaline, I think it's called. And when Rich was on his way back, Dr. Jannesson called Darren and me, spoke with us for about two hours. I swear, Clara, no one cares about our veterans more than that man. He's an absolute godsend, and I hope the VA starts paying for every vet to get that treatment."

"Really? What did Dr. Jannesson tell you?"

"Well he explained how it worked—or how he thinks it works, I suppose. No one knows for sure. But he warned us that Rich was pretty far into his depression, and he was afraid the cetraphaline may have come too late to have a reversal effect."

"And then what happened?"

Liz sighed deeply. "Rich felt better for a few days. He told me so. But then he took his own life a couple weeks later. I called Dr. Jannesson to tell him, and the man was practically in tears at the news. Hand on my heart, Clara, he sent us flowers. He didn't have to do that."

* * *

Clara chatted with Rich's mom for a few more minutes before ending the call. She sat at her desk for a while after that, processing the information she'd just learned in an emotional state somewhere between paralyzed shock and burning rage.

How many vets had Jannesson poisoned? Clara didn't know, but the fact that Rich and Thoma were her own people made her want to find him and slit his throat. She wasn't a platoon leader anymore, but felt a responsibility over her men that was second only to her maternal instinct to protect Aiden.

Picking up her phone, she called Kyle.

He answered immediately. "What's up, girl?"

Clara could hear the background noise of a TSA announcement, and realized Kyle must have been at the Nashville Airport, on his way back home.

"Kyle," she said, "I just talked to Rich's mom. He saw Jannesson two weeks before his death."

"You don't say. How'd Jannesson find him?"

"He didn't. Rich's parents found Jannesson, and paid for the treatment. They think Jannesson is some great doctor, and are blaming themselves for not finding him sooner."

Kyle paused before he responded, the background noise filled with chatter from the airport terminal. "Well, Clara, that's...interesting. Very interesting, after last night."

"What happened? Did you talk to Sims's girlfriend?"

"Did I ever. Gorgeous on the outside, but the ugliest person I've ever met on the inside. And coming from me, that's saying something. But she talked, and I found out everything I needed to know."

"And?"

"Jannesson contacted Sims directly, claiming to be sent on behalf of the VA. Sims went to Savannah for treatment a week and a half before his suicide. That's not all—she said the only story Sims ever told her about Afghanistan was, and I quote, 'the same one he told the doctor,' about him and another guy carrying a pregnant woman's body. Ring any bells?"

Clara's mind flashed to the rubble of the mosque, where Sims carried out the first civilian body with the help of another man from the platoon.

"My God," she said, "Sims and Alan carried that woman's body."

"Exactly. And I'll bet you a bottle that Sims mentioned Alan Smith's name to Jannesson, because Jannesson showed up at Alan's VFW a few months later."

Clara leaned back in her chair, trying to make sense of the one startling contradiction in the evidence against Jannesson. "But Alan had a successful treatment. If Jannesson is experimenting, why did Alan come out clean?"

"I've been thinking about that, and I don't have a good answer. Maybe Jannesson is experimenting with vets here and there, and our platoon got unlucky with word-of-mouth referral."

"There's no way," Clara said. "Two out of thirty-eight seeing him before their deaths is a statistical anomaly, and Jannesson couldn't be operating this long if he had a large number of vets dying after his treatment. I'm not saying there aren't others, but he's working his way through our platoon for some reason. We've tied him to Rich and Sims, and it's a virtual certainty that Thoma saw him too. That connects Jannesson with every suicide except for Dakota, but she's the last person who would kill herself, and at this point I think it's obvious he treated her too. The question is why."

Kyle was silent for a few moments. "I got no idea. I honestly don't."

"Well, we know enough. I'm going to the cops. Right now, today."

He sounded hesitant. "You think they'll believe us?"

"I think I know one who might."

She got off the phone with Kyle, then hastily typed the pertinent information they'd discovered—the names of the platoon suicides, which ones had been treated by Jannesson and how long before their deaths—and printed a single sheet. Then she rushed to her walk-in closet to get dressed in business attire. Tying her hair into a tight bun, she applied just enough makeup to look polished and professional. She needed to look the part of a bright and intelligent woman, not some crazed housewife pitching a conspiracy theory.

Grabbing her purse and heading downstairs, she set foot in the kitchen and heard the clatter of dog toenails. She'd forgotten to feed Thor, she realized, and quickly moved to the cabinet to retrieve his food.

But when she rounded the kitchen island, the creature she saw there wasn't her son's puppy.

It was a shaggy brindle dog, its mangy fur crossed with a coil of razor wire now hopelessly embedded in its flesh. The dog's eyes were wide and wild, tongue lolling as it watched Clara.

This was the Afghan bitch, the dog she'd shot in the trash pit. There was the wafting stench of garbage and blood, the decay of death amid ash and diesel fumes.

Clara stood dumbstruck at the sight—the dog wasn't attacking, or even advancing.

Instead, the bitch looked to her with helpless animal eyes, begging for Clara to kill her, begging to be shot.

Clara's hand drifted to her hip, feeling for a pistol that wasn't there—she was still in her business attire, no longer a powerless witness reliving some past event. This was her kitchen, this was the present, but the Afghan bitch stood there just the same: whining, wheezing, mortally wounded and craving the endless peace of death.

When she didn't wake up in bed, Clara took one hesitant step backward, then another, feeling for the counter beside her as she backed toward the door to the garage. With the kitchen island between her and the dog, the smell of diesel and scorched garbage faded...but she could still hear the creature wheezing, gargling for breath in a blood-choked throat.

Finally Clara's hand was on the door handle, and she eased it open and stepped into the garage, pulling it shut behind her. The handle was cool and smooth; her BMW waited obediently behind her. Clara reached for the square button on the wall and pressed it, and the rolling garage door began shuddering upward to reveal the morning sunlight blazing on her manicured front lawn.

When was this dream going to end? Clara didn't know, and it wasn't until she went through the motions of walking to her car that she realized this was no dream. It was a waking hallucination, something that had appeared real to the point of being indistinguishable from reality.

She slipped into the driver's seat, slamming the door shut as if the car's interior could protect her from the horror. But the horror was no longer outside of her, no longer safely ensconced in the sleeping hours when she'd wake up to find it was all just a dream. She placed her hands on the steering wheel, grasping the smooth, rounded leather surface as if it held some key to her sanity.

Clara pressed the car's push button start, and the engine came alive with a reassuring bark.

With a resolute breath, Clara backed out of her garage and into the sunlight.

22

The officer manning the front desk of the Charleston Police Department headquarters was sitting behind a sheet of bullet-resistant glass.

"Clara Swanner, here to see Sergeant Dennis. He's expecting me."

The officer asked for her ID, and she deposited her driver's license into the receptacle. He checked it and then made a brief phone call before handing it back.

"You can have a seat over there, ma'am. He'll be with you shortly."

Clara turned to the seating area the officer was pointing toward and thanked him.

She crossed the lobby and chose a couch with a coffee table, sitting with her legs neatly crossed and trying to portray an image of professionalism. But her posture felt hollow and forced; she was telling herself that she'd have to be quite careful now, have to patently ignore any sights and sounds that were of Afghanistan and not her home city.

But at present, there were none. Instead she sat in a spacious and well-appointed lobby, the passersby normal officers and citizens in suits and police uniforms. She hoped that luck would hold until her meeting was over. She had exactly one chance to pitch what she and Kyle knew to be true, and couldn't afford to come off as a crackpot.

There was only one cop she felt would understand—Sergeant Raymond Dennis, one of the responding officers for her reported home invasion. He was the only one in the Charleston PD who already knew she was a veteran, knew she had PTSD, and could ascertain from the splendor of her home that she wasn't some lunatic wandering in off the street.

Officers continued to pass through the lobby, casting sideways glances toward her. She knew from their looks what they were going to say once she'd left. Clara was an attractive young female with a wedding ring who was asking to see a male officer by name. She knew that the moment she departed, Sergeant Dennis's fellow officers on both sides of the gender divide would be mercilessly taunting him about the nature of her visit.

And upon seeing him enter the lobby, she realized that thought had occurred to him as well.

He looked irritated, and Clara felt that it was probably more attributable to the withering ridicule he'd face than to any interruption of his duties. But Sergeant Dennis did an admirable job of donning a mask of professionalism, greeting her courteously as she rose to shake his hand.

"Mrs. Swanner, good to see you. Please have a seat. How can I help you today?"

Clara sat as he joined her on the couch. She began, "Thank you for meeting with me. I'm sorry to show up unexpectedly like this—I realize how this looks, and I apologize in advance for any grief you take on my behalf."

She'd intended for the comment to lighten the mood and establish rapport, but Sergeant Dennis said nothing, sitting in the chair across from her with a neutral expression.

Clara continued, "I need to come clean with you first. I was a platoon leader in the military, and involved in a major combat engagement in a village called Pantalay. That's the one where a mosque was destroyed by an airstrike—maybe you've heard about it on the news."

"I haven't."

"Well the identities of everyone in the platoon have been kept out of the media, except for the KIAs. The military deemed everyone involved to be at risk for retaliation."

"And you think that retaliation is occurring, do I have that right?"

"Yes," she said. "There have been four deaths to date, all deemed to be suicide."

"But you think they're murders."

"I do now."

He nodded. "Terrorists? US-based extremists?"

"No. There's a man providing PTSD treatment to veterans, and we've linked him to three of the four victims."

"Who is 'we,' Mrs. Swanner?"

"Me and Kyle, my former platoon sergeant."

Sergeant Dennis shrugged. "So what's the link?"

"This man's name is Marcus Jannesson." Clara reached into her purse, procuring the page she'd printed and unfolding it on the coffee table. She noted with approval that Sergeant Dennis had procured a notepad and scrawled the name down. Plucking a pen out of her purse, she set the cap next to Jannesson's name on the page.

Clara said, "Jannesson has changed his name once, and his medical license was revoked for experimenting on patients. I didn't know any of that when I was treated, but immediately afterward I began having terrible nightmares. And hallucinations. Including the...the incident you responded to, where I thought my home was being broken into."

"Where is this doctor—this former doctor—based out of?"

Clara hesitated. "Savannah."

"Then why aren't you talking to Savannah PD?"

"Because they won't believe me any more than you probably do right now. But I know from our previous conversation that you understand the impact of PTSD, and believe me when I say that the effects I've been experiencing are not that. Not at all. I think Jannesson injected me with something besides the specified treatment."

"And what was that treatment, exactly?"

"Cetraphaline."

Sergeant Dennis frowned. "Cetraphaline goes by the street name of Vitamin C, or Cookie Cutter. It's a club drug, Mrs. Swanner."

"It is *abused* as a club drug, I know. But it's been shown to have effectiveness in treating psychiatric disorders, including PTSD. That's why I received the treatment in a clinical setting."

"Voluntarily."

"Yes, voluntarily."

He raised his eyebrows. "Then you were made aware of any side effects."

"Yes. For cetraphaline, which was the only medication I gave my consent for. But the dosage put me in a trance, and I think I was administered something else while I was under."

"But you can't prove it."

"No, I can't prove it—but the fact that I've been experiencing effects that are not consistent with cetraphaline use, and that Jannesson has experimented on patients in the past, and that he's definitely treated at least two of the four suicides—"

"Three."

"Excuse me?"

"Mrs. Swanner, you previously stated that you had linked Jannesson to three suicides, not two."

She shook her head, uncrossing her legs. "Well the third was told about Jannesson by another member of the platoon who'd received the treatment, so it's safe to assume a high possibility that he received the treatment before his death."

"And that other member was one of the suicides?"

Clara shook her head. "No, he's still alive."

"That would seem to disprove your claim."

"Only if Jannesson treated all of his patients the same way. But he hasn't —or at least, I don't think so."

Sergeant Dennis cleared his throat and leaned away from Clara. "Mrs. Swanner, forgive me for sounding callous. But twenty-two veterans kill themselves every day, and that's just the official count of those enrolled for VA treatment. Personally, I've responded to ten, maybe twelve, vet suicides. And that's just in Charleston, just in the course of my duties as a police officer. You see what I'm getting at?"

"I think I do, but I'm talking about four suicides within a platoon of thirty-eight members present in Pantalay Village. We're now in the realm of a statistical anomaly, and while only two of those suicides definitely saw Jannesson, there was a third who killed himself a few weeks after being told about his treatment—"

"By someone who received that treatment and lived to tell about it."

"Well, yes."

"So if the identities of everyone in your platoon were kept secret, then how could Jannesson possibly have known who to treat?"

Clara leaned forward, eager to explain what she'd learned. "That's the million-dollar question. And it turns out that the parents of the second platoon suicide were researching treatment options for their son, Rich Johns." Using her pen, she tapped his name on the paper. "And they reached out to Jannesson directly. Rich must have mentioned some names, because after he got the treatment, there were two more suicides." She slid the pen to the names of Jason Sims and Joshua Thoma. "Sims, who definitely saw Jannesson, and a fourth named Thoma, who died a few weeks after hearing about him. You look into Thoma's suicide, I can virtually guarantee you'll find that he received the treatment as well."

"What about the first? If the second suicide, Rich, gave names to Jannesson, then how do you explain the first suicide?"

"The first was Dakota Goldsmith, an embedded journalist from *The New York Times*. She'd been self-medicating with opioids, and overdosed after leaving a note. We haven't found a link between her and Jannesson—not yet. But I was very close with Dakota, and out of all four deaths I can assure you that she was the last person who'd ever end her own life. I promise you, whatever caused the other three to kill themselves, Dakota got it first."

Sergeant Dennis was frowning now. "And you believe you've received that unidentified substance as well."

"I know I have."

He smoothed his pant legs and sat back on the couch. "Then the first person you need to see isn't a cop, Mrs. Swanner. It's a doctor."

Clara felt her argument crumbling beneath her feet. She admitted, "Well I have, and—"

"And they found nothing in your system," he finished for her.

She gave a short sigh. "No, but that doesn't mean there's nothing there. Jannesson is smart; he used to be a neurosurgeon and has apparently been getting away with this for some time, and his clinic has a DEA license for pharmaceuticals of all kinds."

Sergeant Dennis craned his neck. "How does his clinic have a license if he doesn't?"

"That's a great question. He transferred all his authorities to another doctor before the medical board stripped him of his license, and now he's operating in the gray area as a clinic employee."

"The 'gray area' isn't illegal, Mrs. Swanner." He checked his watch. "Now if you'll excuse me, I really do have other business to attend to."

"Please," Clara said, the desperation rising in her throat like a wild animal fighting to get out. "I know I'm right about this. He's going to keep getting away with this unless someone believes me."

She quickly folded the page and held it out to him, the square of paper trembling in her grasp. "This is everything I know right now. Please, just...look into this."

He hesitated before taking the page from her. "I will, Mrs. Swanner. But I have many other things to look into first, so please be patient."

He looked over his shoulder and said, "Jerry?"

A uniformed officer walked to Clara's side and said, "Miss, it's time to go."

23

Jeremy was dicing peppers and onions that evening, the *thwack thwack thwack* of his chef's knife sounding against the cutting board. Aiden was coloring at his table, and Clara felt her heart sink when Jeremy spoke.

"Aiden, buddy, why don't you take your art stuff to the dining room table so Daddy and Mommy can talk?"

"Okay," Aiden replied easily, scraping a stack of papers from his kid table and carrying it away with his box of markers.

What was Jeremy going to say next? She didn't want to have a deep conversation now. Clara felt uneasy in the kitchen—she stood not three feet from the spot where she'd seen the mortally wounded Afghan dog that morning, where she'd smelled the burned trash and diesel fumes and gradually faced the dawning realization that it was no dream.

But there wasn't a trace of hallucination now. The corners of reality were sharp and vivid; she was in her own luxury kitchen, situated on the ground floor of an opulent, three-story home in a neighborhood and city that she couldn't have dreamed of in her youth.

That made her disquietude all the more unsettling. No one who lived in a place like this could begin to comprehend the dark alcoves of her thoughts and memories, of the insanity that threatened to swallow her whole at every waking moment.

"You okay?" Jeremy asked once their son had left. "You seem a little...I don't know, like you might be getting sick or something."

"Oh, it's just a little headache. I think I might be getting my period again soon."

Jeremy stopped cutting. "Didn't you just have your period a couple weeks ago?"

Had she? Clara wasn't sure. The days and nights were running together now, the lines between reality and fantasy, suspicion and fact becoming blurred and nebulous. Trying to recall the past brought only a juxtaposition of people who didn't believe her or were otherwise unwilling or unable to help—Ryan Frahm the attorney, Sergeant Dennis of the Charleston PD, and now her own husband.

"You know what?" she said. "You're right. Maybe it's just a headache from allergies."

"Or maybe," he said as he resumed cutting vegetables on the board, "you're just under pressure from the manuscript submission deadline. Isn't that coming up in a few days?"

"No," she said. "Not anymore."

He looked up from the cutting board. "Yes, it is. I marked my calendar."

Why did he never believe her?

"I got a thirty-day extension, Jeremy."

"Really?" He sounded incredulous, and his suspicion grated at her nerves. "That's never happened before."

"They didn't want to move the deadline at first. But I sent them the first twenty thousand words, and they told me it was a masterpiece. Told me not to rush, and gave me the extra month with no questions asked. I probably could have gotten forty-five days if I asked. Sixty, maybe."

"Oh. That's great." He continued cutting, the *thwack thwack thwack* resuming. It was the sound of metal on wood, of blade on bone. "And the writing's still going well?"

Clara shook her head. "It's not going 'well,' it's absolutely spectacular. Turns out that seven or eight hours of sleep a night does wonders for my creative powers."

"And no more dreams?"

The tempo of his cutting increased until it was at the staccato of automatic gunfire.

"Right," she said. "I told you, no more dreams. Jannesson fixed me."

"Doctor."

"What?"

"*Doctor* Jannesson fixed you."

Clara said nothing, noting with an odd detachment that her husband's little corrections should have infuriated her.

But she was focused on the noise of his chef's knife against the cutting board. How many peppers and onions did he need to dice? The sound of his chopping became gunshots in her mind. *Thwack thwack thwack*, each noise a shot fired, a bullet sent screaming into an Afghan village where the killing had just begun.

Jeremy seemed to sense her unease. "Why don't you make yourself a drink?"

Clara suddenly saw her kitchen bathed in blood, the smooth gray walls and marbled granite counters a slate of crimson death. She blinked the image away, and the kitchen was once again a vision of perfection, lit under the scalding glare of circular LED lights pockmarking the ceiling. Domestic perfection, the happy little family with endless finances in a world of utopian peacetime.

"Why would I make myself a drink?"

He shrugged. "I don't know. You seem tense."

The prospect of alcohol repulsed her. She looked to the bar cart, felt the acid rising in her throat at the memory of standing there as Joshua Thoma staggered toward her, knife in hand, naked and dripping blood from his open wounds.

She couldn't recall the last time she drank for pleasure instead of release. Alcohol was a tool now; she'd weaponized it into an instrument of relaxation or sleep when all else failed. And barring the need for sleep, she drank to momentarily absolve herself from the fact that she'd gone from a soldier to some kind of dancing monkey, slitting her veins to pour her soul onto the written page, baring her deepest self to the visceral reviews of critics who bemoaned her use of profanity.

"I'm not tense. I'm fine. Just...fine."

But she was now more than just an author, she reminded herself, releasing the greatest work she was capable of to an indifferent readership who tossed her books aside to pick up whatever was next in the stack. Clara was also Jeremy's little plaything, the sex object dolled up in silk and lace, waiting to be used whenever the need struck him. She was no different from the dog she killed, just a bitch in heat waiting for her husband to take her again.

Jeremy continued cutting. "You're not fine, Clara. This is the worst you've been in over a year. Aiden's starting to notice. He's been asking me about you, asking what's wrong with Mommy."

She barely heard him. Clara was wondering what Jeremy was thinking about when she was on her hands and knees on the mattress, or spreading her legs for him on the counter of their master bathroom—not her, she realized. He was languidly dreaming of those other women, the trophy wives who cast him desirous glances over the shoulders of their own over-weight husbands with gold watches and fat bank accounts.

"Clara?"

"I'm fine," she insisted. "Really, it's just a headache."

Clara couldn't think of anything else to say, now lost in her own thoughts. Jeremy had glanced back at those other women, she knew. Maybe not overtly, but he'd turned to them in his mind, using Clara as a living porno movie onto which he could project his sick fantasies.

What else was he fantasizing about?

"If you say so," Jeremy replied dismissively.

The cutting continued, the gunshots continued, each *thwack* the sound of death, of him thrusting himself into her, of blade on bone.

Thwack thwack thwack and the kitchen was blood again, then clean and white, then dripping with red, each blink exposing the room in a camera shutter exposure that alternated seamlessly between life and death, love and fear.

Jeremy set the knife down with a flat *clack* that made her heart leap. He scooped a pile of diced vegetables into his hands, turning to spread them in the pan on the stove.

Clara stepped forward and picked up the knife. She couldn't take the noise anymore.

When Jeremy turned back to the cutting board, Clara plunged the knife into the center of his chest.

The action had a dreamlike quality to it, as if she were watching herself from the outside, until the *pop* of the blade searing through his breastbone brought her back to reality, to the smell of chopped onions in her kitchen.

She released the knife handle in horror, staggering backward a step to see that it now emerged from Jeremy's sternum, buried up to the hilt.

Jeremy's eyes looked to the knife handle, and then to her, his face a veil of disbelief.

But a circle of blood spread across his shirtfront, congealing into a bloody streak that poured down his abdomen.

"I'm sorry," Clara said.

Jeremy started to fall backward, bracing one hand on the stovetop before collapsing on the floor. He was curled into the fetal position, then flattened onto his back as if lying on the beach. The knife handle pointed upward, quivering with the slowing vibration of his heartbeat.

"Mommy?"

It was Aiden's voice, the sound of innocence, calling to her from the dining room.

"Aiden," she called back, "bring me the phone, sweetie. Daddy's had an accident."

But it wasn't an accident; she'd stabbed him and he was bleeding out on the hardwood floor of their kitchen, and Clara wasn't waking up.

Instead she was watching him, watching her husband die, and the visual details of her kitchen were in stark relief, no longer interspersed with dark fantasy.

"What happened?" Aiden asked, his small footsteps approaching.

She answered in a whisper.

"I just needed the cutting to stop."

Then Aiden rounded the kitchen island, appearing with the phone in his hand. His eyes fell to his father, now lying in a pool of blood with the handle of his chef's knife protruding from his sternum like some prop from a Halloween costume.

Aiden screamed, his shrill cry pulling Clara through an endless fog that ended atop her mattress, a sweat-soaked return to reality as she awoke in bed.

Aiden's scream in her ears faded to the staticky warble of her white noise machine. Pulling off the sleep mask, she felt for Jeremy beside her and found his sleeping form beneath the covers, rising and falling with each breath.

She rose from bed, padding away to separate herself from the dream. Making her way to the master bathroom, Clara turned on the light and set her hands on the sink.

Her hair was matted from the pillow, cheeks hollow with interrupted sleep, eyes rimmed with red. She watched herself breathing jaggedly in the mirror and thought that this vision before her was the *real* Clara, how she looked with all her masks set aside. No makeup, the horror of the most recent nightmare fresh in her face, and it occurred to her that this vision of herself should be her author photo, not some professionally snapped and airbrushed portrait depicting her as a thoughtful and beautiful academic. This state of insomnia and anxiety-ridden despair had produced all of her books, had in fact driven her to write in the first place in some misguided search for constant and never-ending distraction from the realities of her past and present.

She turned on the sink and splashed cold water on her face, trying to remember what had actually transpired at dinner. Had she gone through the motions of being a mother and wife, projecting her best attempt at domestic bliss? Had she excused herself to bed early, citing a headache? Clara couldn't remember.

She recalled meeting Sergeant Dennis at the police station, could remember every word of his glad-handing rejection before she was escorted out. And after that?

There was nothing, just the dream.

Clara dried her face and considered her next move. Now the prospect of alcohol no longer repulsed her. The bottles called to her, summoning her as the only therapy she was ever going to get again.

Clara obliged, leaving the bedroom and numbly acknowledging the whisper of her feet down the stairs.

24

Clara sat alone in the room, under the blinding glare of UV lights. The surface of the table was faux wood, a pattern imprinted on the plastic surface that struck her as absurdly inauthentic.

She heard footsteps outside the door and looked up, but no one entered.

Her wait continued, and she thought back to the morning's events. Nothing out of the ordinary, and that was perhaps the most disturbing thing of all. Jeremy and Aiden had greeted her warmly, providing no indication of what had transpired at dinner. Clara still couldn't remember anything between leaving the police station and waking up from her nightmare, where Jeremy lay dying on the kitchen floor as Aiden screamed.

But Clara had just enough blackout nights to know how to pretend nothing was out of the ordinary, as if she remembered the previous evening so clearly that nothing needed to be said. That was now her default mode —everything fine, no issues with sleep or anything else.

Yet her head now pounded with the alcohol that had allowed a merciful escape into a few hours of sedated sleep, her greatest reprieve since the dreams and hallucinations began. This was it, she thought—she was existing within a trembling, living nightmare. But when she asked herself how much it differed from what had come before, she was unsure of the answer.

Of course, there were no waking delusions before she'd been treated by Jannesson, who was, conveniently, still absent from the clinic for his "family emergency." But what was her alternative to blindly groping for his advertised treatment? Being unable to achieve or maintain sleep, and resorting to alcohol as a tool—how adorable it was, she thought, when she went to bars with Jeremy and his friends and heard them discussing the prospect of liquor shots in conspiratorial tones. She tried not to laugh at times like those. She tried to play the part of the cool wife tagging along, but she was fundamentally different from those men. The levels of alcohol consumption they reserved for wedding receptions were her average week-day, and the effects she felt this morning were just another day at the proverbial office of her life.

And yes, these mornings were always hard; she'd wake with her head spinning, ears ringing even more loudly than usual. But it was preferable to the alternative.

Alcohol was the only thing that made her feel truly sane, like she deserved a place in the world. It erased the vague notion that every one of the men who died were truly better than she was, each deserving to live more than she did and yet succumbing to death by the enemy's hand or, barring that, their own. The news of each subsequent suicide in her platoon made her painfully aware of that, made her feel less worthy of continued existence.

Because Clara had served alongside those men, yes; but as an officer, her year of time at the platoon level was bookmarked by an ascension to staff ranks, to administrative duties as a stepping stone to a company command that she didn't want and wouldn't remain in service long enough to see. What was the alternative, to become the next Captain McHugh? Even if she'd remained in the military after having seen combat firsthand, she couldn't bear the thought of sitting in a tactical operations center listening to the radio transmissions of people in the fight. Nor could she imagine resigning her officer commission to serve in the enlisted ranks, clinging to her last gunfight in the desperate hopes that it wouldn't be the last. The war in Afghanistan was endless, yes, but the prospect of ground combat became increasingly unlikely with each year of US involvement.

So Clara had exited the military without looking back, only to find that looking back wasn't optional, that the demons in her mind continued to swirl.

In this way Clara had continued to exist, earning an off-the-books PhD in pain management. And after a half dozen treatment methods, her only thesis remained alcohol. Everything else had been a waste of time and money, had left her increasingly disillusioned that these so-called professionals had no idea what they were attempting to treat, or how. She could accept if they didn't approve of alcohol, and she could accept if they didn't approve of pills. But Clara could never grasp the mentality that decried booze while upholding a prescription pad, that only approved sedation if it benefited the same pharmaceutical industry that had spawned the opioid epidemic that had claimed countless lives, Dakota's among them.

And in the process of all this, Clara had learned the same truth that countless veterans surely had before her: she was well and truly alone, left to succeed or fail, live or die, by her own hand. No one understood that except those who were similarly afflicted, and many of them rarely talked to one another. Why would they? The alternative was re-immersing themselves in horrors best left forgotten, horrors they'd once willingly engaged in under some forgotten notions of patriotism and duty.

Jannesson's treatment had exponentially accelerated her descent, but that descent was already in progress long before she'd been injected with cetraphaline. Now she had entered a deep void of hopelessness, a dark realm from which there was only one escape.

The office door opened, and attorney Ryan Frahm entered with the papers in his hand.

"Thank you for your patience, Mrs. Swanner. This is Tommy Cook, who will be serving as our notary."

The nervous-looking man behind Frahm smiled shyly, uncomfortable with maintaining eye contact.

Clara didn't stand. "Nice to meet you."

The notary asked for her driver's license, and Clara slid it across the table.

Then Frahm set down his paper and a handful of pens before taking a seat. "I must emphasize again this is really just a stop-gap for proper estate planning. When you're able, it's very important that you make an appointment with your husband to go over your assets in detail so we can establish a trust that will include all intellectual property, including any work you've yet to publish."

"I understand," she said. "Jeremy's been really busy with work, but we should be able to make an appointment within the next few weeks. In the meantime...this is everything I asked you for?"

Ryan Frahm nodded and pushed a short stack of papers toward her. "Yes. These documents stipulate that your husband Jeremy is the primary benefactor for all your assets in the event of your death, with Aiden as the secondary benefactor."

Clara took the papers, glancing at the top sheet. "And that covers my death by any possible cause?"

"Yes," Frahm answered uneasily. "There are no further stipulations specifying accidental death or that resulting from...you know, a health issue. Or anything else. Please take your time looking these over, I'm here to answer any questions you have—"

"That won't be necessary," Clara said, reaching for one of the pens. "Let's get this signed."

25

Aiden was sleeping soundly, his tiny face resting in an angelic state.

Clara always marveled at how peaceful her son looked as he slept. Children had an eternal innocence forever denied to adults, and nowhere was this more apparent to her than in the late hours of the night, watching her son as the pastel glow of his spinning night light orbited slowly across his room.

He was still scared of the dark, and for good reason. Clara knew that fear well now, had seen beyond the perceived terror of nightmares to know what truly awaited in the night. When the distractions of waking hours faded away, all that was left was to look inside, and for people like Clara, that view held fears worse than any dream.

Aiden's fear of the dark had subsided somewhat with the addition of Thor to their family, and Clara looked upon the puppy's sleeping form, now curled up at her son's side. In a way, the dog was like her son—one day he would be an adult, exposed to the realities of life just as Aiden would be in his manhood.

But for now they were both children of their own species, existing in a state of perfection before the world took their innocence as it had her own.

Above all else, Clara felt a deep maternal instinct to protect her son. Motherhood had changed her forever, and while most mothers she knew agreed while waxing lyrical about the unending love that had been brought into their lives, Clara's experience went far deeper. The second she'd heard Aiden's first cries in the delivery room, a new world of emotion had opened to her.

But instead of love, the most profound of these feelings was rage.

She had a protectiveness over Aiden that was tempered by what she'd seen overseas, the realities of how quickly and gruesomely a human life could be snuffed out. And after that point, she'd had moments of anger exceeding all those that had come before. A near fender-bender in a parking lot had become a different event altogether. Before Aiden was born, Clara would shrug off such close calls with a fleeting judgment of the ineptitude of her fellow drivers, carelessly texting or otherwise unaware of the world around them.

With Aiden in the backseat, those events had turned into an adrenaline-soaked rage, an unbidden instinct to *neutralize the threat* to her son's life. Her biggest fight with Jeremy to date had been over just such a trivial occurrence, when they'd nearly been struck by an old man who braked just short of the passenger side of Jeremy's Maserati. Aiden had been on that side of the car, securely buckled behind Clara, and she'd undone her seatbelt and begun exiting the vehicle without a conscious thought.

The words were forming on her lips before she'd even stepped out of the car.

Roll down the window, sir—I just want to talk to you.

She'd kill the old man then, slam his forehead off the steering wheel to buy a few moments of shock and exploit the gap by choking the life out of his wrinkled neck with both hands before moving onto his liver-spotted wife.

Jeremy had shouted, "Clara! Aiden's in the backseat."

She'd been dumbstruck at the comment. Of course he was in the backseat—who did Jeremy think she was about to do this for, herself? Jeremy? Both were capable of defending themselves from the meaningless blows of life, from the idiot drivers like the one she was about to assault, hopefully fatally.

Then it had dawned on her: Aiden was *in the backseat*, awake and cognizant of the world around him, potentially about to be traumatized by Clara's next actions. It had taken her entire force of will to slide back into the passenger seat and close the car door, but not before shooting the other driver a deadpan expression unachievable to anyone who hadn't taken multiple human lives with all the emotional investment of unloading groceries.

Her eyes said, *I will kill you*, and the old man's terrified return glance conveyed that he understood.

Then Clara was back in the car, muttering a half-coherent excuse to Aiden's inquiries about what had just happened. And just like that, she was back in the normal world, gliding along in a Maserati amid an upscale part of Charleston, her confrontation with Jeremy delayed until their son was put to bed.

And now Aiden was in bed once more, sleeping peacefully in a way that Clara hadn't since adulthood, and certainly not since Pantalay. Her foremost instinct remained, as it had since Aiden's birth, to protect her son. But when you'd seen the realities that Clara had, stared into that depth of darkness with an unflinching gaze, there was only one true protection left.

She pulled aside the covers to expose his tiny body, lying barefoot in race car pajamas that she'd picked out after he turned four and outgrew his previous sets. Thor looked up and whined. Clara shushed the puppy, then reached under Aiden's back and legs to gently lift her son into her arms. Gently cradling him—how could children sleep so soundly?—Clara walked toward his adjoining bathroom.

The bathroom lights were on, and she saw the tub as she'd left it minutes before. His bath toys had been cleared away, and the tub was half-filled with clear, warm water. Clara walked alongside it, kneeling on the bathmat to suspend Aiden's sleeping body over the water's surface.

Then she lowered him into the water, slowly, sadly guiding his body downward until he floated on the surface beneath her arms.

Aiden awoke then, his eyes bursting open and finding her with a single word.

"Mommy?"

Clara used both arms to push him beneath the surface, holding his body against the floor of the tub as a volcano of bubbles erupted from his mouth. He thrashed against her arms, now locked at the elbows to keep his body pinned beneath the rippling surface.

His eyes were still open, mouth moving in unheard screams as she held him down. The sounds that reached her were garbled cries that turned to a low, deep growl. It was the growl of a dog, the noise that the Afghan bitch would have made if her throat hadn't been gashed apart by razor wire, and Clara grimaced in silent incomprehension at the noises now coming from her drowning son's mouth.

Clara blinked and she was standing over her son's bed once more, watching his sleeping form with Thor curled alongside him.

But the puppy wasn't sleeping, or even whining—his eyes were fixed on Clara, his jowls puckered in a low, throaty growl directed toward her. She blinked hard, gasping for breath. Then she realized this was no dream; she was back in the real world, standing over Aiden's bed as the night light cast a peaceful spinning glow over his sleeping form.

My God, she thought, My God...Clara told herself that it was just a dream, the most horrific nightmare she'd had but a dream nonetheless... and she turned to quickly leave her son's room as the puppy's growls subsided.

She was exiting his bedroom when she recognized the presence of light where it shouldn't have been. This was her domain, the dark place she resided in when everyone else was asleep, and yet a slit of yellow light cast a glow across the floor.

The source, she saw, was emanating from beneath Aiden's bathroom door. He must have used the restroom in the night and forgotten to shut it off. Heart pounding, she opened the door and reached for the light switch.

Then she saw the unthinkable—Aiden's tub, cleared of his many bath toys, now half-full with clear, tepid water.

26

The Swanner family sat on a picnic blanket in the shade of an ancient oak tree draped with Spanish moss. A warm summer breeze drifted across them, bringing the aroma of flowers in bloom and musical notes from the jazz trio playing in a nearby gazebo.

Hampton Park was Aiden's favorite place in the city. When there was a local event and it was too packed for him to run the trails and clearing with impunity, they'd take him to the adjoining baseball fields to expend some energy, but today was a normal day at the park, and they had plenty of room to themselves.

Families and couples were scattered about, some picnicking and others strolling the trails while enjoying the view. Clara had always enjoyed the abundant floral displays here. Explosions of roses and seasonal flowers bloomed between live oaks, making the park a peaceful place—even for her, even in the present circumstances.

Aiden held the looped end of Thor's leash, which he used to swat away the puppy's attempts to encroach on the peanut butter and jelly sandwich that he'd spent the better part of ten minutes nibbling.

He suddenly asked, "Mommy, why do you have to go?"

Jeremy looked up at her, and Clara gave her son a warm smile.

"Well, buddy, sometimes things get really hard, especially when we're doing something new. Remember how hard it was to ride your bike at first? Or your first swim lesson?"

Aiden nodded solemnly.

Clara said, "But what do we do when things get hard? Do we give up?"

"No."

"What should we do?"

"Keep trying," he said.

"That's right, buddy. So Mommy tried writing a very tricky book, and it's been hard. But you didn't quit the first time you fell off your bike, and you didn't quit when that first swim lesson was really scary. You kept trying, and that's what Mommy's going to do."

"But you can write in your office."

Clara and Jeremy exchanged a knowing glance.

"That's right, buddy," she said, "but sometimes Mommy can write faster when she's all by herself for a long time. It'll just be for one week—then I'll be back, and I'll bring you a surprise. A big one. Okay?"

"Okay."

Jeremy took a sip from his bottle of water. "Just make sure you get some massages while you're at the Wentworth, okay?"

"I will," she agreed. "Every time I need a writing break, I'll be going straight to the hotel spa. It's five hundred a night just to stay there, so try not to think about the final bill."

He grinned. "I won't. You deserve a break, or however much of one you can manage. I'm just glad your publisher gave you that thirty-day extension."

Clara smiled back at him. "They didn't want to at first, but after I sent them what I had so far, they were all about it. My editor said this is my best work yet. I probably could have pushed for forty-five days if I needed it. Sixty, maybe."

"Sure you won't need that long?"

She shook her head. "One week of super-focused writing will get me over the hump. Then it'll be back to the regular routine, and—"

Aiden interrupted, "Dad, can we throw the frisbee?"

Jeremy sighed patiently. "Sure, Aiden."

Clara took Thor's leash from her son, watching in amusement as they carried the frisbee into an open area and began to play. These games were remarkably undramatic: Jeremy and Aiden stood at a distance of perhaps six feet apart. Jeremy would lightly cast the frisbee to Aiden, who'd generally miss the catch before flinging the frisbee in a spastic hurl that could send it in any given direction.

Jeremy would dart after it, return to his starting position, and resume the game to Aiden's unabashed enthusiasm.

Thor whined at the end of his leash, but Clara held firm against the puppy's tugging. He was generally good about staying around the family, but the sight of a squirrel would launch him into a dead sprint faster than Clara could react.

There was one beneficial side effect of her treatment at Jannesson's hands, Clara thought as she watched the dog. For all the agonies she'd faced, the sudden emergence of so many painful memories made a few things clear to her.

One of those was Thor.

Clara realized now why she'd resisted Aiden's pleas to get a puppy for so long. Just as her Cadillac CTS-V had come to symbolize the horrors of war, so too had the Afghan bitch come to represent the abject helplessness she'd felt during the battle. Clara had grown up with dogs; they were an essential part of her childhood. And yet when Aiden wanted the same, she'd thought of a hundred excuses that had nothing to do with the real reason. A dog would shed hair all over the house, would chew furniture, would impede on the trappings of her idyllic life in this Southern port town.

But in truth, that image of domestic perfection had never been Clara's reality. It was a facade, all the interior design and landscaping of her home nothing more than a veneer she clung to so she wouldn't have to look within. She'd built an illusion of life that represented the polar opposite of her military existence, then focused on that illusion by way of snuffing out the emotions of grief and rage, the sociopathic disregard for sanctity of all human life outside of her husband and son.

Even after letting Aiden get the puppy, she'd been resentful of the creature without truly knowing why. But all that changed last night, when Thor had growled at her from Aiden's side. Prior to that, the puppy hadn't shown an ounce of aggression toward anything or anyone short of his chew toys and the occasional park squirrel. But he'd sensed the evil in Clara.

Even now he remained uncomfortable with her, still tugging at his leash in a futile attempt to reach Aiden. Her husband and son hadn't sensed anything truly wrong with her, but Thor had. Clara now felt a deep love for this puppy, who exhibited all the same protectiveness over Aiden that Clara had, but devoid of the bottomless anger lurking beneath the surface. Thor would grow into a massive dog, and while Clara had once disdained that fact, now she embraced it. The bigger the better.

"You protect him, Thor. You protect Aiden until the day you die."

The puppy gave up at his attempt to join the frisbee game, lying down with his ears pointed toward her husband and son.

She watched Jeremy and Aiden now, contemplating the question that had nagged at her all morning: how to say goodbye without saying goodbye?

Clara could think of no better way than this. A final picnic at Aiden's favorite park, a sunlit family moment where Mom was sober, smiling, their family united. This was how she wanted Aiden to remember her forever.

Because her family had to be preserved at all cost—even if that cost meant Clara's life.

She had just enough sanity remaining to know that she posed a very real threat to Aiden, and possibly to Jeremy as well. The homicidal turns of her dark fantasies had pushed her to a threshold of risk that she wasn't willing to cross; she wouldn't spend one more night in her house. Clara briefly wondered if the others that Jannesson had treated—Dakota, Rich, Sims, and Thoma—had undergone similar moments of clarity on their final day. Had they too sensed dark and murderous impulses that drove them to take their own lives before they hurt anyone else? Clara couldn't be sure; Dakota was the only one to leave a note, and it was profoundly moving but not homicidal. Now the sense that Clara was headed toward the same fate as those four seemed very real, even while sitting in this sun-dappled park.

Jeremy and Aiden's game of frisbee was winding down, and they started walking toward her. Clara had already packed for a week's stay at the Wentworth Mansion in downtown Charleston's historic district, careful to take everything she needed for fear of Jeremy trying to deliver some forgotten item. It would be like a mini writer's retreat, she told him, combined with a little rest and relaxation. Her sleep had finally leveled out and the dreams were gone, along with the paranoid delusions of a complication with her treatment—or so he thought.

Only she knew the truth.

Clara and Jeremy had driven here in separate cars, her BMW loaded with her luggage and a backpack containing her laptop. She'd be leaving straight from the park—after all, she'd told Jeremy, the hotel was only ten minutes away.

Aiden returned, settling on his knees by Thor, who'd rolled onto his back for a belly rub.

Jeremy said, "Aiden's getting tired, I better get him back for his nap."

"Sure," Clara said, rising from the picnic blanket. "My check-in is at three, so I'm just going to walk around the park for a few more minutes."

She helped them pack up the picnic, seeing that Aiden was rubbing his eyes; he'd fall asleep as soon as he was in the car, and after arriving home, Jeremy would have to carry him to bed.

She said, "Aiden, you be good for Daddy, okay?"

"I will," he promised. "I'll miss you, Mommy."

She knelt and pulled him into a tight hug, feeling his warm body against hers. "I'll miss you too, Aiden. I love you so much. Never forget that."

Clara kissed his pudgy cheek and forced herself to stand before she was overwhelmed with emotion.

Turning to Jeremy, she said, "I plan on leaving my phone off most of the time. Don't worry if you can't get a hold of me."

He gave a supportive nod. "Whatever you need, Clara. Don't forget to call once in a while and let us know how you're doing, okay?"

"Of course." She embraced Jeremy, giving him a long kiss goodbye that caused Aiden to remark, "Ew!"

And then they were off—Jeremy carrying the cooler, the picnic blanket folded and slung over his shoulder as Aiden skipped ahead, leading Thor on his leash.

Clara watched them cross the sunlit grass, disappearing past the trees. She gave them a ten-minute head start, enough to account for the longest possible process of loading the trunk and getting Aiden situated in his car seat. She didn't want to risk a second goodbye in the parking lot, however fleeting.

27

Kyle sat at the bar, trying not to cringe as he sipped his repulsive drink.

The joint was busy on that Friday night, the background noise of the bar's occupants drowning out the house music. He scanned the bottles lining stadium shelves, each backlit in a way that made the liquid contents glow. Casting his glance sideways, he saw a pair of college-aged guys trying to spark conversation with two scantily dressed ladies seated at the far side of the bar.

The women were out for action, he could tell by their earrings and hair. But their body language told him the men were striking out hard.

He shook his head sadly, taking another sip of the putrid contents of his glass.

It always pained him to see his gender's awkward attempts at chatting up women at bars. They were too clumsy, too eager to rush what should be a very simple and streamlined process.

All they had to do was what he did—first, make her laugh. A self-deprecating reference usually did the trick, followed by asking where she was from, then where she grew up. The goal was to keep her talking, and that was best served by appealing to her ego. Then he'd play a game of talking about the others in the bar that night, making up stories about them that engendered more laughs from his quarry. All the while, he'd be looking for an opening to make the first touch—examining her necklace, placing his hand on her shoulder as he laughed at something she said—to break her comfort zone.

The whole process took two hours at the most, unless the woman had a visible tattoo. In that case, he'd speed up the cycle to finish up within the first hour. Either way, his kill shot was always the same.

Hey, I can't risk a DUI. But I have a huge bourbon collection at my apartment. Why don't you come over and let's finish the conversation?

That line had quite literally worked every single time—at least, when he was back home.

But he wasn't home, so he'd have to make a slight alteration to end up at her place or a hotel. For a man of his aptitude, that was but a minor detail.

A woman slid onto the open barstool beside him, raising a finger to flag down the bartender.

"Hey," she said to Kyle.

"Hey there."

She was in a low-cut red blouse over a black skirt, slender legs crossed and ending in tall heels. But Kyle glanced at her hands, which told him everything he needed to know.

He didn't care whether she wore a wedding ring—that meant nothing in these situations. The key that most men didn't realize was that a woman's fingernails told a story. Bright nail polish meant she was looking for compliments and a one-night stand, and Kyle would respond accordingly.

But this woman's nails bore only clear gloss. That meant she was a businesswoman, and asking about work was the easiest way to keep her talking, even if it was mostly in complaints. Business attire plus perfume was a guarantee a woman was in a hurry, but this one had taken the time to change, so she had all night. Still, he could have her in bed, clothes off, in two hours plus commute time to her place or his hotel.

The bartender appeared. "What'll it be, ma'am?"

"Appletini," she said.

The bartender looked to Kyle. "Another club soda and lime?"

"Sure," he said, looking over to see the woman's forehead wrinkling in confusion.

"Club soda? You on the wagon?"

"Yep." He grinned. "Going on twenty-four hours sober."

She laughed, tilting her head demurely. "Seriously, what's your deal?"

"Have a work call later on tonight."

"On a Friday night? What do you do?"

"Nothing that interesting. But my boss is at a work conference and wants to check in when he's done." He grimaced. "Let me ask you something—you ever want to put a pillow over your boss's face, and just...hold it there until he stops moving?"

The woman giggled. "She."

"Oh, you have a *lady* boss. Well that must be better than having a man —or am I wrong?"

"Wrong," she nearly shouted.

Kyle put on a perplexed expression. "Wrong? I beg to differ, friend. But you tell me about your boss first, so I'll know for sure."

The woman launched into a diatribe about her work, and Kyle stopped listening the second he felt the phone in his pocket buzzing with an incoming call.

The display flashed an unsaved number.

"Hang on, sweetheart, I have to take this."

He answered and plugged his opposite ear against the raucous noise inside the bar.

"Hey, girl."

On the other line, Clara said, "Still no lights on. I think it's empty."

"I told you, it's been that way the past two nights."

"Let's meet up and go over the plan one more time, then head in."

"All right. Be there in twenty minutes."

He ended the call and said, "Sorry, sweetheart. Duty calls."

The woman's lips puckered into a deliberate frown. "Well maybe we can meet up later."

"Don't think so." Kyle forked a twenty onto the bar. "It's gonna be a long night. Later."

He turned away from her without waiting for a response, threading through the bar's occupants until he'd reached the open door.

Edging past a bouncer checking IDs, he stepped onto the sidewalk. The street bustled with young and middle-aged people out for the night, crossing through clouds of cigarette smoke that pooled around smokers clustered outside the bars.

Cars drifted down the cobblestone street beside him, and Kyle moved toward his Jeep at a brisk walk. Orange street lights twinkled on both sides of the road, and across the far side he saw a steam ship making its way upstream. The ship was occupied by a riotous group of travelers drinking and singing on the top deck, its glowing lights casting a rippling reflection across the surface of the Savannah River.

28

For the first time since she'd left the military, Clara felt like a soldier again.

She slipped through the dark woods under the illumination of a nearly full moon, moving to the periodic snap of twigs underfoot as she threaded her way through the trees and brambles. A chanting chorus of frogs and insects covered the sound of her movement, and Clara looked left to see the forest opening to the fairway of a golf course. To her right, she could make out the periodic houses of the neighborhood, alternately dark or lit by back porch security lights. She paused, peering through the trees to locate Kyle's figure as he led the way for her.

Kyle was already familiar with the wooded route from his previous two nights in Savannah. On both evenings he'd followed the woods up to Jannesson's two-story brick home just after nightfall, watching from the trees until the early morning hours for any sign of life. There had been none; wherever Jannesson had gone for his so-called family emergency, he hadn't yet returned.

Clara had gone from a student, to a soldier, to an author. Now she was filling another role she'd never expected: a burglar.

When the lawyers, doctors, and police couldn't help, what choice did she have? Her life was a sliding scale of despair increasingly tilted in the wrong direction. Weighed against the homicidal dreams she'd been having about her own family, how could she possibly wait around in Charleston for a total psychotic break?

Even that was nearly a best-case scenario outside the current circumstances. Clara already knew that Jannesson had targeted Dakota along with three members of her platoon. She didn't know how many other platoon members he was already going after, how many from other units he had hurt in his experimentation, and most of all, *why*. That final question was the most disturbing of all. Facing an enemy whose motives were clear and linear was one thing. The Taliban hate Americans; Americans hate the Taliban. Simple.

But Jannesson was an enigma. Was he simply a deranged scientist who derived a sadistic pleasure from what he did? Or was he using his patients as human guinea pigs? Either would explain the mystery treatments, but neither accounted for why Clara's platoon had been selected for destruction. Maybe it wasn't just her platoon, she thought. Maybe there were others, systematically infiltrated by Jannesson through word-of-mouth referrals by the patients he successfully treated.

Clara knew only one thing for sure: whatever Jannesson's angle was, it ended tonight.

She wasn't planning on killing him when he returned, though Kyle had certainly suggested that. To Clara, that wasn't enough—she wanted to solve the mystery that was Marcus Jannesson, but most of all she wanted to expose him for what he was, not just to herself but to the world.

They'd discussed breaking into his clinic, but Clara had quickly ruled that out. Jannesson wasn't going to risk discovery by keeping evidence in a public place manned by well-intentioned staff members. Whatever proof there was of his crimes, he kept it neatly hidden from the world in the one place he could: his home.

And Clara was going to find it.

Kyle abruptly halted his movement, taking a knee as Clara closed the distance to kneel beside him.

He whispered, "That's our Huckleberry," pointing to a house through the trees.

Clara's first glimpse of Jannesson's home didn't reveal much other than brick wall siding and a second-story window.

Feeling her heartbeat speed up, she said, "Okay. Let's go."

But Kyle didn't move. "Your phone's on vibrate?"

"Yeah."

"You feel that phone buzz, don't bother answering. Just run for the exit. I won't call you unless he comes back or I hear something over the police scanner."

"I got it, Kyle. Let's get this over with."

Kyle led the way to the edge of the woods, and Clara began to see the house in detail.

Two stories, roughly four thousand square feet. There were no exterior lights and the windows were dark, giving the house an ominous, lifeless quality. They didn't know the interior layout, but Clara was only concerned with one thing at present: her entry point into the home.

They heard a vehicle approaching and quickly knelt at the edge of the trees.

Clara could make out the headlights traveling down the neighborhood street, fearful that it would be an officer on patrol or, worse yet, Jannesson returning home.

But it was just an Audi sedan, sailing out of earshot in less than a minute.

Kyle dropped his backpack, procuring a collapsible H-shaped stack of connected metal brackets. He began unfolding it, and Clara assisted him until they'd expanded those brackets into a fully assembled, fourteen-foot-long tactical ladder. Kyle hoisted the thirty-pound ladder easily at his side, then looked at Clara. "You ready?"

"Yeah." Clara nodded, watching the house.

Kyle's last words to her were, "Get in and get out. No need to push our luck tonight."

They emerged from the woods, crossing a narrow strip of lawn toward the back corner of the house. Kyle propped the ladder against a rooftop eave, holding it steady for Clara as she clambered up it. Setting foot atop the roof's sloping shingles, she moved toward a second-floor window and attempted to pull it open. Finding it locked, Clara dropped her backpack to retrieve a crowbar.

The theory was that the second-floor windows were unlikely to have any alarms or glass break sensors. However, if Clara happened to trip a security system, she'd be back in the woods and far from the house long before the police arrived.

She slipped on her empty backpack, then used the crowbar to pry the window upward. The sliding plastic frame groaned as the latch was forced open. There was a sharp *snap* as the bottom of the window sprang free of the frame, and Clara slid it all the way open. She leaned inside, listening for a security system's warning chime. After hearing nothing, she walked to the edge of the roof, gave Kyle a thumbs up, and then hucked her crowbar into the yard for him to recover.

Then she darted inside the window, alighting on the carpet and listening for any sounds of movement. The ringing in her ears meant that required conscious effort, and she prepared to bolt at the sound of footsteps coming to investigate the noise.

But the house was quiet, illuminated only by the ambient moonlight streaming through the window and the tiny green light from an overhead smoke detector.

Clara withdrew her penlight and turned it on, casting a dim red glow as she swept it across her surroundings. She was in a guest room, the bed fully made. Her search of the room was hasty—she doubted anything useful would be here, and quickly found she was right. She turned her attention to the door, slipping into a hall to search for the master bedroom.

It was located at the top of the stairs, and Clara glimpsed Jannesson's room in flashes of red light. The comforter was askew, the pillow rumpled. Unable to contain her paranoia, Clara momentarily removed a glove and set it atop the exposed sheet—to her relief, it wasn't warmed by body heat.

She checked the nightstand drawers for a tablet, finding none. Then she went to the master closet, knowing that if he had a safe, that's where it would probably be, though she was equipped to do little but photograph it.

There was no safe, though she saw dozens of empty hangers interspersed with whatever clothes remained. Wherever Jannesson had gone, he'd packed for the long haul. She quickly checked the drawers, curious about his personal effects but forcing herself to move quickly. Clara needed one thing and one thing only: evidence. Anything that couldn't hold data was of no interest to her, and she moved swiftly through the remaining rooms and closets on the second floor, using her penlight sparingly to check for safes, computers, or filing cabinets.

Finding none, she made for the stairs.

They extended down to the first floor, and up to a bonus room. Thinking of her own office, the inner sanctum where she retreated to escape the outside world, she decided to check the upstairs first.

Clara set foot on a hardwood stair, hearing it creak under her weight. She paused, waiting for a response as she recited her route back to the open window of the guest room—right at the stair landing, then the second door on the left. Hearing nothing, and confident she'd be able to exit in a hurry if she had to, she proceeded upstairs to the bonus room.

She opened the lone door to reveal a long rectangular space, its ceiling corners sloped with the rooftop eaves. Her first glimpse revealed a desk, and as she slipped inside the room, her penlight illuminated a computer monitor atop it, but its video plug was lying there useless. He'd taken his laptop with him, and the desk was cluttered with photo frames and folders, a fountain pen in its stand beside a bottle of ink at the corner.

Clara's attention was momentarily drawn to a row of bookshelves on the wall beside her. She felt a wave of nausea as she recognized a trio of familiar titles—the thriller novels Clara herself had written. She wasn't sure why the sight of her own work on Jannesson's shelf made her so apprehensive, but she quickly forgot about it as her penlight's beam turned to the back wall.

Lined up neatly behind the desk were three filing cabinets. Her momentary elation at the sight turned to unease—these three cabinets surely held far too much paperwork for her to simply pack up and exit. She'd have to be more selective in her search, and she pulled the drawers open in sequence, flipping through files that glowed red beneath her penlight.

They were each labeled by patient name, with section breaks marked by year. Seeing the tabbed labels beginning with 2010, she abandoned the first filing cabinet and moved to the second, pulling open the bottom drawer to see that it ended in 2017.

Clara pushed the drawer shut and moved to the top of the third filing cabinet. Pulling open the metal drawer, she saw the 2019 tab and began flipping through the files. She expected to find Dakota's file first—she had, after all, been the first suicide—but instead the first familiar name she saw was Rich Johns.

Clara unslung her backpack and seized the file. Inside was a neatly typed medical report, and she flipped to the last sheet to find a handwritten note.

Patient JOHNS described exact circumstances of Pantalay as source of trauma. When asked if he dropped the bomb, replied, "No, that was Lieutenant Swanner." Further inquiry confirmed that he knew firsthand because "Sims heard the whole thing." Clarified first name Jason, position = radio operator. Resistant to providing further information.

> *Dosage: 2.5 mL cetraphaline, diluted for minimum effects. 4 mL paracetamol*
> *Death by suicide: 15 days from treatment. Hanging.*

Her eyes lingered on the word "paracetamol." What was that?

Clara stashed the file in her backpack, returning to the drawer and flipping through the remaining 2020 files. Skimming the labels, she found Jason Sims's file. She yanked it free, then opened it to see that the first page was a printout of Sims's LinkedIn profile. The dates of his military service were circled by pen. The next page was an expired real estate listing for his residence in Franklin, Tennessee. Clara flipped past a typed medical report, finding the handwritten note on the final page.

Patient SIMS described the source of trauma as carrying a dead pregnant woman with teammate ALAN SMITH. Resistant to providing further information regarding Pantalay.

> *Dosage: 2.5 mL cetraphaline, diluted for minimum effects. 6 mL paracetamol.*
> *Death by suicide: 10 days from treatment. Self-inflicted gunshot wound.*

She closed the file and slid it into her backpack, returning to sweep the 2021 files until she found Alan Smith's. This packet began with his salesman profile from a car dealership in Virginia Beach. She flipped past a member roster for VFW Post 392, finding the handwritten notes at the last page in the file.

Patient SMITH resistant to providing information regarding source of trauma. Paracetamol testing unfeasible due to fellow vets receiving treatment.
  Dosage: 8 mL cetraphaline, calibrated by patient body weight

The next file with a name she recognized was Joshua Thoma's, and Clara briefly flipped to the last page to find the same scrawled note.

Patient THOMA self-refers, citing effectiveness of treatment for ALAN SMITH. Treasure trove of information. Freely admits Pantalay involvement, confirms SWANNER dropped bomb. Provides names BROWN, RIVERA, and SOLER in relation to source of trauma.
  Dosage: 2.5 mL cetraphaline, diluted for minimum effects. 8 mL paracetamol.
  Death by suicide: 7 days from treatment. Cut arteries in bathtub.

She closed the file and slipped it into her backpack, then continued searching the 2021 files. There she found labels bearing the names of the three platoon members that Thoma had referenced: Kenneth Brown, Steven Rivera, and Kyle Soler. Clara took these files as well, pausing only to peruse Kyle's. It had his business name, work phone number, and address down to the apartment number. Clara's skin crawled with the realization that Jannesson was going to work his way through the platoon's ranks, systematically luring them for an injection with paracetamol, whatever that was.

Next she found her own file, which began with printouts from her author website and every book interview ever published online. She flipped to the last page.

Patient SWANNER self-refers. Hallelujah.
  Dosage: 2.5 mL cetraphaline, diluted for minimum effects. 10 ML paracetamol
  Death by suicide:

·   ·   ·

The space after that was blank, waiting to be filled in. Jannesson was probably checking her local obituaries every day, as he clearly had for the others.

She slid her file into the backpack. Only one was missing, and it was the one Clara wanted most. She couldn't understand why Dakota's information hadn't been filed under the year of her death, and she pulled open the bottom drawer of the final cabinet to see if it was in there for some reason.

And indeed, it was—and Clara saw at once why Dakota's file wasn't with the others.

It was massive, spanning several files and going back the farthest. Flipping through, Clara saw that what appeared to be neat stacks of papers were actually a vast number of photocopies detailing Dakota's life—the copies dated back to pages of her high school yearbook, then hopscotched through contributions to her college newspaper, all the way up to her articles for *The New York Times*. These ended with a piece about Afghanistan, written upon Dakota's arrival to Kabul.

Clara knew why this was the last article—from Kabul, Dakota had traveled to meet Clara's platoon. And the lengthy account of her experiences as an embedded reporter had never seen the light of day. After Pantalay, Dakota had deleted months of work, resigned her position at *The New York Times*, and gone to work for a small local paper.

The final pages of the file were photocopies of her articles for the newspaper, and Clara reached the end to find the last thing Dakota had ever written.

Her stepfather had released the suicide note to the press following her death. It had gained some national publicity amid cries for better PTSD treatment, then quickly been forgotten by everyone except those who knew Dakota in life.

Clara's eyes darted across the handwritten script, recognizing the words she'd read a hundred times.

To those I will leave behind:
　　You will probably think this is because of the events in Pantalay Village.

In truth, my disease was not caused by combat. It began with early childhood sexual abuse, and continued to grow long after the traumatic events of my youth had ended.

My entire life has been spent in the shadow of a great emptiness, a looming specter of solitude from others, and flirtation with darkness and suicide. Even with a loving family, I was truly alone.

I hoped that I could one day step out from that shadow, to embrace life rather than death. But what happened at Pantalay Village has proven to me that will never be the case. If that bomb had never fallen on the mosque, I would have died that day. I recognize that, although it now seems a more merciful fate than the alternative. We traded our lives for theirs, and I can't bear involvement in the pain of children after having experienced it firsthand.

Pills have long been the only thing that brought me peace—and now, they will bring me peace forever.

To all those who will suffer as a result of my actions, know that I am truly sorry. But any of you who have not existed in this dark place cannot possibly comprehend what I have to do now. Therefore, I cannot ask for your understanding—only your forgiveness.

Please forgive me, and know that I am in a better place.

Dakota

She felt a surge of burning shame, knowing the truth about Dakota's suicide—if Clara hadn't forced her friend into the ruins of the mosque, hadn't personally ensured that she saw the bodies of children who died in the bomb strike, then she might still be alive today.

Clara forced herself to focus on the task at hand, flipping the suicide note to find it was the last page in the file—no treatment notes, no excerpts from a patient file.

That didn't make any sense; Jannesson had done more homework on Dakota than anyone else.

She wanted to keep searching the house, to exonerate Dakota from her own death. Casting her light to the far corners of the office, she saw a stockpile of medication bottles arranged neatly on shelves, with wall-mounted cabinets over tables piled with medical supplies. She momentarily considered searching that part of the office as well, perhaps finding a bottle of

Jannesson's paracetamol to steal. But every passing minute brought a greater risk of a cop showing up, and Clara already had the name of his once-mystery drug.

She reluctantly stuffed Dakota's file into her backpack alongside the others. Zipping it up, she turned to leave.

But Clara came up short, seeing for the first time the framed photographs on the desk. In one of them, Clara thought she saw her friend —then she realized the woman wasn't Dakota, but a younger image of her mother, the face bearing the same high cheekbones and sculpted eyebrows. Her hand rested on the shoulder of her daughter, then a young girl of five or six with a frilly, floral-patterned dress.

But the man standing with his hand on Dakota's opposite shoulder wasn't Dakota's stepfather.

It was Jannesson.

Clara felt the rippling tingle of gooseflesh across her arms. A line from Dakota's suicide note flashed across her mind—*early childhood sexual abuse* —and Clara's maternal instinct flared to a white-hot coal of rage.

She moved for the office door before halting abruptly, confused. A shadowy figure stood in the doorway, and at first, she thought it must be Kyle.

Clara raised the light, seeing that the figure was pointing a single hand toward her. The object in his grasp wasn't a pistol, but he was holding it like a gun, and Clara darted sideways as the taser fired.

Two probes speared into her chest and stomach, immobilizing her body into a quaking jackhammer of electrical current. She fell onto her side, unable to move or even think as Jannesson straddled her. His face appeared calm in the penlight's glow, one hand still firing the taser and the other fisted with brass knuckles that gleamed as he drove a hard punch into her face.

29

When Clara awoke, her head was throbbing painfully. She fought through the mental fog, but the very act of breathing through her shattered nose brought dizzying waves of pain.

Clara peeled her lips apart, breaking the bond of dried blood. Her swollen eyelids parted, and she squinted against a blinding glare that made her wince. She was still in Jannesson's home office, the lights now on. Why hadn't Kyle come for her yet? Then she saw that the windows were taped over by sheets of black plastic, sealing the light inside the room. Kyle would have no idea that the lights were on upstairs, no indication that anything was wrong until he tried to call and didn't see her emerge from the house.

Looking down, she saw her shirt was marked by an oblong diamond bloodstain, the congealed result of her broken nose draining onto her breasts and stomach while she sat upright. She was sitting in a rolling office chair just like the one she had at her own desk at home. Clara's forearms were bound to the arms of the chair with wide Velcro strips, her ankles pinned together and secured beneath her seat.

Futilely pulling against the straps, Clara realized that she was trapped. The irony wasn't lost on her—for the past three years, her professional life had consisted of sitting in a chair like this to write. Now, she was restrained against it with no way out.

A hand touched her shoulder, and Clara jumped in fear.

It was Jannesson, now circling to her front. He was dressed in black, his gray goatee and auburn mustache contorted into a frown as he appraised her behind the thin eyeglasses.

"I'm sorry it had to come to this, Clara. But you did it to yourself."

She saw that his receding hairline was now dotted with sweat, probably from the effort of fighting her and then moving her into the chair. He took a seat on the desktop, setting down a small bag beside him.

Clara didn't know how much time had elapsed since she'd been knocked unconscious. But she knew exactly what to do, even amid the terror of her current predicament—keep Jannesson talking, because Kyle would come for her. However long Clara had to suffer under Jannesson didn't matter—it was nothing more than the amount of time between Kyle realizing that she'd been captured and how long it took him to find her.

And then, he would turn Jannesson's death into a party. Kyle had done savage things to enemy combatants, and his bloodlust would come through in full force. Clara wouldn't stop him.

She said, "Dakota once told me she had an estranged father."

"And Rich Johns told me that you dropped the bomb in Pantalay. So now we understand each other."

Clara shook her head. "I know what you did to Rich, Sims, and Thoma. But Dakota would have recognized you—how did you kill her?"

"I didn't kill Dakota," he said. "You did. You killed her when you blew up that mosque, and now I will never see my daughter again. That's why you had to pay the ultimate price. Not your life, because anyone can take a life. No, Clara, I wanted you to bear the full pain that I've seen in hundreds of vets, I wanted you to take the same road my daughter had to travel because of you. Once you'd been to her dark place, I wouldn't have to take your life—you'd do that for me."

"Sorry to disappoint you," she said.

"To the contrary, I was impressed. Quite impressed, in fact. I gave you a higher dose than any of your compatriots, and frankly I was quite surprised when you kept every appointment for our follow-up calls. You must have an incredible tolerance for psychological pain."

Clara nodded distantly, trying to appear resigned to her fate. But she knew what was going to happen any minute now. Kyle was going to come through the door behind her, gun in hand, and then the tables would turn on Jannesson for the last time.

She said, "I already saw the files. I know you injected us with—"

He cut her off. "Paracetamol?"

"Yes."

"Congratulations, Clara, you've uncovered the chemical name for Tylenol. Did you actually think I'd put anything into writing, on the off chance that it was discovered? There is no proof of what I've done to you, no test for what I've injected you with. And no cure. The medical community is fifty years from knowing what I know."

"So that's it? You're out to get veterans to kill themselves?"

He shot back, "I've dedicated my entire *life* to helping veterans. That is my purpose, my passion. That is why I *exist*. But you, your platoon? You people can all burn in hell. And you will, for what you did to my daughter."

"Your daughter was doing what she loved before that battle. Your daughter chose to be there. The only one who hurt your daughter was you."

"I never hurt Dakota."

"Really?" Clara nearly shouted, feeling suddenly enraged. "How about that 'early childhood sexual abuse,' Dad? Or are you going to try and tell me that was someone else?"

Jannesson's face contorted into a mask of rage, his nostrils flaring with such intensity that Clara was certain he'd attack her. She didn't care—she was so pissed off that she felt no regard for her own suffering, only for Dakota's.

But as his body tensed into some breaking point of hatred, Jannesson froze.

He relaxed then, his muscles softening until he was exactly as composed as the first time she'd met him at the clinic.

Then he spoke calmly. "My daughter was a very sick woman, Clara. Her mind was twisted from the moment she was born, and since childhood she envisioned past events that never occurred. She thought I did unthinkable things to her, but it wasn't true. How could I hurt my own daughter?"

"I don't know," Clara said, "you don't seem to have much of a problem harming the veterans you treat."

"With the exception of a select few patients, everything I've done has

188

been in the interests of experimentation. And as with any experimentation, there can be consequences."

"Except your consequences cost people their lives."

He rolled his eyes at her. "Oh, wake up, Clara. Six thousand veterans kill themselves every year, but that's not the key statistic. The vast majority of them are *over the age of fifty*. That means we are decades away from seeing the true human cost for a generation of Iraq and Afghanistan veterans, and I am the only thing that stands in the way of that. Do my methods have human consequences? Yes. But they are far more humane than the alternative—thousands of veterans killing themselves annually while ineffective treatment protocols slog through the FDA bureaucracy. In killing a dozen to find a solution, I can save *tens of thousands*."

Clara knew she should keep him talking, but she found herself at a loss for words. Instead she found her gaze drifting toward the door, toward the blacked-out windows, wondering when Kyle would burst through to save her.

Jannesson followed her gaze. "You can stop looking toward the door. Kyle is already dead."

She felt her heart thudding painfully. "What?"

"Oh, come on, Clara. Did you really think I didn't know he was looking out for you?"

Clara's mind was racing, wanting to call his bluff. She wanted to call him a liar, to tell him that Kyle was hundreds of miles away. But most of all, she didn't want to believe that Kyle wasn't coming to save her.

"You couldn't defeat Kyle."

"Hand-to-hand? Perhaps not. But it's not hard to take a man by surprise when you're waiting inside the window when he slithers into your home. He got the same justice you did—except I didn't need, or want, him alive. So I bashed his head in until there was nothing left."

"No," Clara said, disbelieving. "You didn't."

"Want me to prove it to you?"

"You can't," she said, "because Kyle is still alive."

"Well I'm not going to carry him all the way up the stairs, am I? But just to ease your mind, I brought you this."

Now he reached into the small bag on his desk, pulling out the contents to show Clara.

At first she thought he unfolded a cloth, some kind of bloody handkerchief. Then she thought it was an American flag, the stars and stripes visible in living color.

And finally, Clara realized that it was a strip of human skin, the tattoo from Kyle's forearm flayed off for Jannesson to present to her. He did that now, setting the patch of skin and blood onto her lap, the American flag now faded to a sickly gray. Clara tensed in revulsion, feeling the tears welling in her eyes until they spilled over, melting warm trails through the dried blood on her shirt.

Jannesson said, "Now if you'll excuse me, I must dispose of the body."

Clara was sobbing, managing to choke out a single question.

"What are you...going to do with him?"

"There's a swamp not far from here, just off the side of the golf course. I'll puncture your friend's lungs with an ice pick so his body sinks, and then dump him in the swamp. Whatever the gators don't finish off will be eaten by crabs."

She couldn't speak now, crying with her eyes fixed on Kyle's flesh in her lap.

Jannesson walked to the far side of the office. "You really should have killed yourself, Clara. Because now you can't, and by the time you've gotten what you deserve, you'll be begging me to do it for you."

He returned to her side then. "Probably no one would hear you call out, but to be safe, I'll leave you with something to pass the time. How about some more, shall we say, 'paracetamol?'"

Clara looked up to see him holding a syringe, the cylinder filled with a clear fluid that formed a single drop at the tip of the needle.

She began hyperventilating.

"What is that? *What is that?*"

"Wouldn't you like to know, Clara. But it's better that I show you."

The needle pierced the skin on her shoulder, and Clara began to scream.

30

Jannesson pulled the needle from her arm, then took a step back.

"That ought to do it."

Clara pinched her eyes shut, feeling her body trembling in anticipation of whatever horrors were about to commence. She pulled against the restraints, but her limbs were hopelessly restrained to the chair.

"Should be any second now," Jannesson said. Then he switched to a Southern accent and said, "I'd love to watch the show, but I have to get rid of your friend before sunrise."

"My...friend?"

She opened her eyes to see Jannesson reaching for the strip of Kyle's skin in her lap. But his forearm now bore a rectangular wound, the flesh within its corners exposed and bloody. The rest of the arm was tattooed, though, and Clara realized that Jannesson was no longer Jannesson.

He was Kyle.

She looked up to see his face, and gasped in shock.

One side of Kyle's head was bashed in, a gaping void of skull fragments and brain matter. His eye socket was a bloody pit, the eyeball dangling on his cheek by the optic nerve. The other eye looked down to the piece of skin in his hands, turning it around to see the flag.

"That hurt," he said with a giggle. "The man is strong, I'll give him that."

His intact eye examined Clara. "He got your nose, huh?"

"Yeah." She nodded. "Yeah, Kyle, he got my nose."

"Well, you'll still be a beautiful girl. It'll heal fine, once you make it out. You'll just look a little bit different, that's all."

Clara's nostrils were flaring in barely suppressed panic.

"How do I...how do I make it out?"

He shook his head slightly, the loose eyeball twisting on the nerve.

"Ain't gonna be easy." Kyle set his patch of skin on the desk, then reached up to the side of his head to probe the hole in his skull with his fingertips. "He got me good, didn't he?"

"I thought you were dead."

"I am," he said simply, "off to see our boys in the dark place. Rich and Sims and Thoma. They're all waiting for me, and they're waiting for you. Try to avoid joining us, to the extent that you can."

"How do I get out, Kyle? What do I do now?"

"I'll tell you what you *don't* do. You don't engage that man in hand-to-hand combat. He's got that old man strength, you know?"

"Yeah." She nodded. "I know."

Kyle walked to the far side of the office, scanning the shelves and opening cabinets.

"Let's see here. He's got all kinds of pills and bottles, lots of needles. I'm sure he plans on taking you for a real ride. But you don't tell him nothin'. You're the only one who's gotten this stuff and followed up with him, far as we know. Whatever you find out about how this evil works, keep it to yourself. He's going to try and turn you into an experiment, so don't let him."

His footsteps circled behind her, then stopped at the door.

"He's got the door locked, girl. Might need to bail out a window."

He walked back to her front, looking at her restrained forearms with one good eye and then squatting to see how her ankles were bound to the chair. Clara gasped at the sight of the hole in his skull—the contents were now a sloshing mess of fluid, the visible brain a fleshy mass of pink.

Kyle stood. "Got you bound up pretty good, girl. You won't be squirming your way out of those Velcro straps, I'll tell you that."

"How do I get out of this, what do I do?"

Kyle looked to the ceiling, as if he heard something. "Aw, he's putting me in the swamp."

"Right...now?"

"Yeah, girl, right now. Water's warm, at least. I guess he'll be back soon."

"Please don't leave me, Kyle. Please don't leave."

"Starting to get real cold. Don't have much longer. Off to see Rich and...and Sims..."

His body was shimmering now, translucent as he appeared whole again, his head intact, both eyes watching her. He looked to his arm, saw that the American flag tattoo was back.

"I suppose this is it. You get him, Clara. Get him for all of us. Find a way. Find a way."

Then Clara was in freefall, descending through a smoky void of darkness that howled around her. A blinding flash of light, and then she was a passenger in her own body, watching herself digging through rubble, searching for bodies. But she could tell this was a dream—this wreckage was not the dusty mud bricks of Pantalay, but powdery chunks of drywall and scraps of wooden beams.

Pushing aside a pile of wreckage, she caught her first glimpse of something that had been living. It wasn't skin, it was hair—she swept the white powder aside, exposing a patch of brindle fur.

"Oh, God..."

Clara rose and grasped the chunk of drywall, flinging it aside with uncanny strength to expose what lay beneath.

Aiden's body was a lifeless and broken rag doll, his eyes open and white beside the remains of his puppy.

Clara shrieked and scooped her son into her arms, standing to sob uncontrollably.

"Aiden, Aiden, I love you, baby, I love you so much..."

A voice shouted behind her. "We found Jeremy. What's left of him, anyway."

She spun to look, Aiden's limbs swinging limply as she turned.

Her husband's body lay ten feet distant, his face covered in white dust, one arm draped across a shattered wooden beam.

Standing over him was the homeless man she'd seen in Savannah, his eyes milky and opaque as he showed her the cardboard sign in his hands.

VETERAN. BLIND. HOMELESS. GOD BLESS.

The view all around wasn't a ramshackle Afghan village, it was a landscape of green lawns and swimming pools, the grand Charleston houses of her neighbors standing all around.

The wreckage was no mosque; it was her home.

Clara staggered over to Jeremy's body, falling to her knees to set Aiden down beside him. She leaned over to clumsily embrace their cold bodies, panting incoherently between her sobs.

"We'll be together...the three of us...always together..."

The blind man said, "I tried to tell you, Clara. Now you're a homeless veteran. All he's got left to take is your sight."

Clara looked up, her vision blurred by tears. The man's eyes were still white, but the body and face were now Jannesson's. The sign was gone; he took a sip from a coffee mug, smiling down at her.

31

"How are you feeling?" Jannesson asked.

Clara looked up from the wreckage of her home, seeing that she was now back in Jannesson's office, strapped to the chair. Or was this a continuation of the dream?

She tried to speak, but couldn't—her mouth was gagged by a piece of cloth tied around her head. Jannesson pulled it out of her mouth, letting it fall around her neck before taking another sip from the coffee mug. Was it morning already? She couldn't tell; the windows were still taped in black plastic, the only light in the room artificial.

Then she let her head hang, seeing the floor of Jannesson's office littered with the rubble of her destroyed home. She blinked it away, saw the actual floor once again, then blinked again to see Aiden's body lying beside Jeremy at her feet.

Closing her eyes, Clara forced herself to breathe. She was seeing now through a great fog of fear and adrenaline, unable to move even if she'd been free to do so. She told herself this was all a dream, but she couldn't tell anymore—had she ever broken into Jannesson's house, or was she going to burst awake at home, in bed?

She managed, "What did you inject me with?"

Jannesson chuckled. "The only thing you should be concerned about is whether it's reversible. Unfortunately for you, it isn't. Every amount you receive further alters your brain chemistry."

Clara swung her head sideways, seeing the far side of Jannesson's office with its medical supplies. The blind man was standing there in the corner, holding his cardboard sign. She looked away.

Jannesson leaned against his desk and continued, "You people never cease to amaze me. After everything you've done overseas, you're more comfortable in combat than your own home. You can't relate to anyone but each other, and yet you all exist in pockets of isolation to kill yourselves off in solitude. No wonder there are twenty-two veteran suicides every day. It's up to me to stop it."

Clara said, "You lost your...license."

"But my work was far enough along that I don't need a license anymore. I've already found the answer that no one else has. The VA isn't helping anyone, and the best thing the medical community can come up with is to give every vet with PTSD a pharmaceutical lobotomy in an attempt to mask the symptoms. Pills for anxiety, pills for depression, pills for insomnia, pills for pain. More pills to counter the side effects of the first, until vets are strung out on six to twelve prescriptions just to function. And as much as big pharma appreciates having its pockets lined by the government, that's not going to work."

"Then what is the answer?"

"For you? There is none. When I'm through with you, you'll be—"

"Begging for my death," she replied, her mouth dry and craving water. "I know. But what is...the cure?"

"Still interested in saving your fellow vets? I hate to disappoint you, Clara, but you don't have the medical background to understand even if I told you. And after reading the glorifications of violence that you call your novels, I can tell you for a fact that you don't have the intelligence, either."

Clara's thoughts were adrift, processing Jannesson's words in snippets of clarity like glimpses of trees through a thick and endless mist.

"Tell me," she said. "I'm already dead. I know that. What is the...what is the cure?"

"To understand the cure, you have to understand the *problem*. More specifically, where that problem lies. It is within, and that is why modern medicine is not equipped to handle it."

"What do you mean...'within?'"

"You saw, Clara. I didn't give you much cetraphaline, just a taste, but you saw beyond the veil."

"What veil?"

"The illusion of physical reality."

Clara was uncertain whether she was hearing him speak or hallucinating his voice, increasingly unable to discern whether he was in the room or if she was dreaming, alone.

"I don't understand."

"The ether of the cosmos, Clara. You saw it, you passed through it, even if but for a moment."

"You said it was...subconscious."

Jannesson was speaking quickly now. "I credit the subconscious because I cannot give the true solution to a society blinded by false sight. We are all of us projections of the same being, and once you see that, what can possibly trouble you about the past? There is no past, or future. There is only *now*, everything in an existence of total and complete perfection. That is the truth of our universe, and it is a truth that every avatar from Jesus to Buddha has attempted to impart.

"That is why none of this matters. I am making your earthly form suffer for what you did to my daughter's earthly form, but in the end, we all return to the same place of peace and light. I will elevate the consciousness of humanity through my work with veterans, because they are the most desperate to *see the truth*. Fear is the lowest state of vibration a being is capable of emitting—it is total darkness, and those who rise above it can ascend toward the light of absolute reality.

"I will lead the tortured masses out of darkness. Veterans are but the first step toward the loving beauty that I will reveal to the world. That is my work, my purpose. And if I cannot accomplish it in this lifetime, I will do so in the next. I will continue my work across time, until the universe knows only harmony, and peace."

He went silent. Clara was afraid to open her eyes, afraid of what she'd see if she did.

She asked, "Is this...real? Am I dreaming?" She wasn't sure whether she'd spoken the questions or not, and Jannesson gave no indication one way or the other.

"In another lifetime you will join me. Your intentions are pure, but you have not ascended to a plane sufficient for assuaging the anguish of mankind. That is why we were brought together in this life, Clara, you and I. I am elevating your consciousness so that in future lives you may return to become a harbinger of change. Humanity is nearing the point for its next great leap of enlightenment. And you will help me bring it."

"What...what happens then?"

"Then the process begins anew. A new universe reborn into darkness, so that it may learn the meaning of light over eons of time. Always evolving toward perfection, Clara, just as you and I are. All things in total harmony."

Clara looked back to the corner of the room—the blind man was gone, and in his place was a fold-out bed. She wondered if she was hallucinating the bed, but after blinking repeatedly it remained in place, and Clara was certain it hadn't been there before.

She closed her eyes and spoke groggily. "The bed...what are you going to do to me?"

Jannesson's tone became clinical. "That's for your LP," he explained. "Your lumbar puncture."

"What?"

"A spinal tap, Clara."

Clara swallowed. "Are you going to kill me?"

"Before I get my samples?" he asked. "Of course not. The cell count in cerebrospinal fluid increases dramatically after death. Postmortem samples are useless for analysis, and analysis is exactly what I need from you. But don't worry, Clara. When the time comes, I promise you won't feel a thing."

For some reason Clara couldn't muster a response to the prospect of a needle entering her spine, or of him killing her afterward.

Instead she asked, "Why did you rape Dakota? Why did you rape...your daughter?"

Silence then, darkness.

And when he spoke again, his voice was closer, lower.

"I told you, Clara: I didn't."

Then a stabbing pain in her shoulder—he was injecting her, the pain lucid and real, and just as Clara was certain that she wasn't dreaming, she lapsed into the void once more.

32

Clara somersaulted through an infinite expanse of blackness, hearing a thin whistling sound that grew louder until it was a shrill, howling wail that made her ears hurt.

Then came the blast, a deep reverberation of light and sound that shook the ground and cast its booming echo across the landscape.

The reverberation faded to silence, a deathly stillness that brought with it a pale vision like fog—only this wasn't fog, Clara knew, it was a tawny cloud that reeked of dust and sand and the sickly, molten plastic scent of high explosives. A wave of heat washed over her and faded along with the cloud, and as the sand lifted she saw the destruction of the mosque at Pantalay.

Then the cloud of sand lifted further above the rubble, revealing a single figure standing atop the carnage, facing away.

The figure turned, and Clara saw that it was her.

She was naked other than the sheer babydoll and lace panties that Jeremy had bought her, hair down around her shoulders. Her face was adorned in full makeup, bright red lips parting in a dazzling smile.

Thor was at her feet, eagerly tugging strips of flesh from a human arm that extended from the rubble, its hand lifelessly clutching a mud brick.

Then the dead began to rise, the enemy fighters clambering out of the wreckage to stand, then falling prostrate before her. The elderly and the children followed, emerging from the rubble to see Clara before falling to their knees in worship. Clara saw the pregnant teenager in her burka rise from the destruction, assuming the same position of reverence as the masses now prostrated before her.

They began to chant in unison, the same words spoken over and over as if in prayer. The chant was in Pashto, but Clara understood the words.

Queen of Death. Queen of Death.

And then Clara felt a deep, horrifying chill, a fear that shook her to the depths of her soul.

"You don't have to look, you know."

The view drifted sideways, and she saw Dakota standing there, her hair covered by a checkered cloth that wrapped around the sides of her face. She appeared exactly as she had in Pantalay before the bomb fell, her DSLR camera in her hands.

Dakota gave an embarrassed smile. "Well, I guess you *do* have to look. But you don't have to *see*. I'll show you."

Raising her camera toward the rubble of the mosque, she snapped a picture of the Queen of Death standing atop the destruction. Checking the camera display, she tilted it into view and said, "Here."

The camera's digital screen showed Jannesson's desk, the view from Clara's chair.

"It's not really there. And you can feel. Try."

Clara flexed her right hand, and saw the lingerie-clad specter of herself do the same. But Clara felt the armrest beneath her hand, even as she looked down to see the baked mud street below. She couldn't see her own body. Her view was of Pantalay and the horrific worship at the building remains, but she could move her muscles and feel the resistance of the chair supporting her.

"That's enough," Dakota said sharply. "You need to remain still, very still, until he's gone. He doesn't know."

Clara thought she understood—was Jannesson still in the office with her? She had no way to tell.

Dakota continued, "You heard what he said, Clara. You saw the bed in the room. He's going to run, and he can't take you with him—he can only take your samples. That's why you can't move in front of him, not while you're under. Because he can't move you to the bed without untying you from the chair first."

The Queen of Death began a slow, alluring stripper's dance, lowering the straps of her babydoll off one shoulder, then the other. It fell to her feet, exposing her body now clad only in lace panties. Beneath her, Thor continued to chew the human arm amid the chant: *Queen of Death, Queen of Death.*

When Dakota spoke again her tone was conversational, as if none of this were occurring before them. "And he wears those glasses for a reason —he's blind without them. Don't forget that, Clara."

Clara wanted to speak, but she couldn't; she wasn't there, merely a point of perspective observing the scene around her, watching Dakota.

She willed herself to speak, but had no voice. And so she thought instead, focusing her mind on a single question.

What should I do?

Dakota looked to her with hazel eyes, and smiled.

"Tolerance."

Clara didn't understand, and kept thinking the question over and over in her mind with increasing panic, trying to reach this apparition of her friend. *What should I do? What should I do?*

Dakota was grinning broadly now, her sculpted eyebrows raised in delight. "Tolerance, *tolerance*, Clara! Can't you see? Don't you get it—"

Her last word hitched abruptly, her mouth yawning into a wide, gaping maw as Dakota's face withered to a skull caked with black flesh, her eyes becoming hollow pits.

Then she was dead, a shriveled corpse in a rotting dress, skeletonized hands folded atop the family Bible that Dakota's mother had buried her with. Clara saw all this because she was in the casket, looking down at her decaying friend before ascending backward through the soil until she was soaring high over the nighttime cemetery.

33

Jannesson flew into the office at a near-run, startling Clara as she awoke from her dream.

At least she thought she was waking, but this time, there was no groggy, half-conscious fight to full consciousness. She was fairly alert almost immediately, surprised by the speed of her recovery. Had he injected her with less, or was her body building up a...

The thought faded, giving way to a memory of Dakota in her dream. *Tolerance.*

Was such a thing possible? Could her body be building up a tolerance toward the treatment?

She couldn't consider the question for long. Jannesson was racing past the fold-out bed toward the medical area of his office, flinging open a cabinet. His back was to her, but she heard him knocking over bottles in a rush to prepare something. If her mouth weren't gagged, she would have asked what he was doing, but she got her answer a second later when he spun around, using one hand to grab a stainless-steel side table and roll it toward her chair.

His other hand held a syringe.

Clara's eyes darted from the table to the needle, and she shook her head quickly, pleading with him to not give her another shot.

Jannesson arranged the table next to her, locking the wheels in place.

The syringe remained in his hand, needle pointing toward Clara's arm as his thumb remained on the plunger, ready to stab her.

She was still shaking her head, but Jannesson wasn't looking at her. His eyes were unfocused, head facing the far wall of the office. Clara noted with a repugnant sense of dread that the syringe wasn't filled with the clear liquid he'd injected her with previously—instead, it was a murky brown.

Clara used to think that nothing could be worse than whatever medicine he'd concocted to send her into a vortex of terror with each treatment. But now she realized there was one thing worse: a needle stick with something new, something unknown.

He thrust the syringe in her face, the needle trembling in his shaking grasp.

"You make one noise," he whispered, "*one sound*, and it's over. You understand me?"

Clara nodded, breathing quickly through her nostrils, thinking that she didn't understand at all—even if she'd wanted to scream, her mouth was gagged.

And then, she heard it.

It was a deep, deliberate pounding noise coming from downstairs, the sound of someone hammering on a door.

Then she heard a man's voice, distant and muffled, but loud enough for her to make out the words.

"Doctor Jannesson, this is the Savannah Police Department. Open your door, sir."

Jannesson whispered again, "Not a sound, Clara, or we're taking our medicine together. Half for you, half for me. If they break down my door, we'll both be dead before they reach the stairs."

Clara nodded slowly, thinking that even if she'd tried to scream with the gag in her mouth, the sound wouldn't reach the officer at the front door. Her eyes were fixed on the needle, her body gripped by a paralyzing fear of being injected.

The knocking resumed again, then stopped. Jannesson used his free hand to procure his phone, thumbing the screen and staring at it fixedly.

He shook his head angrily. "There's two of them, and they're walking around my house. They're looking in my windows. This isn't good, Clara, not for you."

Clara realized then what Jannesson was watching through his phone: video feed from cameras around his house, cameras hidden from outside view. During his reconnaissance of Jannesson's house, Kyle had hidden in the woods and used binoculars to search for cameras covering the backside of the property. He'd found none, and now Clara knew that Jannesson had been watching as he waited for them, that he saw their every move as they crossed the lawn.

She wondered if the cops would be able to make out the signs of forced entry on the second-floor window that she'd pried open. If they did, they'd have probable cause to make entry into the house—and Clara would die.

Because she didn't need any confirmation to know that Jannesson was crazy, but she could see now that he wasn't bluffing about the death needle in his hand, could tell from the despair on his face and in his voice that he wouldn't hesitate to kill her, and then himself.

Clara heard the faint slamming of car doors, then an engine turning on and fading out of earshot.

Jannesson took a shaky breath, his trembling hand setting the uncapped needle on the stainless-steel table beside her chair. Clara felt a sense of relief that the danger had passed, at least for the time being.

But Jannesson ripped the gag out of her mouth, pulling it down around her neck and bunching the cloth into his fist to choke her.

"Who did you tell?" he hissed.

Clara tried to shake her head, but the pressure on her throat cut off her air. Blood surged into her brain, her lungs screamed for oxygen. Her arms were jolting involuntarily against the Velcro restraints, making a failed bid to gain control of her airway.

She gasped hollowly, struggling in a futile attempt to pull air into her throat, until her field of view began to fade to darkness.

Jannesson released his grip on the cloth, and Clara pulled a single long breath into her starved lungs, feeling a wash of relief. But Jannesson's hand cocked back into a fist, and he drove it hard across her cheekbone.

Clara's head was ringing with the impact as he shouted, "*Who did you tell?*"

But she couldn't answer—his strike had ignited her broken nose into an explosion of torment that sent waves of pain shuddering across her face.

She sensed the coppery taste of blood at the back of her throat, and swallowed it down so she could keep breathing.

Jannesson grabbed her jaw in his hand, lifting her head to him.

His eyes were ablaze with fury, his face red and wild.

"Answer me."

Clara said, "What happened to all your 'ether of the cosmos' talk?"

"Shut up," he hissed.

Those two words were spoken at a near-growl, and he threw her head to the side. Then he stepped back, seeing his hand was slick with her blood and mucus. Disgusted, he wiped his palm against his pant leg, smearing a bloody streak down his thigh.

Jannesson was pacing now, crossing his office in quick steps to one end and then the other, passing Clara's seat like a snared predator.

Clara sensed that the best thing she could do was comfort him. She said, "I didn't tell anyone. It was me and Kyle, that's it."

He didn't break stride.

"Then how would they know?"

"They don't," she replied, her entire head spinning in pain. "If they knew I was here they would have sent a SWAT team, not a patrol car. You can still walk away."

"Oh I *will* walk away. You won't, but I will. My flight to Vietnam leaves in three hours, and after that I'm never returning to this wasteland of legislative overregulation. But my search for the cure will continue."

Jannesson stopped pacing, his eyes drifting with a faraway, unfocused look. He was muttering something to himself, words Clara couldn't make out.

He stopped whispering to himself then, looking to the bed and straightening his posture as if he'd had a sudden revelation. Then he used both hands to grab the gag around Clara's neck, trying to force it into her mouth. She resisted, turning her head and trying to clench her teeth. Jannesson slapped her hard, then slid the gag back into place.

Satisfied, he strode back to the medical area with its cabinets and needles. Clara was shaking her head without any attempt to do so, making choked screaming noises against the cloth stretching her mouth apart.

He returned with a new syringe, its barrel clear with transparent liquid.

Her eyes darted to the stainless-steel table, almost wishing he'd chosen that syringe instead. The brown liquid, the death needle that would end this nightmare that had invaded not just her dreams but her waking hours as well. Each was as bad as the other now.

Jannesson spoke his final words to her before stabbing her with the needle. "It's time for you to go, Clara."

Then the needle was in her arm, the liquid pouring into her blood-stream yet again, and she wondered what—

Silence.

Clara's hearing cut out completely. Jannesson was still there, stepping back with the empty syringe, watching her to see how she'd react. He had a scientist's curiosity, a genuine intrigue about what his lab rat would do. For a fleeting moment, Clara didn't care. She didn't think about the spinal tap she was about to receive, or how she'd die afterward. Because the world was completely muted, an astonishing stillness that almost moved her to tears. She was listening to true silence, something she hadn't heard in the five years since Pantalay had irreparably damaged her hearing.

The never-ending, high-pitched ringing was gone, and that alone left Clara in a momentary state of profound peace. She looked to Jannesson in astonishment, thinking, my God, man, can you bottle *this* particular effect? The vets would make him a millionaire, if he wasn't already. Because none of the audiologists Clara had seen could do this.

Instead they all spoke the same words, words like *high frequency hearing loss, permanent, irreversible*, the absurd term *tinnitus*, usually paired with some query as to why she hadn't simply paused during the fight to put in the foam earplugs that the military had so graciously provided. Their understanding of the effects was limited to books, just like all the therapists she'd seen. None of them knew what it was like to have their head turned into a constant, ringing bell.

The silence was beautiful and profound, unencumbered even by Jannesson watching her, his mouth hanging open in anticipation of...what?

Clara didn't know, and didn't even particularly care. She basked in the silence like a frigid reptile that had just found the first rays of sun, by then a half-remembered vision of peace, of life-giving force. She felt a single hot tear spill over an eyelid, the fathomless depths of tranquility overwhelm-ing. *Silence.* Each flicking second brought with it waves of peace that shook Clara to her emotional core.

Then sound returned to her, but not the sounds of this room. A thin warble entered through her right ear, passing through to her left with vibrations of noise that were subtle, familiar. This was the sound of her white noise machine, drowning out the constant ringing the same way alcohol quieted her body's throbbing hypervigilance. Alcohol for the ear—if you can't fix the disease, then drown out the symptom—and Clara was lying in a bed.

She pulled off the sleep mask, seeing her darkened bedroom and feeling the heaviness of a weighted blanket atop her. This was home, this was Charleston, and looking over she saw her husband's sleeping form beside her. She placed a hand on his shoulder, feeling the warmth of his body, and for a moment she embraced the illusion—she was home, this whole trip to Savannah just another tortuous dream.

Then Jeremy rolled over to face her, his voice heavy with sleep. "You want to have sex?"

"Yeah," Clara answered, without knowing why. That was her default answer, the one box she could check in a long list of wifely duties usually left unfulfilled. Because Clara's mind was racked by the symptoms of post-traumatic stress, but she was at her core a sexual being, and Jeremy was a good lover.

She pulled the blanket off, the bedroom air cool against her skin. Jeremy rolled on top of her, his weight reassuring, the feeling of protection, of safety, and yes—even domination. He kissed her neck and Clara gave a breathless sigh, feeling her body come to life against his. The warmth between her legs began to spread into her belly, her breasts swelling.

He lifted his head to find her lips, and Clara returned the kiss eagerly, greedily.

"I want you inside me," she whispered.

"Okay," he said, swallowing. "I'm going to undo the straps now."

Clara's mind jolted with the awful realization of the truth—she wasn't home; she was in Savannah, strapped to a chair in Jannesson's office. And against the rising swell of panic, Clara fought to keep her body calm as Dakota's voice flashed through her mind.

You need to remain still, very still...He doesn't know...

Doesn't know what?

She pressed her palms flat, feeling the smooth armrests of the chair even as Jeremy continued to kiss her. Clara could only summon reality in fragments now; her consciousness was in her bedroom with her husband atop her, but there were whispers of a chair supporting her weight, the sensation of breath against her face, a hot breath that didn't belong to Jeremy. Dakota's voice again. *That's why you can't move in front of him, not while you're under.*

He was going to take off the straps. Could Clara resist? Escape? She tried to see the truth, to glimpse Jannesson instead of her husband, but the world all around was her bedroom. Then the smell turned putrid, a hot stinking animal's breath in her nostrils, and her husband was no longer her husband. Now it was *her*, the Queen of Death in her makeup and her panties and a babydoll top, eyes gleaming white against the darkness.

She felt a tugging sensation at her ankles, but the feeling was coming from beneath her, not from her outstretched legs on the bed but from those restrained upright in a chair. It was a ghostly impression, an amputee's perception of feeling in a limb that was no longer there, and Clara fought to orient her physical body amid the endless expanse of this fantasy.

Then she was back in Afghanistan, a sun-scorched hell where human beings had murdered each other for power since the beginning of time. The sandy expanses of Pantalay Village spread before her. Was this before the battle? After? She couldn't tell, but it certainly wasn't during the fight— the streets were quiet and empty, Clara the lone witness aside from a figure leaning against the wall beside her.

It was Sims, wearing his full dress uniform and smoking a cigarette. He closed his jaw, allowing the smoke to billow out the exit wound at the back of his skull.

"Neat little parlor trick, eh, ma'am?"

Clara said nothing. She couldn't speak, wasn't even there—her body wasn't in Afghanistan, only her perception, and then she felt her feet spreading apart in the real world. Jannesson had released her ankle restraints; he must have.

But her view was fixed on Sims as he took another drag, puffing smoke through his mouth, nostrils, and back of his head all at once. He held the cigarette upright, examining its glowing ember with his one good eye.

"They say these things will kill you."

Sims pinched his cigarette by the filter, then inserted it ember-first into his mouth until the glowing cherry emerged through the hole in the back of his skull. Clara tried to wiggle her toes, and distantly felt the fabric of her socks within shoes. The sensation occurred a world away, registering only vaguely in her mind as she watched the wispy tendril of smoke from Sims's cigarette.

Then she heard Dakota's voice again.

Tolerance, tolerance, Clara! Can't you see? Don't you get it—

Clara was certain of it now. Jannesson's repeated dosages of this drug had inoculated her to the effects. Her mind was still lost in a haze of terror, but she had motor control absent from her previous hallucinations. She wasn't a passenger in her own body; she was now an active participant in the nightmare around her.

Somewhat.

Her mind and body were still separated, disjointed from one another. She tried blinking and caught flashing glimpses of herself restrained in the chair, Jannesson's hands pulling away the Velcro straps from her right forearm. Dakota knew this would happen.

Because he can't move you to the bed without untying you from the chair first.

Then Sims was back, pressing the cigarette ember into his Adam's apple with a chortling laugh. The transition between mental fantasy and physical reality was seamless—one second, she saw her right forearm free, attempted to move the fingers of that hand and observed them responding as Jannesson began undoing the strap around her left forearm. The next instant, she was peering into Sims's horrible eyes against the backdrop of Pantalay Village.

Clara fought to keep her body limp, betraying every primal instinct to resist until her left arm was freed from the chair. She blinked and saw Jannesson fumbling with the final strap.

Then Aiden's voice called out to her.

"Look, Mommy! Look!"

He was waving excitedly with one hand, the other clutching a bloody knife. Thor lay dead at his feet, throat slit.

Clara blinked again but she could not see reality; there was her son standing over the dead puppy, dark arterial blood oozing from his gashed neck. Aiden opened his mouth as if to scream then, but the sound that emerged wasn't his voice—it was the rip of Velcro breaking free.

Mustering all the strength she could manage, Clara drove her right fist toward her best estimation of where Jannesson's groin would be in the real world.

Her son and the dog disappeared from view, replaced by a fleeting image of Pantalay's resurrected dead worshipping their queen.

But Clara felt her knuckles impacting Jannesson's crotch with astonishing force, and the chanting in Pashto merged into a single human scream of pain. It was Jannesson's voice, a shrieking wail of agony and disbelief. Clara heard a thudding footfall to her right—he was going for the death needle beside her—and flung her arm sideways to flip the stainless-steel table over.

It hit the ground with a crash and Clara was trying to stand, moving blindly to her feet and using her memory of the room to sidestep right. But her vision was still filled with the blurry images of Pantalay Village, the rubble of the mosque, when Jannesson threw her into the wall.

Flying backward, she tripped over the fallen side table and struck the wall hard, barely having time to brace herself before the impact. Then she fell, her visions of Afghan sky jolting into a momentary view of the room—and Jannesson standing over her, turning to the corner with his eyes cast downward.

He was looking for the death needle on the floor, the only true threat that Clara represented to him anymore—she couldn't win a fight unarmed, but if she got that needle in her hands, one prick would kill him in seconds. Clara spun around, using her legs to scissor his ankles in an adrenaline-fueled burst of strength. Jannesson lost his balance and fell forward, pulling himself on his hands toward the brown syringe lying a few feet distant. Then the syringe vanished, her view once again filled with the filthy dirt roads of Pantalay.

Clara scrambled to where she'd last seen Jannesson, feeling his legs and clambering atop his back to futilely choke him from behind. But it was too late; he was still moving toward the needle in the corner, and he'd reach it long before he lost consciousness. Then Clara heard Dakota's voice in her head once more: *He wears those glasses for a reason—he's blind without them.*

Ripping the glasses from his face, Clara flung them to the far side of the office. Now they were both blind—Jannesson's vision degraded, and Clara's immersed in an Afghan village, each negotiating the same battlefield in a fight that wouldn't end until one of them was dead.

Clara was certain that he'd cut his losses and either go for the glasses or flee the room entirely to return with a gun. But she felt herself sliding forward on his back, his hands groping along the ground for the needle. She pulled herself forward with feverish intensity, scrambling over his shoulders and driving a hard backward kick that caught the corner of his neck.

Jannesson grabbed her ankle, pinning her leg against him. Her fingers were splayed, sweeping an office floor she couldn't see. The fingertips of her right hand hit the thin plastic syringe, and she made a panicked grab for it before Jannesson yanked her backward with astonishing strength.

He rolled her over onto her back, and the Afghan sky was gone; she was back in her bedroom now, Jannesson straddling her, hands squeezing her neck. His face hovered over hers, eyes glowing white as he shouted words she couldn't make out.

She drove the needle into his right eye, slamming the plunger as hard as she could.

Jannesson's eye yielded like jelly, first to the needle and then to the syringe, until Clara couldn't force it in any farther.

He shrieked, a shrill sound that made Clara's heart leap as he choked her with all the force he could muster. But his grip was going weak around her neck, finally releasing altogether as he rolled sideways, landing on his back beside her.

Clara scrambled away from him, leaping to her feet as she desperately searched for anything to use as a weapon, but Jannesson remained flat on his back, limbs askew, the barrel of the hypodermic needle emerging from his right eye like the handle of a dagger buried to the hilt.

And then he started laughing.

He was smiling peacefully now, staring at the ceiling with one open eye. Clara's view flickered between him and Afghanistan, though she heard his voice clearly.

"This doesn't matter." Jannesson spoke in a ragged whisper. "I'm free now, but you...if you return home, your husband and son are as good as dead."

He emitted a gargled cough. "There's no way out for you...except...except..."

Jannesson's panted breaths became irregular, some deep and others shallow as they grew increasingly erratic. Finally he struggled to breathe at all, instead emitting a deep, monstrous groan like a dying animal before the sounds transformed into a wet, throaty gargle as he choked on his own saliva.

This was his death rattle, the most horrible noise Clara had ever heard —and when it ended, Jannesson was dead at last.

Clara would have welcomed the sights of Afghanistan to the scene before her—Jannesson's blue-tinged body, the syringe buried grotesquely in his eye. But the flashbacks were gone, her visual field warping as she faltered on her feet and placed a hand on the wall to steady herself.

She had just enough coherence to be certain of one thing: Jannesson was right.

Clara pulled the gag from her mouth and swayed forward on shaky legs, moving toward the corner without knowing why as she slid one hand on the wall beside her. The noises of her movement echoed like distant bells ringing in her skull. Jannesson was dead, but his damage to Clara was complete, and she felt no desire to call the police, or her husband, or even await rescue—whatever her mind had been before, it was now so far gone that she'd never return to the fold of society, or family.

She arrived at her destination, the office corner she'd been seeking before she consciously realized why.

The cabinets and shelves were stocked with medical supplies, and by focusing on one label at a time, Clara could make out the medication names. She found oxycodone and lifted it from the shelf. This would give her Dakota's death, a blissful lapse into eternal freedom. She needed a guarantee, an ironclad assurance that Jeremy and Aiden would be forever safe from the horrors that had overtaken her mind.

And for all the imagined gravity she'd envisioned suicide possessing, now that she stood here it was almost painfully simple. For all her abilities as a novelist, Clara lacked both the capacity and the desire to compete with Dakota's final letter. She knew what hers would say before she ever wrote the words. It was more about her platoon than herself or even her family, because those were the facts that mattered to whoever would find her. It would be short and concise: *Marcus Jannesson killed Rich Johns, Jason Sims, Joshua Thoma, and Kyle Soler. Kyle is in a nearby swamp. Sergeant Raymond Dennis of the Charleston PD has the answers.*

Should she bother penning a note to Jeremy and Aiden? She considered it and then decided that she couldn't. To explain *why* would require explaining the monster they'd lived with, the haunted mother who had fantasized about stabbing her husband, who had filled Aiden's bathtub and stood over his bed without realizing it, prepared to drown him.

No, she decided. It was far better for them to remember her from their last memory together, the family united for one last picnic at Hampton Park, smiling and happy in the shade of an ancient oak tree draped with Spanish moss. The rest could be left up to interpretation, assuming Clara had been lost in some misguided search for truth and justice in the wake of what had happened to her platoon.

Because above all, she could not, she *would* not, bring this evil home to her family. This evil had become her, it had taken over her being, and there was no coming back now.

She turned the bottle of oxycodone over in her hand, the pills rattling with no more maliciousness than the children's vitamins she fed her son.

Then she looked back up, seeing the now-exposed bottle that had been behind it on the shelf, and focused on the label.

Cetraphaline.

Clara came up short then, considering her first treatment and the surreal dream world that she'd entered. It had uncovered profound revelations into her own psyche and dark associations that had followed her back from war, and that seemed particularly meaningful when she recalled the words from her file, from the files of the other platoon suicides—*diluted for minimum effects.*

She retrieved a fresh syringe with shaking hands, tossing aside the protective cap and inserting the needle into the bottle. She had no idea how to calibrate the proper dosage based on body weight, and she didn't care. There was nothing left to lose.

Clara filled the needle with as much cetraphaline as it would hold and carried it to her chair. There was nothing restraining her now; she sat of her own free will, studying the tip of the needle. Could you overdose on cetraphaline? She suspected you could, and if that happened to her now, it mattered precious little.

Pulling up a sleeve to expose her shoulder, she stuck the needle into her flesh and pressed the plunger all the way down.

Clara winced as the cold liquid flooded into her muscle, then pulled out the needle. She put her arm to the side in order to drop the needle next to the chair, and was opening her fingers to let the syringe fall from her grasp when her vision began drifting, the room around her swirling in a hazy orbit.

34

Clara's swirling vision intensified—she was spinning faster and faster now, her perception a whirling cyclone. She was in the center of a violent tornado, a vivid and terrifying landscape that quaked with painfully bright blues and purples and magentas. Clara felt her lungs seizing up, the horror and panic swelling even as a voice in her mind told her to surrender, to give herself over. She felt the shuddering spasms racking her body, and fought to maintain some semblance of mental control.

Was this death? She didn't know and it didn't matter—the voice said to surrender and so Clara did, willfully giving herself over to whatever was occurring. She laid down all inner walls of mental resistance, allowing herself to be swept away by whatever force now surrounded her.

Then she was no longer thinking at all, only *perceiving*, understanding that she was moving toward the ultimate reality and away from it at the same time, entering a universe of consciousness re-explored. Clara's vision was gone entirely, replaced by a psychedelic starscape of color and light. Her seat became the greatest massage chair in the world—rippling, three-dimensional, gyroscopic, weightless. It hurtled her forward with incredible momentum, flying through an endless space that unfolded before her. She was moving through an infinite effervescence, soaring through reality not as it existed to her, but, she sensed, to all eternity.

This was the mesh of the universe, the forever shifting fractal patterns morphing with psychedelic beauty, pulsating the warmth of unity with all that existed. There was no longer any time, no progression of one event to the next. Instead the space contained all that ever had been, was now, or ever would be. Everything prevailed in perfect harmony, the universe a staggeringly beautiful place of total peace, and total understanding. And in that moment, she knew that the ultimate truth at the heart of everything... was love.

Clara asked if Aiden would have a long and fulfilling life. A voice answered in her mind, *You tell me, Clara*—will *he have a long and fulfilling life?* She repeated the statement as fact, and then asked the same question for her husband, Jeremy. The response was the same, a question that she restated as fact. *Jeremy and Aiden will have long, fulfilling lives.* Then the voice spoke again, a single statement that swelled with a powerful sense of truth: *The three of you will always be together.*

She hesitated at this, then asked the universe of her mind how she could possibly overcome the medication that Jannesson had administered. There was a wave of pain in her head, signifying she was asking the wrong question. The voice said, *You are only at the outset of your journey. Your whole life has been building up to this. Pantalay, Aiden, the journey. Push through.*

Clara's being was transported deeper into her mind then, the kaleidoscope of color and pattern flying by with immeasurable speed, until she entered an infinite, black, dimensionless expanse. This was the heart of the universe, she sensed, and it was the most beautiful thing she had ever seen. There was no movement, no thoughts of any kind, only endless peace and total clarity.

Then she existed in human form once again, standing in a peaceful forest amid the chirp of songbirds overhead. She turned to examine her surroundings, hearing a burbling brook in the distance, and her view shifted across moss-covered tree trunks until she saw a figure standing beside her.

Dakota.

She was wearing a simple dress, her hazel irises clear and lucid. Her face was angelic, sculpted eyebrows and high cheekbones rising as she broke into a smile at the sight of Clara. They were united, pulling each other into a tight embrace, hot tears streaming down Clara's cheeks as she held her friend. "Why did you do it?" she asked. "Why did you leave us?"

Dakota set her hands on Clara's shoulders, and her response was calm and quiet.

"I'm in a better place now, Clara." Then her eyes widened. "Are you?"

Clara had a flash of understanding—she'd metaphorically died that day in Pantalay Village, allowing herself to die at war by failing to move on. Looking into Dakota's eyes, she knew that the power to continue living didn't exist in medical treatment or therapy. It was all inside her, and she had the power to change it for herself. Whether it was easy or hard, whether she did it sooner or later, didn't matter to the universe; the change had to occur from within, or not at all.

The true peace was there all along, inside herself, merely obscured by a maelstrom of thoughts and memories that clouded her true perception.

But through it all was an eternal light that spelled true salvation from her anguish. She needed merely to stop resisting and embrace the truth, however much effort that required, and she'd be free—truly free, released from her torment. That was all any of us had to do, she thought, because in the end we were all the same. There was no military or civilian here, not even man or woman. The pains she grappled with were not veteran issues, but human ones, and the source of salvation was the same.

She nodded to Dakota and whispered, "I understand."

Dakota released her hands from Clara's shoulders, and she smiled again before looking upward, as if sensing some disturbance.

"What is it?" Clara asked. Then she heard it too—a faint, eerie howl that rose and fell somewhere in the distance.

Dakota seemed to understand, and she said, "Goodbye, Clara."

"No, don't go—"

But her friend was gone, the forest replaced by a starscape that Clara traveled beneath at impossible speed. The wait continued, increasing in volume until it became an emergency siren and the starscape faded to reveal the roof of an ambulance.

She was on a stretcher, breathing shallowly as the vehicle rocketed forward.

Dakota spoke urgently.

"Stay with us, you're doing great."

Clara looked over to see not Dakota but a female EMT attending to her in the ambulance. The EMT leaned over her and removed a respirator from Clara's face. "How do you feel?"

35

"Mommy, wake up!"

Clara pulled the sleep mask off her face, seeing morning sunlight streaming through the windows. Aiden was beside her bed.

"Hey, buddy," she said. "How'd you sleep?"

He gave her a thumbs up. "Are we making my birthday cake tonight?"

Clara smiled. "Yellow batter with chocolate frosting, just like you asked for."

"I want sprinkles too—rainbow ones."

"I think we can make that happen," Clara said as Thor thudded into the room.

The dog stopped beside Aiden, laying his block-like head on the comforter—her son's inseparable friend was a puppy no more. Clara patted the animal's head, giving him a scratch behind his ears as Thor closed his eyes in pleasure.

Jeremy approached from the walk-in closet, tightening his tie knot.

"Hey, babe, how'd you sleep?"

"Not bad," Clara said, rising from bed to kiss her husband's cheek. "Took me a while to go down, but I pulled off six hours."

"Not too shabby," he said, looking to their son. "Aiden, let's go downstairs and let Mommy get ready. Bring your werewolf."

"Daddy," Aiden objected, "Thor's not a *werewolf*, he's a *dog!*"

"Could've fooled me. Let's go."

Clara checked the nightstand clock and said, "Let me jump in the shower, and I'll be right down."

Jeremy nodded. "Take your time. See you down there."

After her family left, Clara walked to the bathroom and turned on the shower. As the water heated up, she examined her face in the mirror.

Her eyes were clear with a decent night's rest, but her nose was canted slightly to the left. That little adjustment had been courtesy of Jannesson breaking it in his office, and it now served as her daily reminder of the events that were now almost a year distant. Clara detested the new look, but it was, she reasoned, better than losing an eye to a needle filled with a lethal agent. In that sense and many others, she'd emerged as the victor in Savannah.

But Kyle had died in the process, and that loss would forever weigh heavily on her soul, alongside the deaths of Rich, Sims, Thoma, and Dakota.

She undressed and entered the shower, letting the hot water wash over her body. Every day felt like a fresh start now, and after her captivity in Savannah she still felt a sense of novelty with almost every successive wakeup in her Charleston home.

Clara had later learned that Jeremy suspected her location after she disappeared, and his pleas to the Savannah PD eventually yielded the visit to Jannesson's home that she'd overheard while tied to the chair.

But as for the ambulance that had arrived to carry her away, that was Clara's doing.

She had no recollection of making the call, but at some point in her self-induced cetraphaline trip, Clara had apparently dialed 911.

Against the operator's feverish requests for information, Clara had spoken four words over and over, eventually going silent until police and paramedics could trace the call and arrive to find her comatose on the ground, along with Jannesson's body.

I want to live.

Following her evacuation by ambulance, she'd been taken to the hospital and monitored closely. The subsequent investigation revealed Jannesson's injectable recipe for suicidal and homicidal ideation—a mix of pharmaceuticals that produced an enhanced elevation of paranoia, violent tendencies, and hallucination meant to elevate existing anxieties to the breaking point.

And to her surprise, she found that the drug's effects were long-lasting, though not permanent—Jannesson surely knew that too, which was probably why he used his final breaths to convince her to kill herself. Clara was transferred to the psych ward of a Charleston hospital for a month of close supervision. During that time, the nightmares had dwindled until they stopped altogether, and Clara had eventually been cleared for release.

In the months that followed, she resolved to become a source of strength for others, starting with her family. Doing so meant working through her own issues first, and so Clara was back in therapy. She met with her counselor weekly to talk through all her repressed memories, to discuss her setbacks and how she could better manage her emotions and tend to herself. At first, Clara felt both humbled and embarrassed by the process, but she knew the work was required to keep her family, so she kept at it. For her, it was the first step in a cycle of healing that she would have to actively cultivate for the rest of her life.

Sometimes that cycle felt like a regression, sometimes the anguish was so deep that forward progress seemed elusive if not impossible. But Aiden depended on her now, and Jeremy did too—the truth was that they *wouldn't* be better off without her, no matter how much she believed that at times. Whether by death or divorce, her loss would deal a crippling blow to their existence, and would impart new pain upon others rather than helping to guide them through their own difficulties.

In the end, Clara could bear the difficulties of her own past—as Jannesson said, she had an abnormally high tolerance for psychological pain—but she could not bear to inflict any more miseries upon the innocent. She'd joined the military in part to protect those who couldn't protect themselves, and while that intent had gone awry at times, it remained a part of her being that she couldn't divorce herself from no matter the hardship.

The real cure for PTS, she'd come to learn, was the same as the meaning of life: there wasn't one. Still, she was cured in the sense that she now realized there was no mystical way to absolve a human of everything they'd seen and done, or had done to them. She'd stopped looking to the outside world for answers, and started looking within. There, she'd found the torn threads waiting to be mended, and she began treating them with her own personal threads of meaning: writing, meditation, nutrition, exercise, and the support of her fellow human beings no matter how flawed it was at times.

Because her fellow humans were her real hope, and she was theirs; they were beings in this existence together, and while alcohol could—and still did—provide a temporary respite, it was now only a small cog in the machinery of her continued treatment. She still had sleep disturbances, but her hypervigilance was drastically reduced, and when insomnia struck she no longer resisted it. Instead, she'd write late into the night, allowing herself to sleep in the next day to recover.

There had been progress in the medical community as well. Using seventeen million dollars from private donors, Johns Hopkins had opened a new center for psychedelic research. The team of six full-time faculty and five scientists ran trials with psilocybin from mushrooms, MDMA, LSD, ketamine, and cetraphaline on volunteers with medical histories of depression, addiction, and posttraumatic stress. Research was ongoing, and the initial results were incredibly promising—but Clara knew the truth. Psychedelics like cetraphaline may be a valuable tool for some, just as they had been for her. But they were only one of an indeterminate number of options that people would have to try, or not, to find an individual combination that worked best for them.

Clara's suffering at the hands of Jannesson had been picked up by the media, garnering national and international media attention. Soon thereafter, Clara's publisher swooped back in to offer her a book deal, as had several other publishers with offers of ghost writers, co-writers, and huge marketing plans for the memoir.

In the end, Clara had chosen a small, upstart publishing company that had agreed to her only three demands: that they also publish her now-finished literary fiction novel, that she write the memoir herself, and that her royalties go to PTS research. She didn't need the money; Clara had more than enough, and with so many suffering, this was her best means of giving back. The raw manuscript was perhaps not as professional as a co-written work, but the successive rounds of editing had cleaned it up to a polished finished product that she was proud of. The book, titled *My Dark*

Silence, had spent five weeks on *The New York Times* Best Seller List, and the first printed copy now sat on the shelf in her office.

Her conclusion in the book was this: in the end, there was no solution. And there may not ever be. Every person had to find their own path to salvation, the combination of factors that best achieved balance in their lives. And once they found it, as she had, they had to stick with it—there were no "cured" people, only cured *acts* consistently performed to achieve balance.

Because everyone had their personal horrors to live with, whether from combat, or childhood, or auto accident. The sources were endless, and ultimately it didn't matter how someone acquired their trauma. It only mattered whether they overcame it. Ignoring and repressing *was* an option, but not one that served to express the feelings of fear and hopelessness. Repression did nothing to help families or friends, or to help the afflicted heal. That true path to recovery was different for every single person, and it was endless. While no one could change the past, everyone had the potential to move beyond their darkest hours, using their journey as a source of strength to guide themselves forward, stronger than before. And until the afflicted moved past their own trauma, they couldn't help those who depended upon them to guide them through theirs.

Emerging from the shower, Clara toweled herself off and quickly got dressed. She took a final glance in the mirror, her canted nose seeming like an inconsequential price to pay in the wake of what she'd learned about herself, about life itself and overcoming trauma. After years of struggling with the invisible wounds of war, Clara was finally the mother and wife that her family deserved. Whether that was easy or hard changed on a near-daily basis, but Clara was finally in control of her life.

She left her bedroom and trotted down the stairs, joining Jeremy, Aiden, and Thor in the kitchen to get ready for the day.

The Spider Heist
Spider Heist #1

As an FBI agent, she specialized in hunting America's most elite thieves. Now, she's become one of them.

Blair Morgan's world is in shambles.

After being used as a scapegoat by a corrupt former boss, she is unceremoniously fired from the FBI. Now, with her reputation, pride, and years of service stripped away, Blair just wants to start over.

But when a chance date turns into a mysterious job offer, her past comes crashing back to haunt her.

In a flash, Blair becomes entangled in a high stakes bank heist. Her status as a former FBI-agent-turned-hostage transforms her into an instant media sensation. And the unwanted attention makes her a target for ruthless killers that will stop at nothing to silence her.

Caught in the crosshairs, Blair must confront her past before she loses her freedom—or her life.

But there is something strange about this team of bank robbers. They aren't who they seem. And as a deadly SWAT raid closes in, Blair discovers that she may not be either...

Get your copy today at
severnriverbooks.com/series/the-spider-heist-thrillers

ABOUT THE AUTHOR

Jason Kasper is the USA Today bestselling author of the Spider Heist, American Mercenary, and Shadow Strike thriller series. Before his writing career he served in the US Army, beginning as a Ranger private and ending as a Green Beret captain. Jason is a West Point graduate and a veteran of the Afghanistan and Iraq wars, and was an avid ultramarathon runner, skydiver, and BASE jumper, all of which inspire his fiction.

Sign up for Jason Kasper's reader list at
severnriverbooks.com/authors/jason-kasper

jasonkasper@severnriverbooks.com

Printed in the United States
by Baker & Taylor Publisher Services